The Pressure Drop

The Pressure Drop

PETER FINCHAM

PublishingPush

First edition 2022

ISBN 978-1-80227-392-2 (paperback)
ISBN 978-1-80227-391-5 (ebook)

Published by PublishingPush.com

Typeset using Atomik ePublisher from Easypress Technologies

'Time has gathered us here by coincidence. I admit I have spent some time in confusion…. Riddled with my own self-destruction… The bold raging flame of your heart is making me stay.'

'Co-incidence' - I am Kloot (2005)

For my wife, Jennifer, and our fabulous girls,
Maddie, Grace and Joan.
You all amaze me every day. Individually and together,
we can do anything.
But mostly this is for 'The Boy', our boy, who left us far too soon.
We are so lost without you Freddie.
Sleep well My Son & 'Thank You For The Days'.

Chapter 1

Although flights had resumed quicker than initially expected, it had still taken Ste several days to get a seat on one of the few flights heading home, enabling his escape from a city still gripped by an all-consuming fear. As the plane took off, he gazed down across a world much changed by the horrors. Although the dust cloud had now broken up, to an eye as familiar with the city as his, the gap in the skyline, which had taken no more than an hour to create, had quickly come to mean so much more than the concrete itself. And Ste knew that like the skyline, he too had been immediately, permanently changed.

Aside from himself, it was not just the view that had changed. He had left what had always been an energised and hedonistic city, as one now engulfed in an unrepentant sense of terror. It was the sort of paralysis to normal life that was natural when heavily armed soldiers are visible on every street. An occupying force following a coup d'état would have been less noticeable.

The subways closed and then re-opened as the unqualified alarms continued to come and then go, with a predictable irregularity. No one felt safe, the anticipation of a further round of Armageddon always imminent.

On video, the events which he had witnessed were represented in seconds; but in real life, they had taken an eternity. His own slow-moving stagger through that eternity continually played out on repeat in his head. Ste could still touch the individual grains of dust as they rained down on him and the unholy visions that had lodged in his mind's eye several days before refused to morph into a different view.

He remained consumed by the shocked cries and sorrowful tears from the thousands of bystanders who had witnessed his own struggle. Whatever internal battle Ste was fighting, he still believed that no one could see past his thickest skin. He told himself that no one could see where he had been, and they'd never understand if they could. So *just keep running mate*. Because then, when Ste had run far enough, it could start to be okay again. Out of sight, out of mind.

He made an immediate vow to never return.

As the plane veered North-East, out over the vast expanse of sea, he took a moment to think of her. Instantly, a different source of pain washed over him. A set of painful waves of regret for what had gone on. He was paralysed both in mind and body. She had been the one who called him 'Darling' and he had sent her away for no crime greater than trying to help. It had only taken him a moment to realise he needed help; her help. But by then, she was gone.

As his view of the city disappeared for a final time, he remembered what she had said to him - that '*everyone wants to be loved*'. That may have been the case once. But now, Ste Lewis had no interest in being loved. From now on, he would be an island. Not those fun Mediterranean ones which were blanketed in sunshine and good times throughout the summer months. Those islands were the fun ones which he was used to visiting several times each year for long business weekenders, where he would be at the centre of the place where people travelled to; a place which made the tourists feel like life could be no better.

No. He was not one of those islands.

Now, he would be the sort of island that stuck up from the depths of the North Atlantic, onto which random fishermen would plant their flags in order to support their various intransigent claims of legitimacy to work the surrounding waters. There was nothing on those grey, lonely islands. They were desolate and depressing, as well as dangerous to everyone who tried to land.

From now on, Ste would be Rockall. His was the wretched island on which no one would ever again want to plant their flag.

Chapter 2

1990

"I'm so sorry, Tina." Stephen Lewis could not express his sincerity in a more succinct way.

"I've known him since we were eight years old and he's never taken his clothes off on stage before."

Tina Garner had made a rare decision to leave London and head for Portsmouth on a cold, rainy Tuesday night in November to support the band's breakthrough gig; it had been worse than awful. Johnny, the band's eighteen-year-old drummer, was off his head on something far too strong for him, and although the other three kids battled on, the terrible sound that struggled out of the decrepit house PA would have created insurmountable issues for even the most experienced band, let alone a group of four mates not long out of the sixth form.

From the opening notes, it was clear that one of them was out of tune. The awfulness was compounded by the lead singer not being able to decide which of the keys to go with and, in a feeble attempt to bridge them with harmony, he found one somewhere off the register that made the whole thing sound even worse. It was cringeworthy, and as they struggled through their opening numbers, half of the small audience were already calling it a night, prompting Johnny to shed his clothes in an act of desperation that he dedicated to the 'Gods of Rock.' It was the camel-breaking straw. The house lights went up and the PA shut down, ending the horrific event before the end of the first set.

"Stephen…"

"You can call me Ste…."

Tina sighed, once again appraising this bloke who, despite being no more than a kid, had managed to get her down the A3 through his sheer force of personality. An agent of her standing did not usually spend her time encouraging raw acts like these lads - and she never went to venues this far out of town. But there was something impressive in the way Ste had come across when he hand-delivered their EP to her office a month before. She'd taken a gamble on this band, but standing in the near-empty venue, with a long drive home ahead, she knew the gamble had backfired. They were finished.

Ste was heartbroken. He knew what was coming. Ever since he and the singer, Ben, had stolen a bottle of Oranjeboom from his dad's cellar before recording the worst version of *Stand by Me* ever put onto a D-90 tape, Ste had been on a journey to what tonight stood for. He accepted he was not going to be the musical face of any band himself, so had thrown himself into the promotional and management side of the enterprise – tonight was meant to be the successful culmination of those years. It should have been so different from the death knell it turned out to be. He was embarrassed, his humiliation irrecoverably increased as the band began a full-on fight on the stage behind them. He'd had enough.

"Just fucking stop it!"

It was bad enough standing in front of Tina, apologising for their collective failure, without his four bandmates marking the permanent demise of their band with this shit.

"I knew I should have gone to Uni."

After a short lifetime dreaming about what tonight should have been, his initial association with the music business saw him flat broke and the manager of a band that was trying to kick the shit out of each other.

Tina, embarrassed for him, had begun to drift towards the exit, trying to make as quick a getaway as possible. She didn't want to add to his problems by telling him what he already knew. Like her, he had gambled on the wrong horse. For her, this wasn't about the band. She had joined the company as a receptionist ten years before. In a tough business, she'd clawed her way through the positions until she landed the role she'd set her sights on. She headed one of the best A&R departments in the industry. Although times were changing, Tina was one of few women to have carved a name for herself on that side of the business. She surrounded herself with hard-working, interesting people untainted by the self-aggrandised nonsense that many of her industry peers were consumed by.

This trip to Portsmouth was about more than the band on stage and was as much to satisfy her curiosity about this bloke who had earned her attention with his charming persistence. Ste had a charisma held by the frontman, not the chap who booked the gigs and put up the posters.

She'd lost interest before the first song was murdered. Harsh as that was, the industry was too cut-throat when it came to music. So, her attention was now concerned with Ste. Changes had to be made to her staff. She'd fired one of the juniors in the office for being shit and lazy, and she had a vacancy to fill and she was coming away from tonight with something to show for it.

He really did know his music; therefore, he knew, even before the first chords of the night, that they were screwed. The omens of doom were cast when he saw it was Deaf Barry doing the sound. He had the look of a beaten man and smiled at Tina with weary resignation.

His earliest memories were set to a permanent soundtrack of hits pulled together from the Radio 1 playlists he would listen to from under the covers, late each night. Annie Nightingale, Tommy Vance or the Kingmaker, John Peel, broadcast from the pulpit of his church, sending the choice of sounds to a divided nation languishing on its knees. He lamented that he'd been born just too late to catch Led Zeppelin playing Kimbells, a small nightclub in Southsea, in 1969 or to get an extra's role in *Tommy* when The Who filmed on South Parade Pier six years later. The classic live albums of the '70s were the gigs he'd never got the chance to attend and he wished for a time machine to transport him to them. But the world only moved forward. *Back to the Future* isn't real and rather than lament not being part of the past, what he focused on was helping shape what the masses listened to in the future.

"Ste. You know I have to say 'Thanks but no thanks' when it comes to the band. And you understand why, don't you?"

"Look, Tina, thanks for coming. I know you came a long way to see those wankers and I really appreciate it. If I ever have a chance to return the favour, please let me know."

The lads on the stage were still arguing and Ste's dreaming was over. The fighting had stopped only because there was nothing left to throw but the group was finished. They were now left to aggressively berate each other with what insults had yet to be thrown while they inspected their superficial war wounds. Ste had no more words. He was done.

Surprisingly, however, Tina had still not left the building.

"If you're as serious as I think you are about this industry and really want to make a start on that repayment, then how about coming and working for me? Do a good job and we could call it 'favour returned'? I might even pay you."

Ste wondered if Tina was talking to somebody else. He pointed his middle finger at the centre of his chest, mouthing the word 'Me' in disbelief at his sudden upturn in fortunes.

"It is you…. Oh yeah," Tina mimed back at him.

He cracked a smile for the first time all night. He could leave the chaos that had erupted behind him—behind him. Deaf Barry was pulling cables across the stage with enough force to cause damage. Ste instinctively moved to help him, but Tina put her hand on his arm.

"This isn't your job anymore, Ste. I'll see you next week."

Chapter 3

Thatcher was now gone, finally ousted from the pedestal from which she'd orchestrated a decade of division. But the world was in no less of a mess with the circus performer's son in charge. Looking over the Solent, Ste sucked in what he hoped was the last breath of sea air he'd take for some while, excited to be trading the cleanliness of the coast for whatever pungent aroma London was likely to suffocate him with. He was trading salt for soot. Was it true that the Underground turned your snot black? Moving away meant leaving the community he had grown up in; a place where everybody knew everybody else's business. He was transplanting into a city of impersonal crowds, where the homeless masses huddled around a flame at night, desperate to keep out the cold in the 'Wild West End'. He had no fear. It spelled opportunity and a fresh start. He was suddenly a grown-up person with a grown-up job.

Arriving in the city, he quickly navigated his way past the flaming oil drums under the bridge outside Waterloo Station. He was nineteen, and, within a week, had relocated his life to London, landing a dream job that promised all the opportunity available for him to be able to do something meaningful with his life. His days of reading NME to be told what music he should be listening to were over. He was going to tell NME what they should be listening to. Ste Lewis made a resolution - like Sting in *Quadrophenia*, he was going to be the face.

Rather than heading straight to the flat Tina had sorted him for his first month in town, he walked the mile from Waterloo to the office near Denmark Street, a place where the last beatniks glided around their town in a hazy denial that the '60s were over. Les Cousins on Greek Street had now been closed for two decades, but that meant nothing to these ghosts of a different era. No matter how hard the Twelve Bar Club tried to keep the spirit alive, the world had a different energy. Kids walked around the Centrepoint building, guitars in hand, looking for the path to success by whatever means necessary. One or two would make it, but only those who were exceptionally good or extremely lucky. That band which was drafted in and heard by chance on a good night when the record company had somebody down for a different band who had unfortunate technical difficulties. The demo tape that caught the talent spotter off guard enough that they listened to more than the opening thirty seconds, and by doing so heard enough to take a chance. Only the one-in-a-million bands, in the right place at the right time, would make it. The rest would fall by the wayside and spend their lives busking in the tube stations. Some would get into NME once; maybe more than once. But most failed to get anywhere near the heights that they set out to.

Ste settled into his new world, defying the heckled doubts of his mates from home. He would never go backwards. He wouldn't need to go down the tried and tested route of a university education and student lifestyle. It wasn't pride that meant he would never consider it as Ste was not a proud man; just a bloke who was confident in his abilities, purposeful and deter-mined to succeed at whatever he set himself up to do. His mates were living in the small student communities of Bristol and Leeds, but doing the Otley pub crawl was nothing in comparison to getting a backstage pass for when Morrissey played in London.

He knew his role was at the bottom of the pile, tasked with taking on acts who were at the bottom with him. It was hard graft, but with great benefits. Tina provided a guiding hand to help shape his path and things started to work. Some of the bottom-dwelling bands he inherited made the right noises that got them into the magazines that mattered and with success, came success. Having moved to London as the last chimes of Thatcherism faded, by the time President Blair took his place at the head of the table, it was no longer Ste making the calls to the venues; the bigger and better ones were now calling him.

The dark artistic depression of the '80s which permeated every corner of the land as Ste arrived in London six years previous, had been replaced by the golden age of Brit Pop. The country seemed to be smiling again and with it, there was more fun to be had. Oasis was the epitome of a new England; a society where the country pivoted on the sounds of Manchester, taking on all comers to their self-anointed status as the musical Kings of England.

Blur were a different strand of the same ilk, and the intense sounds of The Manics bellowed across the Severn Bridge.

But it was the internet that was generating the greatest change in the way the game was played, and Ste had started to cement his position at the centre of it all. As 'New Labour' opened the gates of Downing Street to the great and the good of British pop culture, Ste was starting to become the face he had set out to be. After years of grafting from a minibus on the M6 with small, rising bands, the established artists were at his door. It was 1997. He was there.

Chapter 4

1997

She couldn't be sure which direction the noise was coming from, or how many rooms away they were, but the familiar sound of hotel cleaners in the hallway was the first thing to jolt Isla from the small amount of sleep she'd had.

All hotel rooms are unfamiliar to start with, but this one was definitely not one she recognised. At least there was a small chink of light under the door showing the most likely escape route. The room smelt of booze and sex, nothing like the odour she would normally wake up to; this was not how Isla's mornings usually began.

That was definitely breathing next to her though, far over on the other side of the huge bed that was too big for a normal room and certainly the sort you found in a decent hotel. Ever so slowly, she moved her arms tight into her sides.

Don't disturb him - whoever 'him' was beside her.

The last thing she wanted was a conversation, a retrospective, a fake plan to get in touch in a day or so. Or an actual plan that turned whatever last night had been into something it was not.

Where the hell am I? And what's that taste?

Isla made the first attempt at trying to remember. Mostly, what she had been drinking to have a desert-dry mouth and a head that was now paying the primary price for the indulgence. You need to learn the lessons of these nights.

Tequila; definitely Tequila. But there had been something else as well.

Don't wake him up. Don't wake him up.

Isla felt around herself, checking for any signs of clothing that she could start to collect up and get on with getting out. Nothing.

As her eyes started to adjust to the darkness, she began to make out the shape of the body next to her. *Not bad! No idea who it was, but you've done well there* she told herself.

This sort of thing was not a habit of hers, but on occasions, when it took her fancy to cut loose and not give a shit, these sorts of things had been known to happen.

Isla was a good-looking girl with a fantastic job for someone of her personality and age, and the opportunity to meet hundreds of new people every day. It was only natural for that to lead to occasional carnage as the world of work would drift seamlessly into fun in a bar and beyond.

Water! Where was the water?

More fumbling around the bedside table. An empty plastic bottle, the small ones that come in those tiny fridges in hotel rooms.

Why did complimentary have to mean miniature?

After the moments of recollection, she was no nearer getting out of the room. Something nagged in the back of her befuddled head that there was something important to do this morning.

Why am I not at home?

She began to attempt what should have been a simple process of sitting upright. She'd managed to sit upright every morning of her life, but this morning – if indeed it was morning – it was going to be more of a challenge than normal. Despite the hangover, physically, it was going to be OK. But the process was complicated by the need to not disturb the sleeping man. The *fit* sleeping man!

Ever so slowly, Isla swung her legs over the side of the large bed, keeping her body low against the mattress so as not to disturb the sheet that covered them both.

What time is it? I know I've got to be somewhere.

Encouraged by an increasing sense of concern that she needed to get a move on, Isla's movements became less gentle; more purposeful. Her feet touched a carpet that was covered in clothes. Hopefully, *her* clothes, and so, using her feet, she began to pull them together, bending down to pick up what she'd managed to muster. There was a door on the far side of the room. Instinct said that was the bathroom and with the clothes clamped tightly to her chest, Isla tiptoed towards the room.

Drink water, have a wee, get some clothes on, and get the hell out.

She figured she'd be out of there in less than 5 minutes.

The sound of the cleaners in the corridor was getting closer. It was a three-way race to get out of the room before he woke up, she woke him up, or the cleaners knocked on the door and made all her efforts to stay quiet totally redundant.

She reached the door, her hand patting it down to find the handle.

What was his name? How have I ended up here?

The questions still had no answers.

This isn't the bathroom! It's a bloody cupboard.

The ironing board started to slide as the door opened and Isla dropped her clothes to stop it in mid-fall.

Which one is the bathroom?

Her eyes now fully adjusted to the dimly lit room; a process of elimination led her back over to where she'd come from; she'd failed to notice the door that had been right next to her all along. Creeping back across the room, Isla breathed in relief as she managed to get into the bathroom and locate and then turn on the light without any significant noise. And a bonus; he was still asleep.

Water In. Water Out. Done.

Relief at both ends. The clothes were a mixture of his and hers. There wasn't a complete set of anything. Decision time.

How important is it to have my own socks?

There was no way she was going to stay in the room longer than needed, so she quickly swilled her mouth with the toothpaste in the tiny tube. She'd leave the toothbrush for the sleeping man; the whole aggressive teeth cleaning might make too much noise.

Why are these things always so small?

SHIT!

The sudden realisation of where she needed to be had arrived. Isla was supposed to have a meeting with her boss. She had no idea where she was, let alone how late she was running.

My watch! Where's my watch? Shit!

She looked at herself in the bathroom mirror. Her blouse was crumpled.

Shit! A stain.

That wasn't going to come out quickly and trying to do so would make it much worse. Isla pulled her jacket tight over her.

Just about covers it. It'll have to do. Now, what the hell is his name?

Once again, she drew a blank as to who was in the other room. It had been nice though, she had started to remember that much, as she veered towards maybe waking him up to say goodbye.

Shit! I need to go – although Isla could not be sure what time it was and therefore whether she was indeed late already!

It really was decision time. Find her watch and the bits of clothing she could probably do without, but any of these tasks increased the risk of waking him. How much did Isla not want that conversation? She skulked back into the room, careful to not open the bathroom door too quickly, risking unnecessary creaking.

Door out – left. Bed – in front. Light switch? Where's my watch?

For the first time since waking up, she made a quick decision. While there wasn't time to turn herself into the majestic princess BA always expect their female cabin crew to resemble, she could at least try to find the 18th birthday present which her parents had given her only a year ago. Everything else set, she flicked on the bathroom light which immediately gave her enough light to play with. The watch was on the table underneath the TV.

He's waking up. Shit! Grab it and run….

She lurched forward towards the table, tripping on a towel disguised as the carpet before dropping the bag she was holding, emptying the contents all over the floor in front of her.

Shit! Game Over!

"Hello, Isla…"

Shit! He's awake. Of course he's awake now. Dumbass. And he remembered my name! Why can't I remember his?

Frantically, Isla gathered what she could from the floor, grabbed her watch and made purposefully for the door without saying a word. As she reached the exit, whatever his name is turned on the bedside light and she instinctively turned and smiled, before catching her first full glimpse of the man she could feel she'd just slept with.

Fit. Long hair. Sexy bod. Hmmm, good work! How old though? Looks younger… surely that's not possible?

Un-tempted to engage, she opened the door and left the room without another glance back. Finally, in the corridor, she checked her watch. Her meeting was in 20 minutes, but she still had no idea where she was. It would be a step too far to ask one of the cleaners which hotel this was. That kind of embarrassment was a little too much to handle in her current state.

They'll think I've been abducted or something. Just get outside...

Looking out of the window, she could see the runway. This was an airport hotel; Heathrow for sure. The Hilton over at Terminal 4. With a bit of luck, she wasn't going to be late. The best she could hope for now was to look tidy enough for the taxi driver to not drive off without her, and then apply in transit whatever concealer had survived her 'dropping bag' moment before.

There was no time to think about what had happened last night. It was the day ahead that mattered. And a meeting with Clarke. Her Boss.

Chapter 5

This was supposed to be a big day for her. Having completed her training on the Transatlantic beasts, things had been looking up and the performance review was supposed to be the confirmation Isla had been looking for that things were changing. While she was realistic as to what that meant, she was hopeful that her desire to get off the short European routes had been heard. She was desperate to see everywhere.

Isla had joined BA straight from college. Whilst unusual for a cabin crew role to be offered to somebody aged just eighteen, Isla had shown the maturity and focus needed for a career in the sky. Flying around Europe was her escape from a potential career administering the Caravan Park holidays that her mum had been selling for Haven her entire working life. Swerving that path was the primary motivation behind her choices for as long as she could remember.

As a kid, the furthest Isla had travelled was the annual family holiday in the Algarve. Her father spent the time talking sport to strangers in the pub, and her mum was permanently attached to the sun lounger on which she would lie for the duration of their holiday. Isla wanted to see more of the world than the tiny corner of British-occupied Spain and a career in the air was the best route to achieving her objective.

On the surface, her folks didn't seem to be happy people, but there was no doubting they were happy with each other. However, their life choices held no appeal for Isla. Despite their solid marriage, it lacked something more. Isla wanted diversity and excitement. The need for romance and energy meant she was going to get out of Hemel Hempstead – fast.

Like most of the staff, Isla was an infrequent visitor to the main BA building on the far side of the airport. Reviews and disciplinaries were the only reason you ever got hauled in to see Clarke.

And Isla knew all the rumours about her boss.

The dirty old dog

He'd had to take a ground-based job after his wife demanded he put the family first, stop doing whatever it was he did when he was away in far-flung places, and grew the hell up once they had started a family. Rumour had it he had women all over the world, and many a mile-high. But the choice between ditching the fun for the family had to be made and he was now a very well-behaved family man. But there was still a glint in the eye which Isla knew would follow her intensely around a room.

She knew he had taken a keen interest in her career, probably a bit more than the others who joined up at the same time. If she'd been around in his prime, Isla had no doubt that they would have had a different type of shared interest.

He's still gorgeous. Lucky wife, whoever she is!

But those days were gone and while they both had to retain a professional dance face during the tedium of these performance reviews, she had never been able to resist a bit of a flirt and he normally couldn't resist responding with a bit of charm.

Being liked seemed important to him. He was an old-fashioned player who still enjoyed the game vicariously through his charges. And ordinarily, in this type of meeting, Isla would have been very front foot and full of life, playing the role of a youthful enthusiast, hanging on his every word. But this morning, she was conscious that if Clarke got too close, he might smell through the perfumed disguise and not be so favourable towards what he found. The hangover had now kicked in and she was properly struggling; no amount of makeup and perfume could help her cover up the stain on her blouse, and she kept checking herself to make sure her tight jacket covered the offending blotch, the damning evidence that she'd not yet been home.

Please be quick!

"So, Isla, you've been scoring well and getting some nice comments about how well you're doing. It all seems to be working out pretty well."

She'd already stopped listening, her eyes drawn to the various pictures of Clarke and his family spread around the small office. She wondered whether one day she'd have a family of her own, forced to make the same decision Clarke had made years before. What had Mr Last Night's name been?

Michael, Mikey, Malcolm… no not Malcolm. I'd never shag a Malcolm! Definitely M something.

Isla chose to smile and nod. An acceptably polite response to most things, especially when you're not truly listening. It was just as well Clarke's face showed he'd had this conversation a thousand times and wasn't really listening either.

Matthew, Matty….

Isla sensed Clarke had drifted into his own world, but was not sure whether his gaze was on her, or if he'd rumbled her dishevelment beneath the veneer of jacket, makeup and perfume. She wasn't quite sure where he was staring but nervously pulled her jacket tighter as a matter of instinct.

Please don't ask me anything!

"So, what is it you want out of this review then Isla?"

Damn! Shit!

Isla could tell that her mouth was once again dry and reached forward to pour yet another glass of water. To the experienced eye, this was a tell-tale sign of a good night.

Stop drinking water. Don't lean too far forward or he'll see the stain. What was his name?

Isla took a moment. The answer was straightforward, but it was all about the delivery.

"I was wondering, Clarke, after a year of doing Europe, what's the chance of some long haul, please? I've done the training for the big ones, but I've not been East of Berlin and with all these new routes. I'd love to get assigned to somewhere different. Like Moscow? I know you're not supposed to request a route, but if there was any chance that I could, I'd like Russia as a starter. Please."

"Hold on, hold on, Isla. I've not asked you in here for you to tell me what routes you want to work. This isn't a democracy."

Isla was desperate to hide her disappointment. But once again she'd disengaged as her eyes continued to glance around the room. There was something strange about one of those family photos.

Max, Martin…. Definitely Maaaa something. What is it about that photo?

"Isla, you've certainly made your mark on the team."

Mark! I knew it was Mark!

There was now a smile on her face, and it was not about this meeting.

Making every effort to suppress the grin, Isla was finally pleased she'd remembered the name of her unexpected shag.

Mark. Mark. Oh Shit! That's him!

"Is that your kids in the photo, Clarke?"

"Yes, my youngest is now nine, but can you believe Mark is now sixteen?"

Sixteen! Six-fucking-teen! How the fuck did I end up with a sixteen-year-old? Oh my God, I've shagged my boss's son!

"I'll tell you about the family another time if you want. But I need to crack on today."

Phew – I think I know a little too much about young Mark already!

Clarke resumed his management pose, eager to get on with things. Pride in his family was evident, but a chat about the kids was the last thing either of them wanted today. He was in charge.

"Isla, I'm going to offer you what everyone wants. You've done well and people like you. Your performance merits a promotion and as your training is complete…"

He paused; Isla was aware this was a Clarke trick, designed to assert his position of power by drip-feeding this news. She didn't have the energy to play games today.

"How do you fancy the East Coast?"

"The East Coast of where?"

"What's wrong with you today, Isla? The US. Boston, Washington, down to Florida. And of course, New York?"

All thought of last night was temporarily forgotten. She let out a squeal of excitement. In post for a year, she was one of the youngest cabin crew in the company and had been given the routes that everybody wanted. These routes were well-trodden and the schedule predictable; a day flight to the US, then some downtime to play. It was supported by a healthy daily allowance before the simplicity of a night flight back. Occasionally, you got the one-day turnaround, but that was no hardship. She couldn't wait to tell her parents.

"Thank you, Clarke! Thank you."

She cast an eye towards the photo once again, the memory of last night already fading with this unexpected good news.

Skipping towards the door, humming the Sinatra classic, Isla realised she had no idea what happened next.

"When does this start, Clarke?"

"I'm glad you asked. We've had someone pull out of the flight tomorrow. It's a two-night layover, which has cocked up everything. We will cover your Milan trip leaving you free for New York. Sound do-able?"

"Yes, yes, of course."

"Oh, and Isla?" She stopped at the door to look back at him. "Do yourself a favour and get some clean clothes before you come here again. You look a bit like my boy after he's been out all night."

Isla had thought she'd got away with it. And although he'd rumbled part of her story, she had stumbled through without damage.

Start spreading the news.

Chapter 6

Having spent more than six years working his way up, Ste had few regrets about the state of his life. But being based in London whilst travelling all over the country in the back of a van for half of each year, he hadn't been able to lay down many personal roots in the city, or anywhere else. Superficially comfortable that he had few non-work relationships, on the few nights he had off work, he would sometimes feel that there was something missing.

Work was all-consuming. There was always a gig to go to. He lived a stone's throw from every serious venue in the city of nine million people. Every night was an opportunity to see a new band, and there was always a chance it could lead to the next greatest thing, although Ste was realistic enough to know it probably wouldn't be. Aside from the bands, there was always a drink to be had with somebody, somewhere, and when there was no work, there was a girl to entertain. There were so many girls to be had. They swirled through his life in a haze of blonde, brunette and fiery red sex. But when the music stopped and the good times faded, the sound of silence was not a comfort, and the darkness that enveloped his flat when the lights went out was as metaphorical as it was literal. He felt no pressure to change anything, but something would eventually have to give.

Life was straightforward. Ste loved the flat he rented above the Cuban Restaurant just across from Islington Green. It was convenient for his needs with the bonus of being at a distance he could frisbee an unsigned seven inch away from Reckless Records from which Ste would support his vinyl habit by exchanging the '*Not for resale. Promotional copy only*' music he'd legitimately pilfered from the office for the classic rarities that thrilled him. Finding Roy Harper's *Commercial Breaks* white label for twenty quid, given that it was never officially released in original format and worth fifty times that, was the most blessed of days. And coming across the original pressings of *Please, Please Me*, Floyd's seminal '*Dark Side of the Moon*' and rare pieces of Bowie vinyl were prizes now displayed on the walls of the flat he called home.

Most of the time he was not alone and didn't think beyond his world of music. His latest band were killing it. The Cormacks were all over the scene. They were a fucking good band, his best band so far, who blew him away on the first listen. There was no need to babysit them. They knew what they wanted and, unlike many other bands that had been in his charge, they had the discipline to achieve success. With his help, they were on the cusp of their move into the big time after dancing around the edges for much of the last year. Some of the embryonic music websites, as well as the established magazine press like Mark Ellen's 'Q', had picked up on the Cormackian vibe.

And he'd just got the news. He was off to New York. It was happening.

Chapter 7

They weren't going on tour yet. This was a pre-cursor to a tour with Ste setting up the appearances to publicise the album and test the water for something in the following Spring. Perhaps a support slot for one of the larger American acts, or, just maybe, a headline tour on the circuit the British bands used as their launch into continental America.

He had developed contacts with the 9.30 Club in Washington and Hammerstein Ballroom in New York as well as all the famous East Coast venues that could pave the way for a trip West or branching North into Canada. But it took work. North American audiences were not going to rock up because a band from England were touring. They had to be teased into the idea that if they didn't get in on this early, they were going to miss out on seeing something at its birth. Americans don't like to be outboasted, and the tactic was to make sure they believed they'd be forever kicking themselves if they weren't at the first Cormacks tour of North America. Ste's idea was the company marketing line. Imagine being in LA and not seeing The Doors at the Whiskey-A-Go-Go. If Floyd, The Stones or Van Morrison played your town and you weren't there, you'd spend the rest of your life listening to your friends relaying their anecdotes about those moments in local history. Just like when Zep played Kimbells back in '69.

The strategy was simple and hardly unique; tactically identical to the one Ste had been successfully using for years with his new bands back in England. He just re-badged it into American marketing language. In these early days of the internet, Ste was in his element and ahead of the competition. He was young enough not to be befuddled by the age-old strategies employed by his experienced bosses and Ste embraced the cutting edge feel of new-age technology. He moved the traditional mailing lists from the letterbox to inboxes, saving the company a fortune and realising the rewards that closer proximity between band and fan could deliver. He had quickly jumped onto the E-bus and engaged with his 'E-nabled' audience that all had either Hotmail or Yahoo accounts, giving Ste the quickest access to them all.

And the music was good enough. The hype in the UK was founded on a great first album and their tight live act, captured on an EP from the Borderline. '*Finding the Crack*' notched well enough for a debut album, spending five weeks in the Top 10. It was only kept off the top slots by the respectable competition from Suede, REM and Kula Shaker. The media streams were promoting the four lads from Dublin, with a sound that conjured up U2—before Bono turned all wanky. It melded with a Celtic intensity and musicianship that bands like The Levellers showed off nightly in sweaty venues across Britain.

Ste was smug about the way he developed the band. His band. He had found them gigging at a near-empty Mean Fiddler eighteen months before, but he made them smarter, tighter and more confident by arranging an intense tour of English venues, playing initially to small, unfamiliar audiences. They had to learn how to handle playing to strangers, learning to successfully deal with the sort of issues that had blighted that awful Portsmouth gig in front of Tina seven long years before. Being on the road gave them the chance to get the songs, the show, and the package right.

And now America called.

Although she was pleased for him that things were moving in the right direction, Tina only agreed to the trip after Ste agreed to a clear outline of what was expected.

"You know you get one shot at this."

"I do, and I won't let you down, Tina. And more importantly, I won't let the band down."

"More importantly? Really."

Tina was expressionless, allowing him his moment.

"You've already given me the contacts and I'm going to show you what I can do."

Smart lad thought Tina. He had played this well, showing deference but confidence. And he had the band at the centre of what he was doing. He gave a shit about people, unlike many of the others she employed in whom she had no faith. Tina remained impressed with Ste; she had been from their earliest conversations that had ended up with her attending that wretched gig.

"More importantly, I won't let the band down. They're doing their bit, and this is where I earn my money. I've been right about them so far and it's paid off. And thank you for everything you've done. Even when you have openly doubted me, you've still trusted me to get it right. If you think I'm gonna be out of my depth or missing opportunities, don't worry - I'll phone you every day to check in and bring you up to speed."

He looked at his boss for a sign of assurance, but Tina remained expressionless, allowing him his moment.

"Make sure you meet with Jarrod straight away. He's a good man and your first priority. I appointed him myself so play nicely. Now, enough of this chit chat. To the pub! We should celebrate."

There were no more words to write and no calls to make. Ste had earned this and The Cormacks were in a good place within a year of joining their company. The new band of brothers was ready.

Before he left the office, he called Ben, just to let his oldest friend know his news as he always did. After the band split, things went off the rails between them with unfounded suggestions that Ste had stitched the band up by going with Tina on his own. But time had mellowed them both out and they were as close as ever. Ben had been re-incarnated as Mr Chips. His days of dreaming about playing a double-fretted Gibson at Madison Square Garden in the style of Jimmy Page were long gone. Now, he spent his life functioning as a tireless devotee to the boys at one of the finer public schools in England, although a guitar was never too far away.

Typically, he reached Ben's voicemail and left a message. He checked his watch and realised his friend, the responsible English teacher and Deputy House Master for the offspring of the exceptionally well heeled, was probably supervising something dull like Fourth Form Prep. It was a world away from this life where the pub was calling.

Chapter 8

The office emptied into the busy early evening traffic jamming the Charing Cross Road. Ste glided through the mass of people struggling to get home, before slipping into The Pillars of Hercules where his colleagues were gathered. Their local was full of Old London character—and always the same characters. It was an out-of-the-way place the tourists wouldn't just stumble into; you had to intend to end up there and even the regulars could easily miss this old watering hole, hidden between the Borderline on Manette St and the western edge of Soho. At the business end of the working day, the real work took over when the liquid flowed. Nobody he knew had any money, but being knackered and poor was the life you signed up to if you wanted the success that could come at the end of it all.

For everyone in this industry, life was an endless round of socialising, small talk, big talk and getting hammered with people you didn't always want to meet again. It wasn't a hard life, but tonight it felt like this was taking one too many for the team. Ste just wanted to go home and reflect, plan and sleep. His colleagues would push on late into the night, again; but they weren't going to America. He was.

He stayed for a couple before making his excuses and jumping on the bus to Islington. He was home by nine and with no reason not to, he gave Greta a call. She lived up the road and they had hooked up a few times. She was okay company, but the best thing about Greta was that she never expected to stay over. He wasn't good at asking somebody to leave before sleep time and was even worse at sharing his bed all night. Greta appeared at the door thirty minutes later with Chicken Shish and they sat on his roof terrace eating the food and listening to London go through its nightly wind-down routine, accompanied by Astral Weeks.

The CD was still playing when Greta woke up. Like Ste, she too had drifted off and quickly skulked away leaving him to sleep in the warm night air. Shortly before 2 am, Ste shivered awake as the cold of a late summer's night won the battle over the lingering heat of the day. Looking around the rooftop and then the flat, he was relieved that Greta had predictably wandered home. Not for the first time, he wondered why he'd wasted another evening with her. On the surface, she was interesting enough; but when they were together, they barely spoke. This was not what he was looking for. While he was in no rush to find loves' young dream, this was as far from that as Ste could contemplate. They were young, but there was nothing dreamy about their unions.

London attracted a lot of lonely people, and while many found love and happiness, London was no panacea for the loneliness that gripped them. This evening was enough for him to decide that Greta wasn't the one. He saw no point in seeing her again.

Chapter 9

Isla felt different about heading to work. While there was no change to the routine which she had grown used to, this morning, Isla could feel there had been a significant change in the way she viewed her place in the world. She felt more grown-up than before her last trip, and having moved up the pecking order, the enthusiasm Isla felt for her job had put her on the brink of combustion. She would be lying if she said that the time she had spent with her parents the previous day had not been a chance to show off just a little. Despite being horribly hung over and tired from whatever exertions she'd got up to with 'the kid', she'd been able to suitably impress her parents with talk of her promotion, so much so that her mum called her sister way over the border in Bedfordshire, before Isla left them to another evening in front of the telly, Her dad focused on whether Ken Furphy, the former Watford Manager, was worth looking up.

"Who's that, Dad?" Isla tried to show an interest. But she hadn't a clue what the point of the conversation was.

"Ken. Ken Furphy. You know, the old manager? Semi-Final Ken. I told you about him. He went to New York in the seventies. Something to do with Pele and the Cosmos."

Her dad's renewed interest in Watford had come about with Graham Taylor re-taking charge of the club she supported her dad in supporting. The Hornets were making a recovery from the ten lean years that had followed the ten fat ones. He'd been going more as a way of re-creating his youth of twenty years before, co-incidentally the last time Taylor managed the club.

Despite their kind words and enthusiasm, Isla didn't feel that her parents understood what made her tick. And she wasn't going to explain it. Her motivation to get away from the insular world of Hemel hadn't wavered. However, it would be cruel to hammer it home to them as her parents were content with their lives. She was just frustrated that her relationship with them wasn't closer, but raw honesty wouldn't be helpful. They continued to perform the time-honoured dance between parents and child.

Isla took a moment to really look around before the plane doors opened. She was already a mess of bundled-up excitement, but she soon relaxed into the job as the first passengers filed onboard. Different plane, different route, but the role still meant babysitting people. One man did stand out though, catching Isla's attention as he bounded towards the back of the aircraft, before taking his seat next to the window, making no attempt to hide that he was a people-watcher. She liked the look of him. He was tall and athletic but in a way that suggested it was natural as opposed to gym induced. He was like a younger incarnation of Clarke, but with less attention to his hair.

Isla was a gym dodger, holding onto an unwavering dislike of the men regimented into their world of strict gym routines. They would often adopt an almost evangelical posture about the lifestyle; endlessly going on about the benefits of protein diets, which made non-believers always feel shit about their own fitness efforts. The irony was that many of them were full of steroids and coke. But this bloke didn't look the sort, and he had a lovely scent. That was something that mattered in a big tin full of sweaty people. He looked maybe five years older than her, too young for transatlantic business travel, but the smart/casual jacket and jeans combo seemed too high brow for a holiday. Her ability to read a traveller based on clothing may need some refinement on these longer flights.

"Excuse me, Miss?"

Her dreamlike state was interrupted by a large American woman who was pulling on Isla's arm to get her attention. She was already talking before Isla had had the chance to acknowledge her and Isla realised this was her first encounter with an OAT – 'Obese American Traveller', legendary on these US routes.

"Excuse me, Miss. What time will the food be served?"

She had been warned about the OATs.

America – Land of the Free to grow as large as you fucking want.

"Good morning, Madam; welcome on board. We will be bringing the first round of food after the drinks have been served. But nothing will happen until we've taken off."

"When will that be?"

If you sit down and shut up, it will be far sooner

"It depends on the captain and the weather, Madam, but in about an hour. The safety of our passengers and crew has to be our priority."

Isla had learnt the required response to this line of questioning early on in her career. It was far simpler to play the safety card than try and explain that the food would be out when it was out. And no amount of badgering from a rude fatty would make a difference to the Captain's directive on when that would be. There was no please or small talk from this lady; just the first of a long line of rude OATs enquiring and then demanding to know about their food and drink.

"I have to eat before my medication, and I have to take my medication in an hour. I need a sandwich brought to me now."

"If you're unwell, Madam, are you fit to fly?"

Isla could sniff this ruse. Nobody gets on a plane under medical direction without making suitable contingency plans around food. This was a well-employed trick to get her food prioritised and was part of the Day 1 scenario training on 'How to deal with difficult customers'. Isla's advantage was that they were still on the ground.

The threat of an enquiry into a passenger's health when offloading was still an option was enough for a swift compromise to be reached. Isla kindly produced the snack packet of biscuits which she'd snaffled away for herself, and there followed a nod of mutual agreement that this would do. So far, so good. Happy with the opening minutes of her new transatlantic career, Isla took her seat ready for new adventures in New York. Five minutes later, they were airborne, Isla making a mental note to talk to the fit bloke with the nice smell who was already drifting in and out of sleep. But aside from a large G&T and a tray of airline gruel, their interaction was regrettably non-existent, and, after the most uneventful first flight to the US as was possible, Isla could only hope that the destination was more interesting than the journey.

Chapter 10

It took until the wheels thudded onto the tarmac at JFK that Ste started properly thinking about the week ahead. He'd had a hectic itinerary drawn up by Tina, repeatedly assured that working with the US was no different to the UK. Most things in the music business are done at night wherever you are; but this time, the jetlag would render him useless on the evening of the first full day. He needed to stay awake as late as possible to avoid suffering the consequences of being up before 5am tomorrow morning, giving him a fighting chance of making the evening.

This meant he was in no rush to get into Manhattan, which was just as well, as the long queue that snaked back from the immigration desks was like nothing Ste had experienced before. Even the toughest European queues were nothing more than twenty minutes of slow-moving human traffic. But as twenty turned to thirty, and the half-hour became more than an hour, his excitement turned to irritation. The queue didn't ever seem to move and with the intimidating eyes of the security people and the multitude of cameras fixed on everyone, the hour and a half spent in the queue was one of the longest periods of Ste's short life.

By the time this virgin entrant to America had reached the processing desk, few people from his flight were behind him. He had seen his cabin crew pass through about an hour before. This was a real anti-climax.

"Good afternoon, Sir. What is the purpose of your visit to America?"

"I'm representing a band and we are setting up a tour over here."

Ste was unprepared for the questioning and unsure what to do with the declaration form he had been nursing for the last hour. The heavily built official looked up. The answer had set off something in the officer which made him uneasy. Little did Ste know that he was about to get played with. He was clearly no threat to national security, but as Ste started to panic at having said something that had suddenly made him a person of interest, he noted what he thought was the slightest sign of a smile.

"A band, you say. Aren't there American people already in the United States of America who do that sort of thing? Why is it necessary for you to come here and do a job an American could do, Sonny? Are you trying to put us out of work?"

Ste stammered a few words, but nothing coherent came out. He hadn't been warned that the trickiest part of the business trip to the US would be his entry into the place.

"I'm the band's representative. We can't appoint an American to represent the band until the American agents know there is a band to represent. And if I don't represent them, how will The Cormacks get the exposure in the US to become one of the biggest bands in the world?" Ste hastily rolled into a soliloquy to the amusement of the border guard.

From the broad smile on his face, the official knew he had won this one. He always won.

"Mr Lewis, I'm messing with you, Sir. Welcome to America. And good luck; you'll need it."

The guard chuckled once more, before stamping the passport whilst offering a knowing wink. Ste was finally allowed in for a whole month.

Wanker

Collecting his luggage which was still doing the lonely circular tour of the carousel, Ste strode through the sliding doors which signified the barrier between No Man's Land and American soil. It should have felt more symbolic, but as with much of the day, it was yet another anti-climax.

At least the queue for one of the yellow New York taxis moved quickly. The drivers were controlled through a series of whistles and hand signals, reminding him of the sheep dog trials which the BBC passed off as family entertainment back in the '80s. This was the sort of bustle he was expecting, and he excitedly jumped into the next vehicle telling the driver to head for 'The Hilton on Sixth Avenue'. This was the standard hotel all his colleagues used, booked for him by the agency mainly because of the benefits of patronising one chain which rewarded people like him with ever so minimal travel privileges.

"Que?"

"Hilton. Sixth Avenue, please," Ste repeated.

"Manhattan?"

"New York!"

"Que?"

What was this shit? Is Manhattan somewhere different to New York? And what's with all the Spanish?

Ste started to panic, ignorant of the local geography and suddenly very concerned that this was one of Tina's tricks. Perhaps there was no Sixth Avenue or Hilton Hotel? Ste passed a piece of paper with the hotel details through the plastic divide. Finally, some positive acknowledgement from the Hispanic driver, who passed the paper back before repeatedly nodding his acknowledgement of the destination. The driver was no longer fearful that he would lose the fare. As the car started its crawl towards the city, Ste slouched back into the grubby back seat, finally relaxing just enough to take in his first view of the America he intended to conquer.

Ahead of him, Ste recognised the towering sights of what he now knew was Manhattan, fixating on the numerous world-famous landmarks outside the car window. After emerging from the depths of the Queens Tunnel, he felt an immediate change in atmosphere. Now on Manhattan Island, the slow-moving procession of traffic was even more stop-start than the road in from JFK; a constant battle through the jaywalking pedestrians and flashing lights all set to a soundtrack of irritated car horns. It was as if he were a competitor in a loud, lifelike game of *Frogger*.

The driver snaked along thirty-seventh street, all the way to sixth and fifty-third, where a brick canopy hung over the Hotel's drop off zone. Ste had arrived later than he'd expected to, but there was still daylight and, in a city new to him, there was lots to do. Before he'd paid for the ride, he was pounced on by the hotel staff with offers to carry his bags. Wherever he was visiting, he hated this part of travel. Just because he wasn't on his own patch, he didn't suddenly lose the ability to open his own door, carry his own bags, press the button on the lift or find the way to his room.

Thanking the bellboy for his time, Ste moved through the revolving glass door into the well-lit foyer and to the check-in desks manned by the United Nations of eager receptionists, keen to meet his gaze.

"Good evening, Sir. Welcome to the New York Hilton Midtown. How can I help you?"

As Ste turned and looked around to confirm he was the intended recipient of this mouthful of salutation, he noticed a pretty young woman sitting on one of the heavy foyer chairs. She was clearly watching him, and, on catching his eye, waved the tiniest of acknowledgements in his direction. Urgently wracking his memory for who it could be, Ste couldn't place her. He met hundreds of people, often after a few drinks. But here, in New York? He had no idea who it was or why she was paying him attention.

After checking in, he noticed that the lady, whoever she was, was still looking at him. It would bug him all evening unless he found out why this stranger was waving to him. He would have to find out.

"Hi there! I'm so sorry, I haven't got my best head on and am a touch disorientated. Do we know each other?"

"Well, not exactly. It's just that I served you on the flight earlier on." The lady, not much older than a girl, had started to blush. "Wow, this is embarrassing. I wasn't sure if you recognised me and it's clear… that you don't."

It was now Ste who was feeling the embarrassment. In his profession, it was important to never forget a face, but to be fair to him, their engagement had been hardly significant, and he'd been in and out of sleep for most of the journey.

"So, this is awkward," Isla joked. "Shall we just forget it happened?"

Not a chance! She's gorgeous!

"No! Not at all. I'm really sorry about being off the pace. I'm usually much more reliable. Have you been to New York much? I'm guessing cabin crew stick to the same routes, so you must come here all the time?"

"Nope! I've just moved off the European routes and this is my first time here. So…" the woman lowered her voice, looking all around her. "I've snuck away from the rest of the crew as I wanted to explore things for myself, if you know what I mean?"

"I love the sneaking off thing. I travel a lot too and can't tell you the number of times I've wanted to do the same. Seeing something for the first time without having a running commentary makes it a more personal experience. It's my first time here, too. I've just lost my US virginity."

"So, we're two virgins together then."

Excellent. Flirty and beautiful.

Both blushed a little as they looked down, then away before instinctively catching each other's eyes in their own.

"I expect your off-duty time is limited. What are you doing hanging around a hotel lobby talking to the likes of me, when this city is waiting out there for you?"

"Well, it was you who approached me!" Isla quickly replied.

They both laughed, already having hit their strides.

"One of the reception staff is bringing me a discount card for an Italian place in Greenwich Village. He mentioned his cousin. Every hotel receptionist has a cousin who can help with something."

"Well, I'm pleased to have interrupted your wait. My name is Stephen, but everyone calls me Ste."

"Isla. Pleased to meet you, again. Does the first-time count?"

"Who cares? We've met now. Aren't you tired? I slept on the plane, but you've been working since God knows when."

"I'm young, free and single and in one of the world's great cities. I'm going to explore until I drop and that may or may not be in this building."

Ask her out. Ask her out.

Ste took the plunge. There was nothing to lose.

"You, err, you want some company? I don't mean to impose, but I'm about to do the same. Just without the discount card."

Isla's face lit up. Nice smell man had displayed an interest. There was no awkwardness in the conversation. This could be fun.

"Yes, I do. I'd like that."

"Great. Hold tight and let me dump my bags. Count to a hundred and I'll be back down."

Suddenly excited at the prospect of the evening ahead, Ste raced away having made a beautiful new friend with whom to explore this fantastic city. Bring it on.

Chapter 11

As a result of his expected upgrade, Ste had a room with views across the whole of South Manhattan; but his interest in looking out over the city had been significantly reduced after meeting Isla. He tingled with excitement at the evening ahead.

Although he'd recently seen Greta on a couple of occasions, theirs was not an association based on either stimulating conversation or emotional togetherness. Theirs was a strictly nocturnal friendship. Most of his friendships were through work, inevitably leading to endless shop talk instead of meaningful, personal conversations, typical amongst groups of real friends. The few lifelong mates with whom he still had contact all had less in common with each other as every year passed. Their rare drunken socialising was always the same. Predictable conversations that focused on their collective histories whilst getting quizzed about his job. He desperately tried to ask interesting questions and start proper conversations about his friends' lives, but they were all ploughing the same tedious pre-ordained paths, and the conversations would always return quickly to where they started. Ste missed the days when his friends could all talk as equals, having real conversations about their futures. The evening ahead could be the start of a friendship that could fill a gap. And the fact that she was gorgeous didn't hurt in the slightest.

He didn't want to screw this up before he'd had a proper look, so rather than risk her drifting into New York alone, he dumped his bags, threw some water on his face, and administered a couple of squirts from the travel-sized bottle of cologne onto his neck, before hastily rushing back to his new friend.

As he approached her, he had already started talking about the evening ahead. Isla swung round mouthing something Ste couldn't quite make out. She wasn't alone. There was a bloke next to her.

Bugger!

Isla fumbled around in her pocket, producing the discount card for the restaurant.

"I've got it."

Ste instantly remembered why she'd been waiting there. The guy next to her stood up without hesitation, snapping the card from her fingers with a confidence that suggested he was the Alpha of the pair. Ste vaguely recognised him from the plane. But the intensity of his stare was beginning to invade his already tired senses, and as soon as he started talking, Ste was immediately exhausted by him.

"Yes, this is a good one, Isla. I've been there. Shall we all go there together? I know a great bar around the corner on Bleeker Street which I've been meaning to revisit. Shall we spend this evening together? Can we?" The bloke didn't take a breath.

What the hell is this?

This was a call only Isla could make. It was her first trip with her new colleagues and there was now a real sense of awkwardness, as Isla evidently didn't want to put a wedge between her and the Alpha male who now lurched over her. With panicked eyes, she discreetly looked at Ste for an indication of his preference, but there was nothing in his face to help her. Ste had learnt to master giving nothing away, and in this instance, he was nervous about stepping into an unfamiliar world. Nevertheless, Isla needed his help, so, moving forward, he introduced himself to a stranger from British Airways for the second time in ten minutes, firmly shaking the limp hand of the man who loudly introduced himself as Jeremy.

"Thank you for asking me along. I'd be delighted to join you both. I'm not meeting my colleagues until first thing tomorrow, so I think I can find the energy for a meal."

Jeremy led the way with flamboyant, camp gestures before telling a half-arsed story about passing through the revolving doors alongside somebody connected to the theatre. As stories went, it was unimpressive.

Jumping into a cab at the rank, the driver wound through the neighbouring streets, before running alongside the Hudson and throwing a left towards 'The Village'. Jeremy was a veteran of the city, jabbering on incessantly about its more liberal night spots while Isla and Ste gawped at the size of the buildings looming above them. They were like ants in the land of the dinosaurs in this new land which they were both seeing for the first time. Ste was surprised that the steam rising all around them, emerging from the earth through the drains, was an actual thing and not just something TV shows like Taxi had invented. Seeing was truly believing.

"Stop here," yelped Jeremy, who, without taking a breath, had talked about himself since the cab left the hotel rank. "Please stop, driver." He was now begging, with a gaze fixed firmly on the two muscle men about to disappear down some nearby steps underneath a set of rainbow lights.

"Can we go in there, just for a snifter? It's fabulous and you won't be disappointed."

Isla and Ste shared a look. This could be their chance to get rid of him.

Jeremy thrust a ten-dollar note through the grate before darting towards the bar. While Ste and Isla were still getting out of the taxi, Jeremy had already danced past the bouncer and was now inside.

"I guess he wasn't really asking," Ste quipped.

"I'm sorry, Ste. I only met him for the first time on the flight out here and didn't know how to tell him to fuck off without it being career-limiting. Please promise me that my first evening in New York isn't going to be in a gay bar with British Airways' most annoying member of staff?!"

They agreed to go in for one and see what happened. However bad the techno sounds coming from the inside were, how crap could one drink be?

"ID, please." The doorman didn't look up.

They showed their passports before moving forward, a route that was blocked by the leather-clad arm of the bouncer who reached across the steps. He fixed his gaze on Isla.

"Miss. This is America. You can't come in here for another two years, but in 1999 you'd be most welcome to come back and join us. Sir, you are welcome to go in. You will be a very popular patron."

It hadn't occurred to Isla that she was not allowed to drink in New York until she was twenty-one, two years away. With the speed of her move onto the Transatlantic fleet, she'd not given it a moment's thought. Ste laughed at the inadvertent save. They could now ditch Jeremy and get back to Plan A without regret. Ste nipped in, just to be polite at letting

Jeremy know what had happened. He was quickly waved away, Jeremy being already occupied in flirtatious conversation with somebody more suited to his desires.

Ste and Isla were now on their own.

Chapter 12

According to the card, the restaurant was an old school Italian Pizzeria. Arturo's had been open for forty years which seemed to be cause for celebration in this city; the equivalent of somewhere in London having a history traceable back to the time of King James. As they walked close together through the warm, late summer evening, a shyness had descended between them. However, the silence gave them the opportunity to look some more at the vast city, allowing them to be really present in the chaos of the global smells and cultures.

The overpowering aromas coming from the food carts positioned on every corner were complimented by people who talked in more dialects than Ste could count. They could have been anywhere in the world. A man was ordering Falafel in Arabic next to a Burrito van with signs all written in Spanish.

Ste broke the silence. "So, tell me about you then, Isla…."

"What's to tell? I can guarantee you'd have no interest in hearing about growing up in Hemel Hempstead. What is it you want to know? Oh, and I counted to a hundred while I waited for you to dump your bags. You're not as quick as you think."

"Speed isn't everything, Isla, but nevertheless, I'm sorry for the misjudgement and resulting delay."

The shyness had not lasted long.

"But you're right. I've no interest in Hertfordshire except when I go there for work. Do you know the Pavilion in Hemel? I put on a gig there recently. Have you been?"

"Dacorum Pavilion. Of course, I've been. What else do you think there is to do in Hemel, aside from taking the train to somewhere better?"

Isla explained why she'd always wanted to get out as soon as the chance presented itself, not admitting that she still lived there. They chatted about her and the few real-life experiences she'd had, and before too long, the lively streets suddenly exploded into the West Village, and Bleeker Street, the epicentre of Greenwich Village. This was the New York Ste had been itching to feel, home to the infamous venues which formed many of his most evocative second-hand memories. The days of Joni Mitchell rocking up and doing an unannounced set were long gone, but the spirit of those days smothered these streets, even if the venues were now increasingly marketed towards the tourist trade. Live music was still everywhere, and as they passed the infamous Kenny's Castaways, Isla interrupted the silence. She was aware that Ste had drifted into the immersive atmosphere of the street.

"Ste, I don't mind if you'd prefer to do something else on your own. I know you're here for music and I can go off and do something myself if you'd rather." There was a tinge of regret in Isla's voice. But her offer was genuine.

She's surely joking. As if I want to give up on this already!

"Well, that's a kind offer, Isla, but really, there's no need at all. It's good to be out with someone who's neither trying to sell me a vision nor get me to do something for them. I've all week to talk shop. And the week after that. We've got tonight and I'm far hungrier than any need I have for a music fix. The food on your plane was crap."

"So, let's stick with Plan A and eat at the Italian. Come on, then, if you're hungry."

They were walking close enough that their hands could touch. They were only a few yards from the restaurant and Ste wished that it was further, enjoying the walk and sporadic chatter the two of them were sharing. Going out for a posh dinner wasn't something Ste generally did. At his age, most of his friends saw eating as cheating, choosing to save their money for booze. Sit down meals were something he did for work. This chatting was nice though. Quite a different evening to the one he had been expecting.

There was a long queue outside the restaurant and if pressed, he would have said that he didn't want to join it. They could carry on walking and maybe he'd get to hold her hand. And maybe more.

But they didn't discuss not stopping; and under the watchful gaze of the

Basilica opposite, they instinctively joined the back of the queue. Ste filled in some of the gaps in his story, while Isla delved into her fear of being stuck working for the Haven Holiday company in Hemel Hempstead. She almost spat out the alliteration

"Haven Holiday Hemel Hempstead"

and Ste wasn't sure if there was humour intended, but Isla seemed happy being able to offload her angst into the evening air.

The sound of a piano drifted through the door. The evocative tinkering of Little Italy now accompanied each of the conversations throughout the queue.

Despite their fears, they were soon seated inside, and the immediate request for their drinks order suggested the restaurant would be conveniently oblivious to Isla's age. The walk and queuing had been worth it. Ste didn't want to drink alone, and even Isla was experienced enough to know that a proper Italian meal needed proper Italian wine.

"It's a good job I don't have an early start tomorrow," Ste murmured across the table as he polished off the first of many glasses of the house Chianti.

"Didn't you say something about a breakfast meeting?"

"That wasn't all bollocks. I was just laying my exit strategy from your mate. I've got a breakfast meeting, but it's not until later."

"You know he's no mate of mine. As it happens, Ste, I don't have to be anywhere for most of the next thirty-six hours." She felt like a kid who had bunked off school without any idea what she was going to do with the time.

The initial couple of drinks provoked a childlike silliness. They released their inner kid as they told each other things about their youth, like watching 'Why Don't You?' in the summer holidays.

"Surely," Isla interjected, "if you were to 'Switch off the TV and go do something less boring instead' there would be no one watching the show?"

Ste's humour was more adolescent, mimicking his mother's reaction to the dirty sheets that every teenage boy is accountable for.

The impression was good enough that Isla spat a mouthful of red wine across the table. She thought she'd won the battle to keep it in, but looking down at the table, she'd clearly failed, spraying the pressed white tablecloth with what used to be an appealing house wine. She was mortified. She'd blown red wine through her nose in front of somebody fanciable who she'd only just met.

"I am so sorry, Ste. It's so embarrassing. I'm not normally this classless!"

"Don't worry, Isla, that's the funniest thing I've seen in ages. Can you do it again?"

This was going very nicely indeed.

Chapter 13

Ignoring Isla's genuine attempts to pay her share, Ste settled the bill, totally forgetting Isla's discount card, before they walked out onto a much quieter West Houston Street. It was nearly eleven pm, and given the time change, their body clocks were screaming at them both that it was now four am.

"Cab or walk?" It was Isla who put the question.

"I think if I walk, I'll fall down and sleep somewhere before I make it back to the hotel. Do you mind a cab?"

"Oh, thank God. I can't walk another step but didn't want to look as though I was bailing. I'll pay for this."

"Lovely stuff. Taxi!" he hollered in the most American way he knew how.

The readiness of taxis meant they were in a car within moments. The streets were now full of a different type of person than the earlier stampede of tourists who had crowded the pavements during their walk through the city. They now had an owned feel, as New Yorkers reclaimed their patch for a few hours before it all started again. The rubbish needed to be cleared, the shops that served their neighbourhoods through the night re-stocked with supplies. New York was a place people typically went to have fun or conduct business. Ste had never given a thought to the people who made the city tick or to the doorways of despairing homeless, quietly napping before they were moved on or roughed up. While London had been bad a few years before, New York looked as if it was still losing its battle with despair.

Ste started to drift off. The cab made quick time, and the towering Hilton now leered over them. Isla paid the fare as her contribution to the expense of the evening, and with todays per diem safely stashed away, she promised Ste that next time it would all be on her.

"That's kind of you, Isla, but I get it all paid for when I'm on the road. And I don't get to keep what I don't spend."

"Well, we'd better do something when you're not on the road then. I've had a great night, Ste. You are lovely and I've enjoyed becoming your friend. I'm assuming we're friends, right?"

Ste felt that this had the legs to be a proper friendship, the sort where you could say what you want to.

"I don't want any more superficial shitty friendships, Isla. I've made enough of them through work. You know what I mean?"

"So, does that mean that you want to do something tomorrow night after work? Let me know if you want to. No pressure."

"I told you earlier, my life is good, and I've loved our evening together. So, can I be honest with you for a minute?"

Isla nodded, alerted that something was happening between them, right now.

"When I couldn't get to sleep the other night, I had no one on my mind; there was no one who I could call to talk shit to and that was okay. But if you want someone to talk shit to, as well as the meaningful stuff, then I'm your guy. And by the way, I'd love for you to take me out when we're back home. It will take some doing, given our schedules, but we'll sort it."

It was hardly a declaration of love, but it felt significant. They gave each other a hug. A long hug. Their collective affection was just as it seemed to be. They were two young people who were into each other. And for tonight, it was as friends.

"Isla." One of her colleagues was gesturing for her to join them in the bar.

"Night, Ste, I'd better say hello."

"Enjoy the Club Soda, Isla. You're only nineteen, remember."

Isla stuck her tongue out before joining the raucous cabin crew who seemed to be midway through a long session in the hotel bar.

Ste followed her as far as the sightlines allowed him to. Isla turned, just to check if he was still there. He winked back at her, unsure of everything other than the fact that he desperately needed to sleep.

Chapter 14

After a few hours' restless sleep, Ste was awake for the day at a regrettably early hour. It was only five am and he'd already been up for a half-hour. They'd been right about the jetlag. His body had not been consulted on the decision to go Transatlantic. But there was at least a decent coffee machine in the room, proper filter stuff, not the horrible Nescafe sachets he was used to in the hotels they used on tour in England. Even the Hiltons he stayed in served that instant dross and they were all missing a trick as this stuff was great. He flicked on the TV. Traffic News, onto Weather News, then more Traffic News. How much traffic was there to report at five in the morning? And had the weather forecast changed so much in the last ten minutes that they needed to go through it again? The broadcast was without any merit. The channel finally switched to some other content, largely of Bill Clinton waving before some depressing archive footage of Princess Diana who had suddenly died a few weeks before. Americans had wholeheartedly adopted the grief of the British in the absence of their own historical institution whose drama they could lament. The news reels continued to run footage of emotional New Yorkers reflecting on their own memories of somebody they had never met, and who knew nothing about her other than what they were fed by people with a news cycle to fill. Beyond that, there was no international news despite the US having active military engagements all over the world with the UN and NATO. There was nothing to educate or even inform America about what was going on in the world. The TV was a procession of mindlessness and Ste switched it off, training his mildly hungover stare out of the window, quietly absorbing the early autumn Manhattan morning.

With hours to kill before his meeting, he reviewed the weeks' plan of action. The first meeting was with Jarrod, the man on the ground in New York that Tina had told him to work with from the off. They were having breakfast in the Hilton's restaurant at eight-thirty. Looking at the detail within his diary, he cast a first glance over the arrangements for the meeting, and the sudden realisation that it was not scheduled to be at this Hilton, but at a completely different one, located miles away down near Wall Street.

Who sorted that out?

Looking out of the window once more, Ste now understood why there seemed to be travel updates on the TV every other minute. The streets had suddenly jammed with the delivery lorries that provided the fuel to feed and water the millions of New Yorkers, and the taxis and the limos which ferried the early risers to where they needed to be. Given his early rising, Ste could use the time to walk through his first New York morning rather than join the traffic or metro. It was a beautiful clear day; the sun was already in the sky and a warm breeze drifted up along the East Coast from the Caribbean. He showered and made himself presentable, before starting the four-mile walk to the sister Hilton at the foot of the island.

The smells of falafel and burrito from the night before were replaced with the morning vendors serving up egg-white omelettes and coffee, the fuel that would generate much of the manic energy that would quickly overtake the city's streets. At this time of the morning, the streets were comparatively sedate, a collection of regulars exchanging pleasantries with the same vendors five mornings a week in the way creatures of habit visit and then ponder around their favoured watering holes the world over.

But the streets were becoming more hectic by the minute. As he wandered South, his pathway through some of the world's most famous towers was hampered by the heightened need for awareness to avoid collision with fellow pedestrians, all of whom were trying their best to avoid the human traffic that seemed to follow no recognisable set of rules. This was in addition to the cyclists who viewed everybody else with spit-filled hatred. There was no time for anyone else's welfare, a far cry from the more relaxed walk of the previous evening. On these streets, it was clearly a game of survival of the fittest. New York continued its speedy migration into its daytime persona, but once beyond the Empire State Building, it seemed to ease off. Union Square Park had a much more relaxed feel before his path took him through the Village and up to the restaurant he'd enjoyed with Isla last night and with Ste now more comfortable with the route he was taking, he started to reflect on the night before. And Isla.

Although she was only nineteen years old, they had signed up to be friends. It had been a really fun evening. And not for the first time, Ste reminded himself just how gorgeous and funny he felt her, and how she was a huge case of 'Wow'.

But although nothing had happened between them, so much seemed to have happened. Caught in his own mind, he realised that he was looking the wrong way for oncoming traffic and stepped into the road. A loud beep woke Ste up and he jumped back onto the path before any harm was inflicted.

The walk down to Wall Street was accompanied by the street types, yelling into their phones, supported with body language suggesting importance at work. Ste quickly surmised that it also acted as a disguise for impotence at home. This was an ugly place. Not architecturally, just spiritually. It was Avalon for people who came from all over the world to work here—but these were not his people.

He hoped Jarrod was a good guy to work with, not like all these wankers. He'd been told that they had met once when he was over to meet Tina, but he couldn't remember him. Tina did not suffer fools. She'd told him Jarrod was one of 'them', and what Tina said, especially about things on this trip, was the Bible.

Chapter 15

Although it had taken well over an hour to walk to this meeting, he was still early. But Jarrod had already arrived and made an immediate beeline for him the moment Ste walked through the hotel's large revolving doors. The pair of them looked out of place, surrounded by hordes of average-looking businessmen in expensive dark suits, mostly sat alone engrossed in either the Wall Street Journal or their thoughts. The dull murmur hanging over the room was quickly interrupted by the energetic presence of the American heading towards the Brit.

"Hey, man, so good to see you again." Jarrod approached, arms out, bear-hugging Ste like an old friend who had come home after a long time away.

It was either a good act at remembering him, or Ste had forgotten more than he thought. Jarrod came across as sincere, despite being so very American in his OTT-ness for this time of the morning. They exchanged pleasantries and in doing so, Jarrod explained that he had arrived early as the ferries from Staten Island were running to time.

"So, remind me, why are we meeting here?"

"They told me you were staying here, at the Hilton."

"Right name, wrong place, mate. I'm up near Broadway."

Ste doubted the mistake, assuming Jarrod was playing a little game by arranging things to his own convenience to make sure he wasn't late for a meeting with Tina's envoy. Why risk the rush-hour New York traffic which crawled through the centre of Manhattan if you didn't have to? He had Jarrod's card already marked for any repeat in the future.

Having talked shop for what seemed like hours, the pair moved on to the arrangements for how the new band was going to be launched in the US. Ste outlined the plan as he understood it. First, they'd hit the big music cities in the North East, and then countrywide. Maybe by next Spring?

"Next Spring? No, not next Spring. This Autumn, Ste. As in 'Right Now'. Who said anything about Next Spring?"

What the fuck is going on?

"Wow, Jarrod. I assumed we were planning to do something, you know, down the line. I didn't think we'd execute it right away. The band aren't even here."

"Not here? They must be, my friend! I've lined up tons of press shit for next week. This was a pre-meet to getting on and doing this stuff. You're not in England now! Things are moving quickly, and you need to get them on the phone right now and get their arses to New York. Today."

What is happening? This isn't the plan!

The effects of last night's drinks were now kicking in, and Ste began to feel quite queasy. This was unexpected and he looked like an arse. Did Tina know about it? Who had put these plans in place and not told him, other than Jarrod?

He asked Jarrod if they could relocate to the office and quickly.

"Jarrod, I need to be sure before making these calls. Who came up with this plan?" Their cab crawled towards Midtown. Ste was unsure if he was being set up, had missed something, or if this was a giant cock up.

"I've sorted everything since you said you were coming out. The message I took from it was that the band were coming, too. You said 'We.' I thought I'd been clear about things, Ste."

"I always say 'we', even when I just mean 'me.' So, no. Not clear at all. This is an epic cock up."

Ste was pissed off and felt undermined by the misunderstanding. What a total fuck up. And he didn't trust Jarrod one bit.

Once at the office, he took a room for some privacy to make the calls. He rang Tina who was fast approaching the end of her workday in London.

"It's Ste. Did you know what Jarrod had planned out here for my bloody band?"

"What's up, Ste? A bit hectic for you out there?"

"No, it's not hectic, Tina. It's a cluster. It's frigging disrespectful. I thought *I* called the shots. Unless you told me something different, this trip was supposed to be about laying the foundations for something next year. I've been here five minutes and I'm told that everything is already arranged, and I now need to get my boys out here, today."

"Okay, Ste, you need to calm down. See this as an opportunity. In this game, you must be able to adapt and think on your feet. You're no good to me if you cave every time one of the pieces move."

"An opportunity. Really. An opportunity to fuck everything up, more like."

"Okay, Ste. I just told you to calm down. Now get a grip and call your band. If they can be out there ASAP, then great. Go with it. No harm done. If they can't, tell them they have to. And if they still can't, we will talk again."

"But what about my role. Am I in charge or not, Tina?"

"Ste, of course you are in charge. You're in charge until I tell you that you're not. So, I suggest you turn this opportunity into what it could be, rather than moan about something it is not. Are we clear, Stephen, or do I have to repeat myself?"

She never called him Stephen. No one at work called him Stephen. The conversation was over. At least these instructions were clear.

That's me told then.

The next call was to Seth, the frontman of the Cormacks and the go-to guy when there were discussions to be had. Seth was intelligent and fair, the one who made things function when they might go off track. For Ste, speaking to Seth was like talking into a mirror.

"You need us there now? Seriously? I know we have passports, but we'll need to sort the paperwork. I presume we'll be flown Business Class."

"Seth, simple question; can you get here or not? Tina will sort everything you need, so don't worry about the details. She has contacts for this stuff and as long as you can get here, we will do the rest. It's a fuck up by me. My fault. But I need your help. Can you just get the boys on a plane?"

Please, Please, Please, Please! And of course you'll fly Business Class!

It was easy convincing a group of single young men that they needed to fly Business Class to America within the next twenty-four hours and Seth quickly confirmed that they were good to go. Tomorrow, not today, but the first logistical hurdle was cleared.

It had been an unexpectedly hectic first day. Ste was wiped out by jetlag and noticed how quickly he was losing his adrenalin once he hung up his last call back to England. Familiar with the curse of jetlag, Jarrod proposed they wrap up and meet the next morning. It was going to be a busy few days.

"Get some sleep. You're going to need your strength with what we have lined up."

Ste groaned. So much for his introduction to America. The place was mental.

Chapter 16

Isla had slept for longer than she thought she would. Her colleague's warnings of jetlag and what normally happens on the first night of each trip to the East Coast really hadn't come true. Although she had woken up several times through the night, she'd quickly found a way for the dark lords of sleep to recapture her. And once finally awake, there were no signs that her body clock was kicking her from the inside out; she felt alive enough to figure out how to fill the coffee machine. Now, this was what transatlantic travel was about! The kind of ground coffee that she never got at her mum and dad's house.

It was already mid-morning and Isla felt a pang of regret at missing much of her only full day in New York, as well as the mild hangover that was a welcome reminder of last night. She wondered what a date looked like if it wasn't that. It could not have been more different to her most recent evening with a Man. Or, in this case, a boy.

What was I doing? He was 16 years old and my boss's son - Mike? Matt? Mark? That's it; Mark.

With Ste, there had been affection. A real connection. Not someone she wanted to creep away from without turning on the lights. Could this be something more than friends? Her male friends didn't bond with her in the way Ste had with her. Self-doubt was never far away.

What if he didn't see things the same way? Am I even his type?

Had she made a fool of herself? She wasn't very good at friendships. Growing up, friendships were thrown together through a combination of the geography of home and school and most of them died as quickly as they came. There were a few that outlasted change, but the mantra she had heard at school still proved to be true. *Friends for a reason, friends for a season, or friends for life.* Every friendship still seemed to fall into one of those three groups. Reasons and Seasons friends had come and gone, meaning she had little to fall back on when it came to what the last one felt like. Lucy was her closest thing to a lifelong friend, but while she stayed on at school for A' Levels, Isla went to college to do her B Tech over in Watford. And now, Lucy was at Uni in Birmingham, while Isla was here looking down on Sixth Avenue. Understandably, they were losing touch, and however much she knew there would always be a place in their hearts for each other, it was unlikely they would reconnect in the way they had done as kids growing up. Dinner in Arturo's in New York, or a pound a pint student club in the middle of Aston? She knew where she'd rather be and, as such, change in the dynamic was inevitable.

This thing with Ste could be the grown-up friendship she wanted. He didn't try to kiss her.

Don't all men try to kiss pretty girls? Does this mean I'm not pretty?

Isla hadn't been on a date with anybody who hadn't tried for a snog at the end of a great night since she hooked up with a kid from school called Mac, and he turned out to be into other boys.

Was Ste gay? Stop it, Isla; not every gay man was as camp as Jeremy.

Isla quickly consigned her questions and self-doubts to another time. She had one day in this huge city and rather than wasting the day thinking about the things she couldn't control right now, she nipped downstairs for the last embers of the breakfast buffet, putting some fruit and breakfast bars into her bag for later. She had no idea how much street food would cost in New York, but her frugal instincts reminded her that she could save her allowance by swiping from the buffet and save it for the excitement of the evening.

Isla was swamped by the crowds heading up to Central Park. She couldn't look upwards for fear of being knocked over or losing her footing. Her pity was mostly reserved for the ones heading against the tide; no one seemed to reserve their mercy for their fellow pedestrians. This reminded her of when she was ten and her mum took her to the Christmas sales on Oxford Street. It was memorable for its aggressive chaos. But this was a Monday morning in September and Isla was now all grown up and supposed to be physically capable of dealing with these things.

Somehow, she made it unscathed across the four slow-moving lanes of traffic circling the park. The 'Imagine' mosaic, known locally as Strawberry Fields, was first on the to-do list. She'd promised her dad a framed photo because he was a huge Beatles fan, especially in their early days when they made the stuff featured in the film *Backbeat*. Having got her dad the film on video as a Christmas present, it was the one thing they repeatedly watched together over several months.

Determined to fully embrace the role of bona fide tourist, Isla made for all the cheesy sights she could, walking around the park looking at the multitude of film locations and taking the accompanying snaps that her parents would recognise. The big locations from Ghostbusters, Home Alone and the one in When Harry Met Sally, filmed at the boathouse where Isla queued for a hot chocolate, nearly collapsing at the seven-dollar price tag. Free from any commitments, she took her time ambling around the vastness of the Park, but soon realised the day had almost gone and she'd seen nothing more than the place where some quirky characters had forever been frozen onto film. It would have been rude not to nip into FAO Schwarz on the park's southern edge to round it all off, seeing where the piano scene in BIG was filmed; but she wanted to see the New York not captured in cinematic history. Ambling around the grand buildings nearby, she saw the Gothic magnificence of St Patricks Cathedral and the Whispering Gallery in Grand Central. Here though, she wished she was not on her own. Everybody else she saw was part of the couple, kind of an important thing when wanting to whisper on one side of the archway for a loved one to hear the whisper on the other side.

I miss Ste.

Isla wondered if he had left her a message back at the hotel. Would she see him tonight? She was hungry and thought ahead to dinner plans. One of the park vendors convinced her she could not claim to have visited New York without eating a genuine New York hotdog, but that was hours ago and the fruit was long gone.

It was late afternoon; she had no idea who was around and whether there were any group plans for the evening. Isla would be returning on the first of the many evening flights out of JFK tomorrow, so would need to be well behaved this evening. In any case, she couldn't go to any bars. Her heart and mind were clear – she hoped Ste had left a message suggesting another evening out. Approaching the front desk in search of any messages for her, her heart sank when there was just one from her mum who had called to wish her well. Rather than appreciate the maternal gesture, it was the absence of any contact from Ste that she was focused on. Maybe she misread things and it was a one-night friendship. He may have assigned her to the category of a *friend for a reason*.

"Can I leave a message for my friend Ste Lewis? I don't know his room number, but if I write it down, can you give it to him, please?"

"Of course, Madam. I will make sure he knows there is a message for him." The desk clerk indicated that this was the most important thing he had been asked to do that day. Isla relaxed and wrote the note.

'Ste,'

One word in, and the self-doubt was back with her.

Do I write Dear, To, or just leave it at Ste?

Isla was already in a state.

How to not sound too keen? And how to end it? Love, From, or just See you, Isla?

Finally, she settled on some words that would just have to do.

Ste, Thanks for last night. Absolutely lovely time. Hope you're OK. Maybe you want to do something? Call my room if you get this and can still remember who I am.

See you. Isla

[no kiss]

The clerk took care to stow the message so that he had Isla's full confidence. His deliberate actions were clearly aimed at getting the expected tip, but Isla hadn't yet developed the trained eye and didn't twig the protocol.

Should I have put a kiss and started with "Dear"?

Having reached her room, she found that a note had been pushed under her door, giving a location and meeting time for her to join her colleagues for dinner. In the absence of a better offer within the next ninety minutes, it was off for another Hard Rock Café experience, a brand that was crap in every way except for their custom of discounting meals for cabin crew. It wasn't a bad perk if you liked the whole experience that went with heavy, well-cooked meat and an exhaustingly manic atmosphere. But was it too much to ask that BA develop some corporate alliances with places where she wanted to eat?

The fatigue from her jetlag, doubled by the frivolity of last night, all on top of the miles of walking around the city, had left Isla exhausted. She lay on her bed just for a moment; but predictably, she immediately dozed off, fully clothed with her trainers still stuck to her feet.

Chapter 17

She woke with a jolt. The phone by the bed was ringing. Even in her bleary state, Isla was hoping it was Ste asking her out for playtime. Where was tonight's adventure going to take them? She picked up without hesitation:

"Hello?"

"Isla, it's Jeremy here. Listen, you are coming, aren't you? We're going soon; just let me finish this drink; I've no idea what it is but it is a dream, and then off we go." In her post-nap grogginess, Isla struggled to follow his high-speed jabbering.

"Jeremy? Okay, hold on, I fell asleep. What did you say?"

"You did get my note though, right? You've got the time and place. We're leaving in ten. Meet you in reception. Bye!"

Jeremy seemed to be only interested in things that navigated towards him. And the 'e' of his "Bye" seemed to last forever, cutting through her semi-awake fuzz. He sounded pissed and much more manic than Isla remembered, which took some doing. The long day off must have already caught up with him. Or maybe he was still on the go from last night. Ten minutes was enough to get herself presentable; after a splash, brush, and a change out of the now crumpled clothes she'd been sleeping in, Isla readied herself for another stab at New York by night.

The lift door opened, and she caught sight of a familiar, albeit weary face across the lobby. Ste looked bedraggled and absolutely shattered. But to her delight, he'd clocked her already and was heading her way.

Yes – he doesn't hate me!

Their faces simultaneously lit up. But the moment of happy recognition was interrupted before a word had been exchanged, as a third, less welcome face imposed himself once again.

"Isla, over here. We're about to leave." Jeremy was waving like an excitable child at the funfair.

"Give me two minutes, please, Jeremy. Just two."

He turned on his heels, aggressively clenching his buttocks in a quiet hissy fit that suggested he was not best pleased with being kept waiting by the new girl. Isla was too irritated to care, and she was eager to speak to Ste.

"Hey, Isla. You're off out then? I guess I'm lucky to get a whole two minutes with someone in such demand! I guess that must mean I've missed out on you this evening?"

"Are you just getting back? That's a long day. Are you okay? You look like shit!"

"Cheers. I feel worse than I look. It's been odd. And the bad news is that our night out in England will not be for a while."

"Oh, why's that?"

"You remember my breakfast meeting? Well, my plans were changed in my first meeting of the whole trip. All plans, off. All new plans, made; mental. Any chance of me getting home anytime soon has now gone. My band will now be coming out sometime in the next two days and then we'll be going straight on the road."

"Until when?"

"You won't believe me, but the truth is…… Christmas! And my bloody visa only runs for a month. Christ, I hadn't even thought of that." Ste reached into his pocket and pulled out a piece of paper with many scribbles on it. Patting himself down for a pen, he found one and added another barely legible scrawl to his long list.

"That's nearly three months. Are you okay? What happens during that time?"

Isla smiled supportively and made the right noises, but she had no idea what he was going through. She could only hope their routes would collide somewhere on this side of the Atlantic so that they could meet up again. Ste was not the only one who could plan.

"Why are you smiling? I thought you wanted to meet up again?" he asked inquisitively.

"Of course, I do. And I'm so sorry things are mental for you. But remember,

Ste, I'm going to be working this route for ages. I'm sure between us we can sort something out."

Ste needed that. He was comforted by the idea that he wouldn't have to wait until Christmas to see her again. He hadn't called people at home to let them know he would not be back at the end of next week, but talking to Isla made it that much more real. He was glad it was her who he was talking to. Her kind, warm smile was what he needed at the end of this exhausting day. His scatty, over-tired brain wandered back to the fact he was underprepared for this evolving situation. He hadn't brought enough clothes to last more than a week, let alone twelve of them. A few nights worth of clothing for September in New York wouldn't be suitable for an October day in New Orleans, let alone Chicago in mid-December. He'd need clothing for all weather conditions. He made another note to the lengthening list on his piece of paper.

Clothing? What I am even thinking about clothing for?

Here was a gorgeous lady with whom he'd spent a terrific evening, and he was thinking about going shopping.

"I know Jeremy is pacing like a caged animal over there, but I've got enough energy in me for a drink, if you're free?"

Jeremy was now jumping up and down as if he needed an urgent wee. Isla knew she couldn't escape him for a second night.

"You know I have to do this with them. I wish I didn't, but if I don't, I'm likely to get a reputation for being a standoffish bitch and I can't work in this game for long with that kind of cloud hanging over me. I'm not off until tomorrow lunchtime, just in case you fancied breakfast with me?"

She pulled a begging face, smiling enough for Ste to know she was taking the piss.

"I'd love to. But it will have to be early. I can't move my first meetings around but give my room a bell when you wake up and we can grab breakfast together. If not, here's my details."

Ste held up his business card which Isla enthusiastically snapped from his fingers.

"You'll find a way to get hold of me through one of those London numbers, or by e-mail. We can make some new plans."

"Really! Breakfast it is. Fantastic. Go and get some rest, Ste. You look like you could use it." Having pocketed the card, Isla leaned in to kiss his cheek. Ste wrapped an arm around her waist, giving her an affectionate squeeze in response. There was a memorable energy to the embrace.

Isla's colleagues had given up gesturing for her to get a move on and watched their newest colleague in action. None of them knew the truth. Jeremy assumed he knew everything and loudly whispered as much to those who were within earshot.

"Night then," they said in tandem. Both smiling, they turned and went their separate ways holding onto the same regret that the evening was not the one they wanted.

Chapter 18

Ste was deflated by the whole day, aside from his brief encounter with Isla. She had been in his mind's eye throughout. He had wanted to hang out with her again tonight, hoping it would have resulted in something more, possibly a hook-up in London before too long. He wasn't used to not getting his own way with the women he wanted to see, and it hadn't crossed his mind that she might turn him down. He wasn't arrogant. It just never seemed to happen like that.

He was yet to give Greta a meaningful thought. She wasn't a priority of any kind, but now, facing months travelling the US, maybe the time apart would save him the termination conversation he always hated having.

The big unknown was whether or not Ste would get to share time with Isla again. Despite what she had said, he knew that there was little chance Isla would be up early enough for breakfast, given that she was only now heading out in advance of the long work shift she had on the flight home tomorrow. Ste knew the chances that their paths would collide again were so slim that it had to be by design. But after just one evening together, he felt something unusual. It was hope. There was no half-arsed desire here. He really wanted more and desperately hoped she'd call in the morning. Maybe they could go to his favourite pub in London when they were both at home? But for now, the best he could hope for was that they would meet up tomorrow before she flew off, and before his world was consumed with a familiar noisy energy for the next three months.

The different energy, which sparked throughout him as they embraced downstairs, had all but evaporated by the time he stumbled through the door into his room. Immediately collapsing onto his bed, he started dreaming of room service. But the effort to even sit up and order something seemed just a step too far. Despite his hunger and desire to not waste a moment of his trip, Ste accepted that tonight was over and allowed his body to immediately, effortlessly drift into sleep. There would be more nights for room service.

Chapter 19

Isla was not being allowed to forget that she was in for the driest of evenings. Having been dragged out to the Diner-Bar just a few blocks from the hotel, the restaurant staff seemed obsessively focused on her table for any signs she was drinking from one of the many cocktail pitchers liberally spread between her colleagues.

As her team got quickly pissed, she found conversation more difficult because of the awful music dominating the room. Isla wanted to talk to her colleagues and make friends, not yell a few barely audible pleasantries across a table over which Jeremy was, of course, holding court. She looked down at the plates of food in front of her. The Special Offer was a large plate of heavy meat accompanied by a huge selection of fried stuff. It was so different from the romantic class of the previous night; a night she had not so secretly hoped would be replicated this evening.

Wine and freshly cooked Italian food, or Diet Coke and…. What even is that?

This job had opened her eyes to the vastness of the world, and the opportunity to experience new things was high on her list of priorities. But this experience was not one of them. She had been to this kind of crappy diner in England more than once. It was fine when she was ten. But regardless of this being the authentic American version, it was no more appealing than the Ponderosa on Watford High Street that she had visited as a treat as a kid.

It was too noisy to talk. The only thing she wanted to do now was to see Ste. Her new friend had given her the tiniest squeeze. And now she wanted to know what that meant. He might have been flirting or it could have meant nothing at all. It was going to bug her until she could explore it because her brief encounter with the nice-smelling stranger had resulted in her craving more. She really fancied him. But she also had to get to know him. Isla wanted him to touch her again and maybe kiss her for real.

Chapter 20

Just after six the following morning, the hotel telephone in his room was ringing loudly. Ste had been up since five and was already washed, dressed and onto his second coffee of the day.

"Good morning. Ste Lewis here." He was formal. Although it could be business, he was desperately hoping that the next voice would be Isla.

"Mr Lewis, this is reception."

His heart sank.

"I am sorry to wake you, but I have a call for you from Miss Isla Kelly. She asked if she could be connected. I am so sorry if I have woken you up."

Yes!

"No bother. Thank you. Please go ahead and connect the call."

A long moment of silence followed. Ste was desperate that it was nothing more than a long connection process and that Isla had not been cut off. The silence was soon interrupted by a soft voice at the end of the line.

"Hello, Ste?"

"You know we really should start memorising room numbers. It would cause a lot less work for the bloke on reception."

"Morning! Yes, you're right. Still got a breakfast in you?"

"Sure. I was hoping you'd call. I doubted you would though. You know it's six o'clock, right? Do you always phone hotels asking to be connected to men you barely know at this time of the morning?"

"Well, I'm not that choosy. In fact, I'm up early as I've just got rid of someone. Forgotten his name already."

"Well, in that case, lucky me. Meet in reception in fifteen, or is that not long enough to wash off last night's fun?"

"Ste, I'm a classy lady who needs time to get ready. I'll see you in ten."

She giggled and hung up. Ste smiled. Although it was still early, his body clock was on British Summer Time and it was not too early for either decent coffee or a chat with a girl who liked him. He pulled his workbag together and went for breakfast.

The frantic New York morning had already taken hold. Large groups of visitors from all over the world jostled around the desk clerks, all demanding to either check in or out at the same time. Among the chaos, the two Brits embraced once again, in the same way that they had done the previous evening. It was affectionate, but not over the line. They weren't there, yet.

"Do you want to go out or stay here? The place looks rammed."

"There's a place a few blocks away that Jarrod recommended yesterday. I'm up for going out if you are."

"Who's Jarrod?"

"The guy who screwed things up for me yesterday, but the guy who may go on to make this whole 'Cormacks do America' thing a huge success. I'm not sure which way it will go or how I feel about him just yet."

"Sounds complicated. But let's go with Jarrod's suggestion and you can tell me all about it."

The forecourt was rammed full of coaches with luggage strewn everywhere in a way that made sense to the people loading it but presented ample opportunity for anyone so minded to make off with something that wasn't theirs. Ellen's Stardust Diner was only a few blocks over, and the walk was no time to catch up on the events of the previous day, but was enough for their minds to race, with occasional glances and warm smiles.

Having slept through the early part of yesterday, Isla had yet to experience New York first thing in the morning, and despite trying to be a casual presence alongside her, Ste was captivated by Isla's captivation, enveloped as she was in these unfamiliar surroundings. The noise of a thousand car horns was unrelenting. The couple paused to look into the tourist shops which would shortly open for the day to sell their tat to the masses. Each of the shops would try to outdo their near neighbour with more appealing prices for even shinier shit. And it would not be until the punters were long gone before they realised that they'd not got the bargain they initially believed they had, and instead, had just purchased a ton of useless, low-quality crap.

Ste and Isla were caught bang in the halfway house between being friends and lovers. Ste had not seen too many love-filled mornings. His numerous sexual encounters were ordinarily simple acts of convenience; shabby, lonely copulations with a girl nice enough to go home with, but not one interesting enough to spend the hours of daylight with, and certainly not one you'd take home to meet the parents. There hadn't been any love to speak of since Senior School, where one of the posh girls from PHS, the nearby private girls' school, had taken a shine to him. She loved the band. But it might have been the idea of being in love with somebody involved in a band which was where her real attraction started and stopped. But at sixteen, he felt like he was in love – if only for a while. And he loved the idea that being involved in music had got him the girl. The feeling only lasted a while, just until she had bowed to parental pressure to focus on her A' Levels, meaning that reluctantly, she stopped having time for him, or the music. Predictably, they quickly fell apart. It didn't matter how you got the girl; the feeling was the same the world over when you lost her. It wasn't as though Ste had turned against the idea of being in love. It was just not his priority given the simplicity of the many other available options.

But he was already determined to see Isla differently from his typical transients. It would require effort, which was new territory for him. Their time together would only come about when they committed to it. But fast approaching thirty, Ste knew it was about time he made some effort at something which wasn't work.

Evidently, he was not alone in this unchartered water. Although captivated by this frantic New York morning, Isla seemed determined to explain a bit more about what she was feeling. Not having been in many truly romantic situations herself, she didn't know much about the ways of love and, like Ste, was struggling to put *it* into a box. But how to sound hopeful without being over-keen and potentially frightening someone off?

There were guide ropes outside the entrance of the diner, ready for the morning throng that would imminently descend at the illustrious, old-style rock-a-billy diner. While seven am was too early for most people, the tourist masses would arrive soon, almost always tired, and certainly hungry, eager to consume and be entertained whatever time of day it was. They arrived just as the doors were opening, and immediately were seated in one of the booths in the centre of the floor. The waitress glided over to them on roller-skates. With Broadway just outside the door, it was inevitable there would sooner or later be some kind of performance. A prominent sign announced that 'Ellen's' had been bringing joy to their customers for ten years. The way Jarrod had spoken about it, the diner was part of New York folklore and had been open for generations.

"I've never seen a menu like this, have you?" asked Isla. "I've no idea where to start. I only want some eggs. Who orders a half-pound chilli burger and fries at this time in the morning?"

There were so many choices that it took some time to even find the breakfast section.

"A few years back, I was booked into a hotel in Milan, a really posh one by the main station. All sorts of people were in there, immaculately dressed businessmen and politicians in the most perfectly created tie knots. They started their day with thimbles of coffee and endless cigarettes. It was the oddest place I have ever had breakfast, partly because no one was eating. And despite being really posh, it was just a fog of smoke."

"What were you doing in Milan?"

"You know the score. Another band, another gig, another hotel. When you dip in and out of places as part of work, it could be anywhere; it's not like you spend any real time there."

Isla nodded. It sounded like a mirror of the last year and the endless racing around European airports.

"The thing was about this place, when I asked for the menu, they didn't have one. They didn't serve anything for breakfast other than coffee and cigarettes and seemed confused by a guest wanting food. Based on this trip, that would never happen in America! I ended up coughing my way out of the place and grabbing heavy bread from the station opposite. Never again. At least the Hiltons all offer something to eat, even if it is the same thing in every country. One size fits all, and all that."

They both continued to stare at their surroundings, captivated at how this recently empty room was now bustling with activity. The previously empty tables had quickly filled up with mostly jetlagged tourists eager to immediately experience the city.

Ste was doing the talking and was trying to keep the flow going. But Isla was quieter than Ste had previously seen her and, having asked if she was alright, she hinted with a touch of sadness that their brief liaison had to end so soon.

"So, you said that yesterday was mad. What happened?"

Ste explained the events of the previous day, alluding once more to the fact that he had to be at the office in a short while. Isla felt bad for abandoning him the night before. The conversation was an unnecessary confessional for two busy people whose lives were getting in the way. Suddenly, they were interrupted by a waitress with coffee and an eagerness to take their main order.

"Paris wins for the rudest," Isla blurted out.

"You what?" Ste was still focusing on the menu.

"If we are doing travel experiences, then I want to play. I may not be as old and wise as you, but like you, I've also had a load of miserable travel experiences."

Once more, they were back to being relaxed in each other's company, as the conversation returned to being a two-way exchange.

"At least the waiters appear in Paris, even if they are the snootiest and least forgiving in Europe. But try annoying an old Scottish woman in Falkirk. At one B&B, I get abused for appearing too English. I swear she deliberately burnt my white pudding."

"White…pudding. What's that?"

"I don't recommend it. Especially in Falkirk. In fact, I don't recommend Falkirk full stop. The things we do for work."

With no white pudding on the menu, they ordered the simplest breakfast choice available, eggs & bacon, and their expectation turned to disappointment at the unimpressive feast. It arrived suspiciously fast and tasted incredibly bland. It wasn't even obvious what type of eggs they had been served. They could have been fried first and then mashed up, or just badly scrambled without seasoning. Whatever it was, they were far too dry and explained the American obsession with Ketchup.

There seemed little point in complaining though, as despite the number of customers waiting for service, the staff suddenly all jumped onto the tables and bar, before performing a Jive Bunny-like Mash-Up Dance.

"I'm expecting Henry Winkler to wander in at any moment," Ste joked, turning to the door in expectation, as the loudest of the staff picked out a customer who was told to holler into the microphone on request. The chosen couple were from either South or Central America and had no understanding of English and, as such, the participation exercise was lost on them. Like the eggs, the early morning entertainment had quickly fallen flat.

"So," Ste took the conversation towards its predictably disappointing end. "I really have to start making a move. I am so sorry this is so short."

"I know. I've only got a few hours left myself, but I've already checked my schedule and will be in Boston this Friday. Then I'm back here at the end of next week. Will you be around?"

"The band arrive here tomorrow. I know we will be around here for a few days, but then we are heading to Baltimore, or it may be Boston. It's still falling into place but I'm sure it begins with a B. So, unless you're back here by Monday, I think I'll be gone."

"Afraid not. I'm not here until next Thursday night. I'll ask for you when I get here; you never know."

"I will have a US phone by Monday and I will make sure to leave the new number at reception. But you have my card, don't you? It's got my e-mail address on it, so please message me. Please!"

They stood outside the diner; the unrelenting weight of traffic continued to crawl past them. They embraced, sharing the sort of polite but affectionate kiss that could easily have turned into much more. Both were determined that this was just going to be a gap in a fun couple of days. Whatever portal they had opened two days ago remained firmly open. There had been a strong emotional connection and both of them shared a desire for more. There was no way anything less than more was going to be enough.

But for now, they were friends, and the departing embrace reflected that.

Ste pulled away first and headed to his office. The business of the trip was about to begin in anger.

As they walked in different directions, they both independently took a moment to glance back. As their eyes met once again, they both knew that whatever this was, it felt real; real enough to already start hoping for the next time.

Chapter 21

True to the schedule, Isla arrived back at the hotel the following Thursday night. However, there was no message for her, even though Ste had checked out several days before, according to the helpful desk clerk.

She kicked herself and hung her head in her hands regretting her carelessness.

When she had arrived home the previous week, Isla settled down to ping off her first message to the e-mail address on the business card he'd given her. But, to her horror, the small business card was nowhere to be seen. She pulled apart all her luggage and still found nothing. Isla remembered having used it as a bookmark on the flight home and her heart fell, as quickly, she remembered putting the book down on the plane, but couldn't remember picking it up again. The book was gone. And more importantly, so was her only way of directly contacting Ste. She tried to remember the name of the record company he worked for and rang what she hoped was his office number. But despite the requests to be put in touch with Stephen Lewis, she got nowhere.

"He's based in the New York office at the moment and is working with the…"

She blanked, unable to remember the apparently unforgettable band 'The Cormacks'.

Record companies are used to girls getting in touch the morning after they've apparently lost a number. The unwritten policy was that unless they gave some sort of codeword, the message was unrequited and contact was to be politely swerved. Nobody ever gave their bunk-ups the codes; groupies were ten-a-penny. It was typical of the male-dominated misogynism of the industry. Isla didn't care what the policy was but quickly realised that her message was never going to get to Ste. All lines of communication between them had now evaporated and she had no way of getting a message to him.

The excitement she felt when entering the hotel had been replaced with sadness. She was an idiot. How could she have lost his card? Her bad mood intensified with the realisation that Ste had not left anything for her. The not knowing was awful. The least he could have done was muster up the decency to say to her 'Thanks, but no thanks.' She had been stood up without an explanation. It seemed so much worse than being dumped in person. She knew her feelings were irrational and she was really at fault. Ste had left the onus on her to get in touch when he gave her his card and that's what they'd agreed would happen. He probably left New York thinking that it was she who hadn't bothered to contact him. However, he could have at least left a *thanks for a great time* message with reception.

Whatever the truth was, it was not going to get him back.

Chapter 22

A few hundred miles away, Ste lay on his bed in a Boston hotel. He had imminent dinner plans with a client in a bar somewhere close. Inevitably, they'd be talking shop whilst watching the Red Sox play out one of the season's final games in Detroit. After a week in the US, Ste had only managed one night to himself and was struggling to keep up the momentum required by the pace of Jarrod's intense schedule. Aside from the workload, his heart felt heavy, and he checked his phone yet again for any new text messages. By now, Isla would surely have received the message he had left at the hotel.

Maybe her schedule has changed and she isn't even in New York?

He refreshed his laptop before glancing again at his new phone. She hadn't e-mailed either.

Even airline stewardesses have e-mail. She said she'd drop me one as well.

Ste was convinced something had happened to her. Too many things were not making sense, especially as the hotel would have given her his mobile number by now. But she hadn't called or texted. He must have done something wrong. He refreshed everything again, slowly resigning himself to never knowing. A tired and deflated Ste started to pull himself together before skulking off to his last meeting of the day.

He could handle being rejected, but it was the idea that Isla was not the woman he thought she was. At least she could have had the decency to say 'Thanks, but no thanks'. He thought he'd made a special connection with her and that she'd be somebody he could have a proper relationship with. Although they'd met only a handful of times, he felt differently about her. Isla had stimulated feelings in him that no other woman had ever managed. A cliché, but despite the embryonic status of their union, she was the first woman he had ever really felt anything for. But it looked as though she was just another woman and he had no choice but to put it down to a brief travel encounter. A friend for a reason when he had hoped for so much more. Given how far it had gone, in time, it would probably not even make the short list of memorable encounters.

The tour was long and, as usual, there would always be other women.

Chapter 23

1998

After the longest three months of his life, Ste had finally made it back from the US just in time for the last of the pre-Christmas parties. The festive season came and went, but before the lights came down, Ste was off on another six-week trip around Europe, the band doing guest spots and all the promotional nonsense that they were expected to do. This was supposed to be the quiet time of year when bands didn't do much live, normally the point where all the industry would take a breath and re-charge. By the time he got back, it was March and the wheels were already in motion for the festival season that always kicked off in June. If Ste didn't take a break in the next few weeks, it would be the end of the year before he could find time for a rest. Tina was concerned that he was at risk of burning out and called him into her office on one of Ste's occasional visits to London. She had barely seen him since he'd headed off to New York the previous September and his trip back at Christmas was when the office was closed, as London shut for business and the workers temporarily, and often reluctantly, relocated back to their friends and family around the country. In Tina's case, it was to her mother in Wiltshire. For Ste, it was the trip down the A3 to his parents; but even there, he had worked non-stop when he wasn't sleeping off the result of three months living and travelling across North America.

He had signed up for a career in this industry and the one thing worse than doing all the hard work was not having that work to do as nobody cared about your bands. Or you. The sudden success across America was unexpected and significant. Off the back of that trip, there was a headline tour booked and the high-pressure follow-up album was slated to be recorded from late March. That would take them all up to the Easter weekend. The release would coincide with the summer festivals which would kickstart a headline tour across Europe. Tina had seen this kind of burnout before and she knew the cost to Ste would be career terminal if it wasn't addressed. All the victims she had encountered, and she knew that she had been directly responsible for many of them, had broken at a critical time in their short, but promising, careers. Recovery was rare. The old maxim about standing the heat or leaving the kitchen was written into the industry HR handbook – if such a thing existed.

Tina was a good boss and would do anything for those who were going to reward her, and she knew that if Ste could hold it together now, he would be bringing the label rewards for years to come. Recognition with The Cormacks would get the label the next band, the financial rewards of which brought them all a step closer to the swimming pool in the grounds of a Santorini villa, and just maybe that half-share of the local vineyard with views of the sunset which she continued to dream about. Tina had started to fantasise over that sort of indulgent retirement and that villa would be the long overdue '*Fuck You*' to everybody who had pissed her off. It would also be an extra special '*Fuck You*' to the long, shitty meetings full of patronising misogynists who doubted her place in the industry. She had a business to run and needed to protect her assets.

"Ste, you've done well but you need to chill out for a couple of weeks. Recharge, smell the roses; you know what I'm saying? Have you got someone to go on holiday with? I'll pay."

Ste didn't register the offer. Anything that deviated him from his diarised schedule and little pieces of paper full of the notes that held his life together was not something he had time for. He replied instinctively, failing to acknowledge the tone of authority Tina had used.

"I'm too busy, Tina. We have so much to do in advance of the album."

"Ste, I'm not asking you to take a holiday—I'm telling you. I don't think you heard me. I'm the boss and you've not stopped. You are going on leave for two weeks. I am sending you to Barbados and the only question I have for you is whether I'm buying one ticket or two?"

This was not a conversation. It was distinctly an order coming from one direction only, with no wriggle room for comeback. It was another instruction in a long line of instructions from Tina that he had come to respect. He carefully put down his laptop, closing the lid with what seemed like carefully choreographed symbolism. He knew he was breaking. Tina had already seen the signs in him, and she had once again called it right.

Barbados in March though. Get in. The flicker of a smile registered as he played back the conversation. There were worse ways to spend time. Should he invite Greta? Against his judgement, he had drifted back into the easy option. He had been seeing Greta since their collective loneliness collided in a jetlagged pre-Christmas trip on his return from the US. Theirs remained an arrangement of convenience which still never got anywhere near setting his world alight. In fact, the best way to describe his thing with Greta was— Boring. There was just no spark, the compromise for them both accepting their comfortable co-existence when their schedules occasionally collided.

The relationship was limited to drinks on Upper Street and sometimes dinner. If the drinks went well, they would end up at one of their flats, but conversation remained minimal, shared interests were zero and they never stayed over with each other after they'd hooked up. He remembered that he had definitely slept with her a couple of times over the last few months but could not actually remember the various periods of pre-amble or any of the actual deeds.

It had to end. Really end this time. No going back. He was done. The long flight to fresh coconuts and local rum was one he'd be taking alone.

"One ticket will be fine. And thanks, Tina."

Ste breathed a sigh of relief. He hadn't realised until that moment just how tired he was.

"Great. You leave in two days. I'll get you booked into the hotel we use in Bridgetown, and the rest is up to you. Get yourself some clothes and a new pair of budgie smugglers. And leave your bloody phone here; that's an order. I don't want you being disturbed."

Chapter 24

Ste had nothing suitable for a holiday in Barbados. He took the train to his parents to salvage some bits from his old bedroom, even though he'd left home almost a decade before. It would have been easier to visit Debenhams, but a trip home could kill two birds with one stone. A few months had passed since his Christmas visit, but all three of them were still raw about his time at home. It had been a disaster. His parents were forgiving, and proud of their son's achievements to a certain extent; but until they saw it for themselves, they had absolutely no idea how hard he worked and were disappointed that after months of no contact, Stephen had slept through the days and worked in the evenings. After a few of these days and nights, his dad finally spoke his mind one evening as they both reached for the kettle. If Ste knew this was how this visit was going to be, he should have thought twice about coming home at all for Christmas! He wasn't trying to be aloof from them, but his parents just didn't understand and he struggled with their disapproval.

Often, it's only when it's too late that the past becomes a thing of regret, but with the dust now settled, Ste was determined to build a better relationship with his folks. Work dominated his life, but the irony was it was the same people who had installed that work ethic into his core who were now castigating him for it. He figured it was all about balance and this was his chance to restore it.

"Do you just clean up after people or is your job something more?" his mum asked, failing to hear what Ste was telling her about his hundred-plus-hour working weeks. So much for trying to reconcile things by being more engaged. He had spent two hours talking about work despite having quickly figured out that there was no point to it. They already had it worked out, of course. Stay calm, Ste, he thought to himself over and over. One day they will be proud. One day.

His visit home was only for the night, but that was quite enough. His parents were old school, struggling to comprehend why a company would pay for an employee's holiday for no reason other than he needed a rest.

"We all need a rest, son. If my company sent me to Barbados every time I looked a little bit tired, I'd have a permanent suntan."

He was sure he overheard his mum suggesting to his dad that he could be a drugs mule. His parents were both grafters and had worked all their lives in a game where nobody gave anything away for free. Using their hands and holding down a job for life in a local components' factory was the extent of their shared professional horizon. They'd met there, stayed there, and, after a while, concluded that there was no point in leaving for more of the same elsewhere. Theirs was an eight 'til four, Monday to Friday existence, the highlights of the week being an earlier finish on a Friday if everyone was good, and the following week's overtime sheet. The unpredictability of the modern world was an alien universe. Ste couldn't impress on them the differences in how things now worked. They just couldn't understand.

Ste loved them both, but he also loved the train journey North out of Fratton at the end of each trip home. This was the jumping-off point back into his own world, with his people, up in London. And this time, it was just him and a bag full of beach clothes that hadn't seen sunlight since the great summer he'd spent messing around on Southsea common before his A' Level results came out. He'd get properly kitted out in Barbados, and not waste any remaining time on packing. He sent Greta a courtesy text, telling her where he was going to be for the next couple of weeks. She didn't reply, which was not unexpected. The no-frills communication style continued to work for them both.

And this was his first grown-up holiday. He'd been on long weekends with mates and a lot of work trips that felt like holidays, especially the ones to the Balearics. But he had never been anywhere on his own to just relax. Maybe he could find time to fish from the back of a boat or learn to dive. Or he could even climb something just for the hell of it. Or he could just sit, watching things happen, sucking on a coconut with a big spliff on the go. Happiness was a tropical island.

Chapter 25

Arriving at Victoria Station, there seemed to be a lot of people heading towards the Gatwick Express situated at the far end of the station. Mostly, they were middle-aged men who, despite it being not yet nine am, were already on the beer. They stood out like any group of blokes drinking cans of Red Stripe would, not to mention they were all wearing England cricket tops.

More out of curiosity than anything, Ste engaged one of the less rowdy travellers about their destination. In a dreadful West Indian accent, the reply came that he was dreading.

"Barbados, man! For the Test Match. We're with the Barmy Army tour and will probably head off to another island after. We'll probably lose inside three days."

Ste's first holiday was going to be surrounded by people he would normally cross the road to avoid; all-day drinking sports fans crammed on a plane before disembarking onto a small island. Why did Tina choose this place, this week?

"*Barmy Army.*"

A cry went up from the Lads on Tour and Ste prayed to whatever Lord was watching over him, that he was not seated next to this lot on the nine hours to Bridgetown.

His frustration with Tina turned to happy relief when he found she'd put him in Business Class, as well as booking him a suite at the Barbados Hilton just outside Bridgetown. At least his flight would be free of the tour groups.

In the Business Lounge at Gatwick, Ste was in the unusual position of having no work to consume him. He thought about Greta—but only because there was nothing else to think about. When they were together, one of them, usually Ste, was either asleep in a blink or interrupted by one of their phones. It was usually his. It never occurred to him not to answer, even if they were in the middle of an intimate romantic moment. Once again, he hoped the relationship would die on its own without him having to accelerate its demise. He still hated endings, however dead they already seemed to be. But as it hadn't yet died on its own, he knew he had to put it out of its misery like a limping greyhound. As thirty loomed and twenty was long since forgotten, he knew it could drag on and become more than it was just through laziness. In a world where it was hard enough for people to hold even the best relationships together, theirs had no chance.

Given that it was a BA flight, Ste made a deliberate check of the cabin crew, as he had started to do since meeting Isla the previous September. He'd not heard from her since they parted in New York, and despite looking out for her at the numerous points at airports and hotels where their paths could have crossed, he'd not even heard the name mentioned. But since he left his number and had given her his card, he assumed she'd long since forgotten him. Typically, there was no sign of her and he was not stalkerish enough to ask the crew on board whether they knew her. That might open a can of worms that could get awkward and if Isla didn't want him, then so be it. It was a shame, that was all.

Some flights were full of memorable occurrences. Whether it was an interesting conversation with someone on board or a dramatic hit of weather, aside from a hijacking, Ste had pretty much experienced most sorts of journeys. He'd even witnessed a bomb alert while grounded on the tarmac at Milan Linate. It turned out to be nothing more than a disgruntled union official trying to hold an impromptu strike. But this flight was yet another filed under the 'unmemorable' heading. The plane went up and he watched *Good Will Hunting* for the umpteenth time. Every viewing made him dream about one day working with Elliot Smith. If ever there was a musician he wanted on his books, it was Elliot Smith, just for his work on that soundtrack alone. It was an incredible piece of art, made up from of a bunch of songs Smith released the year before on a small indie label called *Kill Rock Stars,* which encouraged Ste to keep track of the guy in case he needed newer representation. Someone like him. Even on a business class flight to a tropical island, he couldn't switch off.

Once on the ground, his escape from the airport was fast. With the privilege of a Business Class exit from the plane, he beat the rush to the taxis for the short journey between the airport and the hotel. The view along the south coast road was not the one on the posters, the lack of wealth hidden from the sales pitch the Barbadian tourist board pushed. The only modern building Ste had seen since the airport stood above the small pockets of simple housing surrounding its grounds. It was grand and not in keeping with its surroundings. He was becoming bored of the trappings afforded the business traveller and having lived in Hilton hotels for the last six months, something inside him fancied a bit more rustic on this trip. But how could he complain? He had been flown Business Class to Barbados and was about to spend two weeks in the best hotel in the area doing whatever he pleased.

Chapter 26

"Good afternoon, Sir." A cheery lad approached the car. The boy couldn't have been more than ten.

"Here for the cricket are you, Sir?"

"No. Just a bit of relaxing. I didn't even know the cricket was on until I got to the airport."

"You're fooling me, Sir. Everyone knows about the cricket. You English are so funny. You know we're going to kick your boys all the way home. We're two - one up, and no one's gonna stop Lara. You think Dean Headley is gonna topple the world's best batsman?"

The boy laughed at the thought that anyone could topple Lara, especially not a bowler unknown to anyone outside of Kent. Ste had no idea what he was talking about, but he smiled with genuine affection as he instantly warmed to the young lad.

"Anything else I can do, Sir? I hope I carried your bags satisfactorily. I should stay here while you check in and then help you to your room."

Ste pushed two dollars into the boy's hand and thanked him, hoping he wouldn't have to be more forceful about not needing his help. Ste checked in, and the boy continued to linger in the background, eager for more work from his new English friend.

"Good afternoon, Sir, and welcome to the Barbados Hilton."

The affable desk clerk smiled as he typed another set of customer details into the computer in front of him. Looking up, he became fixated upon the boy who had darted behind one of the larger pot plants, hiding from the staff whilst eager to not lose sight of his latest money-making possibility.

"One moment please, Sir."

The desk clerk was not blind.

"Look, Charlie, I've already told you; you're too young to work here. You need to go home or I'll call your mother again."

"Oh, Sir, I'm not working. I was just helping my new friend with his bags."

"I told you before, Charlie. I can't have your teacher coming up here to speak to me again. You have to go home and then please go to school tomorrow."

"But it's almost the holidays, Sir. And you know we need the money. My Mumma told me it's okay, so you can call her. She'll tell you it's okay, honest."

"You know I can't help you, boy. You need to go."

The lad knew he had lost the battle. For today at least. He made two dollars from Ste and a few dollars more from other guests. While a few dollars meant nothing to them, when added up, it was enough to make a difference for Charlie and his family. He hung his head as he trudged to the door and Ste caught his gaze. If circumstances forced the kid to skip school to work, then he could at least say something nice.

"Give me a minute, would you?" he asked the Desk Clerk.

He caught up with the disconsolate figure, reaching the kid before he made it to the door.

"Charlie, you need to go to school. But I'm here for two weeks and if you want to help me figure things out at the weekend, come back and look for me on Saturday. Okay?"

"Thank you, Sir. I will do that, indeed. For the next few days though, I'll be selling coconuts around the cricket ground. No way I'm going to school when all you tourists are here. But for sure, I'll be back here to see you on Saturday." The charismatic little man had it all figured out. Necessity was the mother of invention.

Ste slipped him another few dollars, assuring him that it was a 'business transaction' and a 'retainer for his services'. Charlie beamed. Ste noticed the patched-up sandals hanging onto Charlie's feet. The kid certainly grafted, inhabiting a world devoid of frills. Here was Ste, enjoying a free holiday on one of the most beautiful islands in the world. He could certainly spare a few dollars and stooped to return the offer of 'High Five' from his newest friend just as a minibus pulled up and the cabin crew from his flight exited the vehicle. Ste was quickly forgotten, and Charlie was once again the first to greet the new arrivals.

Having been caught by this before, Ste turned on his heels and resumed check-in with the Desk Clerk who let him know that everything was pre-paid, including his bar tab. He'd also been upgraded to their best suite overlooking the sea. He'd reached Gold Status with Hilton and BA months ago, but the hotel chain threw all the frills at its regular patrons. He'd been put in the Panoramic Corner Suite. The brochure boasted that it had two balconies and the picture made it look big enough to host a party for the entire cabin crew who were now gathering impatiently behind him.

Ste thanked the Clerk and cast a hopeful glance towards the cabin crew just in case Isla was there after all. She wasn't. Of course she wasn't. She never was, and, as with every previous time he had looked for her, he remained on his own. He seemed to always be on his own in one way or another. While he didn't want for anything material, in this beautiful place, his heart reminded him that he had nobody with whom to share all of this. Under strict instructions to not check his work e-mail, he'd left his laptop at home meaning there was no work to do and Ste's largely one-dimensional life was all rather suddenly on hold. He checked the brochures scattered over one of the many tables around the suite and resolved to learn to dive and visit the caves to the North of the Island as well as developing a decent tan just to show Tina how he really had disengaged for the whole two weeks.

As dusk began to fall, rather than sit watching it from his balcony, Ste decided on a walk along the sandy beach outside. He'd find somebody to chat to and put a spark into his mood. He could smell the Barbadian aroma from his balcony and wanted to eat, drink and smoke it in for himself.

The foyer was busy with another busload of cabin crew checking in, all giddy from their short, but boozy, minibus ride from the airport. The groups of red-faced men moved with discomfort at the end of another long day spent enjoying too much sun and local rum. Some of them were accompanied by their cricket widow wives who themselves all seemed to smell like a sickly combination of perfume, cocktails and suntan lotion. This was the last place he wanted to be, and he tried to move through the rabble into the cooling dusk outside. His escape was halted by the Clerk calling him over to the desk.

"Mr Lewis, Sir, I need to apologise again for the boy. We don't let people, especially children, work here unless they are a member of staff. I didn't want you to think we let anyone in."

He was apologetic, but the disparity between the haves and have nots did not sit well with Ste. He thought of himself as a man of the people, not a card-carrying Watt Tyler apologist sort who marched with the Socialist Workers at the first sniff of an injustice. But in this case, who was helping children like Charlie who needed a leg up just to survive?

He understood that a global brand hotel could not have ten-year-old kids working for them and assured the Clerk that Charlie was both charming and helpful, but he understood. After placating the effusive Clerk, his mind was screaming out for a rest.

For fuck's sake, get me out of here. I just want to relax.

He needed air but was suddenly stopped in his tracks.

Chapter 27

"I thought you were going to stay in touch?"

Ste went from irritated to ecstatic in a heartbeat as he immediately recognised the voice. His heart felt as if it had stopped and he swung round to see a familiar beauty staring at him. Isla didn't look angry, but she wasn't smiling either. If he had to find a word for it, she looked hurt.

"My God. Isla. I said that if I ever saw you again, I swear that was going to be the first thing I said to you. I assumed when you didn't get in touch, as we arranged in New York, that you'd had a change of heart. I left my number for you."

Ste almost punched out the words *'as we arranged'*.

"Hold on, you left your number? I asked many, many times and there was no number for me at reception. I was back the next week and there was nothing. Every time I go back there's still nothing. And yes, I still check. It's the first thing I do! And I look for you on all my flights, but you're never there."

"What about my e-mail address and the office number? I was in the US for three months and every day I hoped to hear from you."

"Seriously?"

"Yes, seriously."

Isla explained about the book and the business card and how she had left a message at the record company but couldn't remember the name of the band and sounded like a stalker and how she had done everything she could.

Ste smiled, trying to bury a laugh that he wanted to let loose, but Isla was in full flow. He knew about the record company policy and the messages he would have disregarded had they been for anybody else. As for the business card, it was easily done. He got it and forgave her, even though there was nothing to forgive. Mostly, he was just sorry for all the time they'd lost.

"I can't believe you are here. You weren't on the flight. And yes, I checked.

Like you, I always check. Coincidence finally got us. What a ridiculous set of events. Losing contact from one side would have meant that at least we still had it from the other. But for both of us to have no luck at all is crazy. I swear I left a message for you when I checked out." His excitement at seeing Isla beamed from his face; he couldn't stop grinning like an idiot. He certainly wasn't lying and put his hands on her shoulders, staring deep into her eyes. He was conscious of rushing towards physical contact but just couldn't help himself. Without hesitation, they embraced with the warmth they had shared in New York six months before.

Isla didn't hold back, reciprocating his warmth, conscious that they were now far physically closer than she had ever expected to be with Stephen Lewis again.

"What are you doing here? You weren't on my flight in from London."

"I wasn't on the London flight. I came from Miami. Now and again, you get a different return and here I am. Two whole days in the Caribbean."

Ste finally removed his arms from Isla, aware that it might be too much too soon. She paused for breath, but clearly, there was so much they both still wanted to know.

"What about you? I wouldn't expect your band to be working here. This is a Reggae Island. There's not much call for your stompy Celtic stuff. What were they called again?"

"You've clearly not been paying attention. Have you not heard how well *The Cormacks* are doing? And I'm not here for work. It's just me, all alone because my boss was concerned that I was knackered and going to burn out. I've been sent here for two weeks as if I've returned from a warzone and need convalescence. She even offered to pay for someone to come with me. But that would mean I had someone I wanted to come with me."

"You don't? No girlfriend yet, then?"

"No. No girlfriend. The girl I wanted lost my number!"

They simultaneously blushed, looking away before their gazes met once again with a smile.

"There was someone I was hanging out with now and again, but it was nothing serious. To be honest, it's run its course. If it wasn't for the fact that when I get home I'll be in the studio with the band for a few weeks and then on the road again for months, I'd do something decisive to finish it.

But there's nothing to finish short of sending a text message and I can't even be bothered to do that."

"You're a keeper if you want to end a relationship by text and can't be arsed to even do that."

"Well, you're not much of a catch either, are you? Can't even hold onto a business card. Truce then - we can both agree that we're losers?"

"Definitely."

They looked at each other, glowing at the quick resumption of their affectionate playtime.

"You've just got here then? It's a shame I must leave on Friday, or I'd take you to the Fish Fry at Oistins. It's mental, and like nothing you've ever been to."

"You've been here a few times then?"

"A few. But it's one of those small places you can get the vibe for quickly. And Oistins is an institution. Everyone goes. It's like Notting Hill Carnival every weekend. You must promise me to go on Friday, even if I'll be in mid-air when you do."

"Well, I am here for two Fridays, so I will. I promise."

Isla's room key was ready, and their brief reunion needed somebody to make the next move.

"Would you like a drink when you've checked in? I assume Jeremy isn't here. He's not here, is he?"

He was only half-joking, checking over his shoulder just to make sure.

"No, there's no Jeremy." Isla paused, unsure how to say the next bit. "There is a Patrick though, back at home. It's not serious, but it would be wrong of me to not mention him after what seemed to be forming with you in New York."

While internally ruined by the revelation, Ste smiled back, careful not to be too transparent and let his disappointment show.

"What went on in New York? Two people met in a hotel lobby, became friends and have looked forward to having another night out ever since?"

Ste thought he had successfully fibbed indifference, but he knew he was gutted that Isla was no longer available. He'd had his chance and fate had blown it for him. He liked this girl and wasn't about to give up that easily. She's said her thing with Patrick wasn't serious and Isla didn't seem to mind being near him again. The race was still on. Nice and easy, Ste. Nice and easy, lad.

"In that case, Mr Lewis, you gorgeous smelling man, I'd love to have a drink with you. Give me thirty minutes and I will see you there."

Isla pointed at two empty bar stools a few yards away and picked up her bags. Ste watched her go, delighted that he was going to be busier than planned for the next two days. He was suddenly happier than he'd been since… since a morning in New York last September.

Chapter 28

Isla took her bags up to the room and changed out of the heavier clothes she had worn in from Florida. Miami had been another crappy American experience. While the beach was nice enough, she was on her own and not speaking Spanish meant she'd found herself on the outside of things.

And she was now kicking herself. Why had she exaggerated the truth about Patrick? What was she thinking? She'd thought about Ste for months and when she finally met him again, she mentioned a bloke who was nothing more than a bit of potential; someone she had only seen a couple of times since they had met at a New Year's Eve house party in Watford. A Junior Doctor at the local hospital, Patrick was a nice enough bloke. But like her, his hours were irregular and their common time off work and in the same location was virtually zero. As such, they'd barely seen each other since that tipsy midnight snog on her friend's freezing cold patio.

But for some silly reason, she hadn't wanted Ste to think that she had spent the last six months cursing his discourteous behaviour around the mobile number. Which of course she had. And she was now immediately regretting making any kind of noise of unavailability. But she now had two days and two nights here.

Forget the Patrick crap and don't fuck it up!

There was plenty of time to set things straight, starting this evening. Return to calm. Enjoy the moment. Who knows what happens next?

When he had touched her in reception, she had experienced a real rush of something that had set her alight and skipping down the hallway, she started to giggle loudly as her mind raced through life's endless possibilities.

Game on.

Chapter 29

Ste had reluctantly been dragged into conversation by one of the middle-aged men who was in Barbados for the cricket. He was rigid with boredom and knew Isla was enjoying his pain as he watched her deliberately slow approach which she knew was extending the discomfort he was currently feeling.

"You see, Si, the problem is the England team just aren't any good." The puffed up, over-ripened face struggled to push out every word, exhausted from a hard day sitting in bars drinking Rum Cocktails.

Si? This old bloke can't even get my name right.

"No good since Gower retired, you know. Did you ever see him play? No one hit a ball through the covers like Gower. And there was real character in that team, but not now. Do you know who has come in to replace Botham?"

The absence of a response did nothing to stop the conversation.

"You're right, Si! No one. Absolutely no one."

Ste had nothing to say, limiting his responses to simple nods and smiles as he sipped his G&T. He was too polite to leave the man alone, and, conscious that Isla was coming over, he tried to change the conversation. But there was no turning this tanker.

Isla looked stunning, in a thoroughly natural sort of way. Her confident walk through the bar in an elegant, flowy dress turned every head. Despite being slaughtered, red-faced man was astute enough to read the situation and realise that three was most definitely a crowd. Without invitation, he turned to leave with drunken ponderousness. Isla still had a moment in which to play.

"Darling, there you are. Boring everyone silly, I presume." She kissed Ste on the cheek and turned to the sunburned man who had finally stopped talking cricket to admire her. "I'm so sorry, has he been boring you with his stories? Do you mind if I steal my man from you?" She winked at Ste. Playing the role of Mrs Ste seemed so very easy.

"Goodnight, Si. Have a great evening. You, Sir, are a very lucky man." He shook Ste's hand and looked Isla over in what could have been interpreted as a bit too intrusive a manner.

"Wow. That was impressive. I didn't think I'd ever get away—Darling, hmmmm. I can handle that! Now, can I get you a drink?"

"Seeing as we are on the island and you are my darling, for the evening at least, I'll have a Mojito, please. Didn't anybody tell you that this is not a Gin Island, Ste? Get on the island Rum this instant; you're embarrassing me."

Ste beckoned to the barman who was making sure his guest was being properly looked after.

"Two Mojitos, please!"

The barman knew Ste's room number already. You don't forget the residents in the best suites, as these were the customers who were not short of a dollar and it was part of the job description to know how to spot where your tips were coming from.

"Please, Sir, take a seat with your friend and I will bring them over."

They could just make out the nearby ocean, now blackened with the darkness of the early night sky.

Reggae drifted from the speakers all around the bar, echoing into the night. The unmistakable sound of Bob Marley serenaded them with a familiarly wonderful base beat. In unison, they said 'Cheers' with the freshly made Mojitos, taking great care not to lose eye contact until they'd had the first sip of their cocktails.

"How's that band doing? Tell me, what's happening? You're obviously making something good happen, given that you're here and someone else is paying."

"They said I needed a rest. After we parted in New York, I did thirty cities in sixty days before spending a month finishing off the business side in Boston. We went everywhere doing shows, interviews and the appearances you have to do to get known."

He explained how the two-week trip had turned into three months, and how he had ballsed up Christmas with his parents because he hadn't really switched off. It was hardly thrilling stuff if you weren't involved, but Isla was keen to hear his news. Ste was just happy to be with her again. He spent his working life trying to put the business first. Here was someone who seemed to want just him, not what he could do for her.

"Are you still enjoying life in the air? With all these cities and things to see, all those people to meet? It's some life."

"Not everyone is as interesting and kind as you, Ste. It's not a bad life, but hard laying down roots anywhere because I'm never in one place long enough. There are only so many times you can be refused entry into a bar on the East Coast and end up having dinner with one of the other younger ones. It will be better next year. I'll be twenty-one and my evenings in the US will be a bit more exciting. Seeing you again tonight was a big and pleasant surprise; how did I cope without you?"

Ste blushed. She'd tried to sound sarcastic, but he knew she was more sincere than she'd intended to be as the rhetorical question hung in the air like a sweet cologne. Replaying her words in his head, she moved on quickly. It was a while since he had reason to remember how young Isla was. American law was a farce. Mike Tyson had been Heavyweight Champion of the World but couldn't go into a bar for a beer. Worse still, there were the thousands who risked their lives in combat for their country but couldn't toast their achievements or, in many cases, their wedding vows, with a proper drink. Consistent law-making seemed low on the list of American priorities. It was absurd.

"There's something I wanted to ask. What's the score with this Patrick?"

Isla paused before answering. She'd put Ste out of his misery soon enough, just not yet. Maybe there was merit in making him work a bit.

"How about we save Patrick for later and get some food? What do you fancy?"

Chapter 30

Ste looked at her as though she were mad.

"Fish, dummy. Of course I want fish. Especially when I'm next to the sea they've just been caught in. Do you want to eat here or head out?"

"We're too far from anywhere good to walk. What're the chances of just staying here and watching the waves through the darkness?"

Ste wanted to know the score with her situation at home but respected her wish to not push things just yet. He beckoned the barman, who was lurking on standby with a pair of menus. Eagerness was not a natural state for any Caribbean barman, except if there was a decent tip to be had. But the English visitors were staying for food, and it could be a profitable evening. He was not going to risk them changing their minds and going elsewhere through his lack of attentiveness. Even in the most relaxed places on earth, money still made things happen.

A local band had started to set up in the corner. Not the best start to an intimate evening, especially when Ste spent his life surrounded by music. He couldn't tune out a band that was right in front of him and had experienced too many bad nights in pubs when the management should have pulled the plug after the first chord.

"I hope they're not too loud," Isla interrupted his distraction.

"We can always move on somewhere else if you like?"

"I'm fine, Ste. But I'm guessing you already hear enough shit music in your job, so you'll be less tolerant than me."

She had him figured out, but they were going nowhere. They ordered food and another drink appeared without request. From the barman's point of view, they were on tab so he was going to keep the drinks flowing.

"Right. Now tell me, what really happened with your number in New York?"

Ste breathed a sigh of relief. He thought there was a tougher conversation about to happen. There was nothing to explain here; it was just a cock up.

"Straight up, Isla. I left it there for you—assuming your name is still Miss Isla Kelly."

"Ste, my name isn't Isla Kelly, it's Kiely. No wonder I never got it."

"You said it was Kelly."

"No, I didn't. I think I'm of sufficient mental competence to be clear about my own name. And, come to think of it, I don't remember telling you my surname."

Isla put her drink down on the table, joined her hands and adopted an upright pose that suggested something serious was pending. Ste considered it for a moment. She had never told him her surname. Ste thought about the mix-up and snapped his fingers recalling that the hotel had connected her call as Isla Kelly the morning they had breakfast.

"So, what would have happened if you'd got my name right?"

Ste wasn't prepared for such a question, especially as the elephant in the room, the subject of Patrick, remained unresolved.

"I'll answer that one after you tell me about Patrick."

"I'll tell you what. Let's put all this talk of Patrick and whoever you have got waiting for your dumping text to one side, just for tonight at least. I hope this is not going to be our last night on earth and we don't have to set everything straight, do we? I'm looking forward to my marlin and that cold white you ordered. I might even share my fish if you want to give me a taste of your Barracuda."

"Suits me. And you're right, we have other nights for all that stuff. The island is beautiful and just look at the stars which have come out to play. Tell me more about what's been happening with you. How many times have you been here and what happened to your US routes?"

"We met in September, right? I spent the first two months doing New York, Newark, Washington and Boston. When hurricane season was over and the winter sun-seekers migrated south, I came onto the Caribbean and Florida routes. It's a fantastic way to spend the winter and I didn't fancy the whole minus twenty feeling of New York at that time of year. So, a long answer to a simple question, but it's my third or fourth time here; I'm losing count of how many times I've been to places. You must feel the same."

"It is what it is, I guess. The novelty of it soon disappears. All that separates a good travel experience from a bad one is speed. Everything else is always the same after the first few times. BA don't re-jig their film or food selection every week and one airport lounge is the same as the next. I just want to get there fast and without much engagement with other people."

"Don't get me started on people. When you get this type of job, you are employed because you say something nice about the passengers and how you like them and are a people person. It means you can tolerate them enough to do your job. Have you any idea how often I am chatted up by someone who has nothing to say beyond a boorish confirmation that they are important? They might as well ask their mum to give a character reference."

"So, given your considerable experience of men and travel, what is the best you can hope for out of a trip?"

Ste took the moment to watch Isla watching him whilst she considered his deliberately leading question. She seemed to be struggling for the right words. Of course, he hoped her answer would be:

'You, Ste. I want to see you on every trip'.

But the pleasurably tense moment was quickly interrupted before she was able to answer. Their food had arrived, accompanied by a new bottle of white which sat on ice in the bucket between them. As Ste poured, he noticed Isla still attempting to start an answer to the question.

However, this coincided with the point the band almost fell onto the stage for their soundcheck, and they both immediately knew that Isla had been saved from needing to answer it. Ste was disappointed—but it would keep. They dived into their food as the soundcheck started and by the time they had finished, the band had rolled straight into the first set without any kind of break, kicking off with the 10CC classic "Dreadlock Holiday". Being a music geek, Ste chuckled at the appropriateness of the opening number given that the England team were in town and the song was written about Eric Stewart and his experiences in Barbados. The lyrics were changed to make the location Jamaica. While not a date-worthy disclosure, he couldn't resist showing off his knowledge.

"I saw Hampshire play when I was a kid but haven't followed cricket since."

"Why Hampshire?"

"It's where I'm from. Southsea in Portsmouth, right by the sea."

"I thought you were from London. Didn't you say once that you lived near Cuba Libra? I love that place."

"I grew up down there. And yes, I live above that restaurant. Have you been there recently?"

"I was there a few weeks ago. Great cocktails, late license – what's not to love?"

"You mean to tell me you've been into my building in the last six months?"

After three months of missing each other across the East Coast of America, fate had put them only yards apart on Ste's front doorstep. Those gods of possibility seemed to be desperately conspiring to make something happen.

Chapter 31

After reflecting on their near miss on Upper Street, Ste filled in some of the gaps in which Isla showed interest.

"I moved to London when I should have been in my first year at Uni." He recounted the story of his boyhood friends screwing up the band, and the guilt he felt as a result of his success, given that the only good thing to arise from the band was his career. His road was one of determination and gutsy attrition but sitting where he was now made it all worthwhile.

"So, Hemel Hempstead. Not known for its cricket. Or anything else. You seem glad to have left it."

"We have a complicated Magic Roundabout. But the chance to move would be nice. I'm still living there with my parents; there isn't much point in paying to live away when I'm only there one or two nights a week. When I am there, I just get the basics done, laundry and job admin. You know the sort of stuff. I might move to Watford before the end of the year. It's a whole seven miles away."

"Life-changing." Ste chuckled to himself. He had only been there once, a few years before, when Pompey had played and it kicked off around the station afterwards. Not an unusual outcome on a Pompey away day, with the 657-crew intent on reminding the locals that they were in town for one day only each year. He remembered watching with interest from the station forecourt as some lads he had been at school with chased a bunch of Watford supporters up the Clarendon Road and into a working men's club. It wasn't really a Mods v Rockers rampage like the one in Quadrophenia, the benchmark for any notable street aggro. It was all rather half-arsed.

Dreadlock Holiday gave way to the usual mix of holiday tunes you'd expect to hear in hotel bars the world over, as the band glided their way through Red, Red Wine and The Merryman's 'Feeling Hot' before they hit their stride with the obligatory smattering of instantly recognisable Marley classics that even the musically ignorant knew. Things went off track as the tempo and volume increased, with the frontman putting everything he had into his version of Billy Ocean's Caribbean Queen, a song that hinted towards the imminency of a musical war crime. As far as Ste was concerned, the set was fast becoming inexcusably bad. He shifted at the change in musical pace and knew they had run their luck. He tried, but he couldn't switch off from the noise. Something needed to change, and despite having the best room in the hotel, he wasn't yet a customer valued to the point that he could arrange for the band to be unplugged.

Ste picked up the baton, desperate to not let his second chance disappear. But before he had got to the first syllable out, Isla beat him to it.

"Do you want to move on somewhere else?"

Chapter 32

Talking in a busy hotel bar was unappealing to them both. Ste was starting to feel the effects of jetlag on top of months of non-stop work, and for Isla, she had spent too many evenings in the sanitised awkwardness offered by these sorts of places.

"Did I tell you about the room they gave me? It's a massive suite with—drum roll, please, if you don't mind, Miss—wait for it, two balconies."

Ste saw Isla blush and backtracked the implied offer. He wanted to be closer to her and hoped that she felt the same, but that did not necessarily make what happened next a sure thing.

"I didn't mean what I think you think I meant, Isla. I'm not trying to jump ahead; it's just that I have a much better music selection upstairs than what we have here. And my own fully stocked bar. I just didn't want to head into the lobby bar again. I really didn't mean to make you feel awkward."

"Ste, honestly, I'm cool with that idea. There is nowhere I'd rather be than hanging out with you, talking some more and listening to the music we both want to hear. You have nothing to worry about, but you know it's on the understanding that I don't want tonight to be something I end up regretting. There is something between us; we both feel it. We both felt something in New York, didn't we? I don't want to talk about what that is right now, but it's all okay."

"Is that because of Patrick?"

"No, it's not because of anyone or anything. It's because I don't want to turn something that feels this nice and straightforward, into something else. Are you okay with that? You understand what I mean?"

While he understood the fundamentals of what Isla was saying, he had absolutely no idea if he would be seeing tomorrow's sunrise alongside Isla or not. Perplexed about what she wanted from him, he realised he was overthinking and resolved to go with the flow. He wanted the physical contact that any man in his position would want. But it was important for him to control himself long enough for their connection to flourish into something bigger. He thought of Greta, but only as a reference point. He and Isla had shared more words and feelings in the last three hours than Greta and he had in the many months they had been occasionally seeing each other.

He gestured to the barman that he was ready to sign for his tab. As a gentleman would, he stood behind Isla's chair waiting for her to stand so he could pull it back and help her on with her light jacket.

"What are you doing?"

"I'm being a gentleman."

"Well, stop it. There's more to being a gentleman than moving a chair. Thanks for dinner. It's been lovely. Shall we go up?"

They nodded their appreciation to the band and barman who was underwhelmed at the ten percent tip Ste had signed for, given that he was in the best suite. The barman may not be so attentive next time.

"I might get a flight to see some of the other islands. I've got two weeks and won't get any more time off for the rest of the year. And I can't see Tina picking up the tab again any time soon."

"You should go to Antigua. It's about an hour north of here and we were there last time I worked this route. It's beautiful and has a lovely vibe. I've heard the Turks and Caicos are incredible but very expensive, so do it while you're on expenses if you can. Don't waste it going to Jamaica. There's nothing there that you can't get far better somewhere else."

They started to share more of their travel stories on their way upstairs, Ste doing his best to hide his overthinking as he searched for any indication of what would happen next. Isla held all the cards and he would play along. He was enjoying the feeling of not making the decisions. For a change, there was an easy equality in every way, except for their room sizes.

He let Isla into his suite, stood back and watched the magnificent seafront vista work its natural magic. Isla sucked in the blackened view from the more spacious of the two balconies, feeling the gentle night breeze tease her skin with its warmth. Apart from the lights following the coastline, the darkness across the water was unbroken with the view across to Bridgetown completely unobstructed. The music from downstairs filtered in as their ears adjusted to the near silence and they stood closer to each other than before. Isla's shoulder touched Ste's arm in a way that was unnecessary given the space, but deliberate. Ste wanted to put his arm around her, but it was Isla who moved first, yet not in the direction he wanted her to.

"Drink? And what about that about music?"

Ste pulled his arm back to his side; he had been left hanging.

"Absolutely. Have you seen all the CDs?"

Ste never travelled lightly where music was concerned, carrying at least one large CD holder to have to hand music for every occasion or mood. It was a heavy way of travelling and Ste often thought that there had to be a better way of taking music with you than carrying it on all these discs. Technology was changing and the internet was evolving; who knew what was coming?

Isla struggled with all the choices available.

"I give up. You sort the music; I'll sort the drinks. Deal? But I am not pouring gin. It must be rum. Mount Gay is only up the road. It's another place you need to visit. There's a whole rum museum and you can see the caves near there on the same trip. Did I tell you about them?"

"You've certainly got the local knowledge mastered. Consider me told. I'll look it up, M'Lady. Is there anything else I should know while you're in travel guide mode?"

"I'll think of something. But you can start by explaining to me who the hell the Toots and Maytals are. I saw a CD with their name but can't say I've heard their stuff."

"You've done it now, heathen woman. This is where I look at you with my 'You're Kidding' face. That band are the greatest thing to come out of Jamaica."

"What, greater than Marley?"

"Of course, greater than Marley. Anyway, he wrote his best stuff when he lived in London."

"Really. He lived in London?"

"Oh, good God, Isla! Where to start?"

"The Toots pre-date Marley by twenty years. They should have got into the Guinness Book of Records for recording an album and getting it out for distribution within a day."

"So, why didn't they?"

"Something to do with not notifying Norris *Bloody* McWhirter on time.

Red Tape – the curse of creativity. What they achieved that night was mental - you need to hear them. Prepare to be blown away."

He pressed play on the machine, and Isla passed him the rum and Coke she'd quickly thrown together.

Pressure Drop came through the speakers and Ste instinctively started to sing along.

'It is you, oh yeah. It is you, oh yeah.'

He stopped, realising how this could be misinterpreted. But Isla hadn't registered the words; she was still captivated by the sensation she was feeling stood out on the balcony. From their arrival a few hours earlier, Ste couldn't believe how the day was ending. If she had come through the hotel doors a few minutes later, or his own journey to reception had been different, they'd have missed each other once again.

The generous serving of Mount Gay Rum was a thousand times better than the branded miniatures left in the hotel rooms he patronised around the world. This was nectar. It was the most romantic place he had ever been and he was in a wonderful room with this truly lovely woman. What he now wanted was to wrap his arms around her and feel the affection he sensed she wanted him to give. If only she hadn't suggested another bloody drink and instructed him to play DJ, he'd already be there. The only thing between them was her reference to Patrick.

Bloody Patrick.

He took a long, thoughtful slurp from the glass before putting it on the table and resuming his search of the CDs, desperately trying to figure out what tune to call upon next with which to impress her.

Isla had started to talk from the isolation of the balcony.

"Ste, can you forget what I said earlier on? I can't believe what I was saying. I guess I am just not used to being in this position. I know we said this could wait, but...."

She paused, summoning the nerve to offer full disclosure.

"Look, there is no Patrick. Well, of course there is a Patrick, but there's nothing in it worth mentioning. I didn't want you to think I had spent the last six months either fawning after you or with somebody else."

Ste didn't reply. "And, I'd really like to stay here tonight, with you, if that is okay?"

She paused once again, waiting for some sort of acknowledgement to her proposition.

"Ste, will you say something, please? Stop pissing me about!"

Tonight, the combination of alcohol, another transatlantic flight and years of hard work had finally caught up with him. Ste lay slumped at the base of the bed surrounded by his CDs, the barely started drink sitting next to him on the table.

Isla took a pillow and blanket from the bed and put Ste in a more comfortable position. She poured herself another drink, pressed 'repeat' on the CD player and went to the balcony with a blanket of her own.

The beautiful, unexpected night was all but over. There had to be another chance for them to finally make this happen.

Chapter 33

Ste woke first, temporarily oblivious of how abruptly the evening had ended. The sun was rising and although it was only six in the morning, it didn't feel early. It was ten o'clock at home and he wondered what he was missing at work and what Tina would do to his bands whilst he was gone. He fixed the first coffee of the morning and noticed that the balcony door was open. Parts of the evening were starting to slowly come back to him—but not all of it. He couldn't remember Isla leaving. Isla, Wow! What a woman.

He changed out of his crumpled clothes and put on a robe, heading towards the balcony to catch the early morning view of the fishing boats chugging away from the bay. When he suddenly caught sight of her on a balcony lounger, his heart started banging like the rusty engines on one of the departing boats. Isla lay fast asleep, and Ste instinctively tightened his open robe which had hung loosely from him, before putting his hand on her shoulder.

She stirred, turning her mouth into a smile as her eyes started to open, before slowly adjusting to see Ste standing next to her. Unlike him, she had full recollection of what had happened a few hours before. And the morning after she had almost given herself to him, she had no regrets. Their mutual smile confirmed it would not be long before they resumed where last night had been left.

Ste spoke first. "Morning, snoozy. Is that dribble coming from your mouth?"

Isla sat up, nervously wiping at her mouth before Ste's smile confirmed he had been joking.

"Ha, ha. Very funny, Ste. And as for Snoozy, What about you, Mr Sleep-on-the-Floor?"

"I am so sorry. I guess everything just caught up with me. Are you annoyed?"

"I stayed, so you figure it out. I hope you don't mind that I stayed here, but you had a balcony, great rum and had some good tunes playing; all things I didn't have in my room. I hope you're okay with me taking advantage of your hospitality?"

"Of course. If you could leave some money out as you head off though, it would be appreciated. These rooms don't come cheap. Look, I really am sorry. I have no idea what happened. It's not the first time I've just crashed when I'm out of battery, but never in front of someone I…."

The sentence faded away before Ste said something he meant.

"The last thing I remember was being appalled at you not knowing who the Toots and Maytals are."

"I listened to them until I fell asleep. And you're right, it's incredible stuff. Have they done much else?"

"Only about twenty other albums. You want to listen some more? We don't have much time together and I'd love to spend the day with you. Music and coffee for now or do you want to go for breakfast?"

Isla stood up and Ste could easily read her mood. They had one day, and they both were glad they would not waste the morning working up the courage to say that they wanted to spend it together.

"I absolutely want breakfast. And I absolutely want to spend the day with you. What did you have in mind?"

"Out there." Ste pointed to the Caribbean Sea a few yards away. "Fancy getting on a catamaran and seeing the island from a different angle? My treat."

With a plan agreed, Isla nipped back to her room to freshen up and pack for the day.

"Come back here when you're ready. I'll get breakfast sent up."

Ste smiled; he wanted to treat her. There was no lingering disappointment about the premature end to the evening and he freshened up while he waited for her to get back. As well as the beaches, there was the hotel pool and Ste loved the water more than the gym when it came to exercise. Isla returned to the suite refreshed, and they ate newly harvested pineapple on the balcony as Ste talked more about the *thrilling* history of Barbadian music. He was in his element. He was happiness personified.

"So, while you were away, I spoke to the man on reception and he's already sorted us out with a boat trip. He called his cousin, of course he called his cousin, and has managed to get us a boat all to ourselves. I figured that we've only got a day and I didn't want to go on one of those loud ones with fifty people drinking all-inclusive the whole time. This one is private, if you're okay with that?"

Isla wasn't given a moment to respond before Ste carried on.

"I hope you are because we're being picked up in an hour."

"I'm not used to such shoddy treatment. And while the company isn't up to much, there's no other boys to play with. I guess I'll have to make do with you."

Ste and Isla were as one, always on the wind-up and full of wonderful sarcasm, banter and laughter.

"Are you ever serious, Isla?"

"You'll have to find out, won't you? And on that subject, given you never finished that rum last night, how about an early morning snifter to get the day started on the right foot?"

Ste was way ahead of her, producing an ice bucket from underneath the breakfast trolley with a bottle of Veuve Champagne and two flutes on ice.

"Mind-reader."

"It wasn't a tough read, Isla. We're in Barbados, it's sunny, we're about to spend the day together. How else could the day kick off, if not with Champagne?—except, maybe, with a kiss?"

"In that case, cheers for the Champagne. And thank you for last night. It was lovely. As for the kiss, I reckon you need to earn that."

"And how do I earn it, if not by giving you the gift of the Toots and a glass of Veuve?"

"Okay, you've earned it. Come here then, darling!"

"Darling! I like that."

Ste stood up and moved towards her. For the first time that morning, the nerves were back.

As their hands joined, the telephone rang.

Chapter 34

Ste pulled away as he was about to go in for the long-overdue kiss. He couldn't enjoy it if the phone was ringing.

"Can I answer it and still have a kiss? It will just be the front desk about our boat trip. I'll let the phone ring out if the answer is no."

"Get the phone, Ste. Like last night, I'm going nowhere." Isla necked the rest of her flute while Ste answered the call.

But his expression quickly changed. He sat down and whispered that he'd be a few minutes. He moved to a position where he could not be heard, and Isla closed the door and went to the balcony to give him the privacy he seemed to need. This was not a call from reception.

Ste slumped against the end of the bed.

After a time, he appeared on the balcony, eyes red from rubbing tears away.

"What's wrong, Ste? You look awful. Has someone died?"

"Isla, I'm so sorry. It's quite the reverse of death. But I have to go back to England. Today."

She jumped up, stunned at the sudden change of events.

"Oh, darling, what on earth can be so important? And what's the reverse of death? If it's work, can't they manage without you for a few days?"

"I'm so sorry. I had no idea." He started to cry again. Isla comforted him before his second revelation. With his chin wobbling, and eyes streaming, Ste composed himself long enough to deliver the body blow.

"Isla. The reverse of death is life. I'm going to be a dad. And I barely know the mother. I'm so fucking sorry."

"Oh, my God, Ste, are you okay? Do you want me to go?"

"Of course I don't want you to go. I don't want either of us to go anywhere other than the boat. But it's just been made clear to me that for me to be a dad to this kid, I need to have the conversations face to face. And immediately."

Isla started to search for her bag amongst the mess of breakfast trays and their boozy morning.

"I don't know what to say to you. I can't say it isn't your fault, because you're involved. I don't understand why you need to go back today, but it's not my call. Aside from that, all I can say to you is good luck. You're really going to need it if you jump to her call like this."

Isla was not sticking around to talk any further and Ste let her go, unable to contain his tears. The loss of whatever it was they had, before they had even shared a kiss, was a hard enough pill to swallow. But in that instant, his life had changed. He couldn't shirk his responsibilities and if he didn't return straight away, he knew he could not say with a clear conscience that he had always put his child first. He knew that the right thing to do was to fly back to Greta and do whatever had to be done in order that he could look his child in the eye and be able to say,

'From the first moment, I put you first.'

However naïve this aspiration was, he was not going to fail at the most important job of his life before he had even started it. It wouldn't be fair to keep Isla hanging, and although his heart was breaking, he didn't raise his head or say anything as she hurried out of his suite. If she had looked back over her shoulder, there would have been no gaze for her to catch.

And then she was gone. Once again, he sat alone on the carpet. But this time, Ste had absolutely no idea of what happens next.

Chapter 35

1999

The group of mourners stood together; gazes respectfully fixed on the four pallbearers as they lowered the coffin towards its resting place. Ste held his father's hand as they shared their last moment with his mum. They hugged each other to the soundtrack of soil landing on the coffin lid, allowing themselves a few seconds of peace before accepting the well-meaning condolences and sympathy from the mourners who had gathered in the early summer sunshine.

'Where's Greta, Son?' Mr Lewis Senior realised he hadn't seen Greta and the baby. Ste shrugged and said they couldn't make the trip to Portsmouth for his mum's send off.

There was no way he was going to lumber his grieving Dad with the truth. It would cause more hurt than any excuse he could concoct. The truth was that Greta didn't want to come. She had no interest in anything beyond their daughter, Amy, including being a supportive partner to Ste after his mum's premature death. Even though Ste was devastated at the loss of his mum, Greta still refused to come to the funeral.

"I don't like funerals; I have never been comfortable around death, and besides, I only met your mum once."

Ste had quite literally begged her to make the journey with him, but she had not even tried to find an excuse, and that included using Amy as part of her justification. They both knew that their daughter was no trouble at all, still so young that she slept most of the time. Compared to many infant horror stories they'd been privy to, Amy was a dream baby.

"There were plenty of chances to meet and get to know her, Greta. You chose not to take them. Anyway, this is not about you, or my mum. It's about me, standing in front of you pleading for you to come. What about me? Do I mean that little to you?"

"Don't be so fucking needy, Ste. Grow up. I'm not coming. I'll stay here with Amy and be here when you get back."

Part of him wanted to take Amy and stay awhile with his dad in Southsea. He was in a relationship with a woman who couldn't support the father of her daughter at such a sad time. His simple search for love and support met with repudiation, and it confirmed everything he knew about their relationship. There was nothing there. There had never been.

Ste had left his dad waiting for a better answer for long enough.

"Amy had a bad night's sleep and Greta has been up with her for what feels like days. It's nothing serious, just a bit of colic. You know how babies are. She sends her love though. Now, am I jumping in with you back to the wake?"

Ste could tell that Lewis Senior didn't buy it but now was not the time. If it wasn't for the handful of photos with her and Amy, Greta would seem like an invention of his Ste's mind. His mum had been suddenly struck down by a serious illness and so, for the last couple of months, his parents couldn't be a part of their family life in London. The devastating illness had taken his mum before she ever knew their granddaughter and Ste blamed Greta for that. Greta had no interest in them. She didn't even seem interested in Ste most of the time. It was disjointed, and for grandparents wanting a relationship with their granddaughter and, de-facto, their daughter-in-law, it was heart-breaking that no effort was made.

Ste had done his best, bringing Amy down several times as the end neared. But Greta never came, and he had always come to them straight from a flight back from somewhere far-flung, meaning he was typically rushed and exhausted. Even at his weakest points, Ste always had an excuse to hand about why something had come up preventing Greta from accompanying them. He tried to protect them from the truth.

"There will always be space in my car for you, Son. I love you. You know how proud your mum and I are of the man you've become and what you've achieved. Now, come on, you can tell me about how Amy is doing. Are those teeth still coming through?"

Ste grabbed his old man in a bear hug. It was not just the loss of his mum that had put him on the edge of tears. Something had to give. Greta was never going to change and, therefore, nothing would change at home unless he took the lead. She never appeared happy with their dynamic either but didn't seem prepared to do anything about it. Now, with a small child to take care of, she suggested that things were 'just fine', and 'for now' she was okay with how things were. Happiness with her partner did not seem to be a massive priority.

Father and son took their seats in the middle of the limousine. Neither of them had the words to make any conversation a better replacement for the few moments of calm.

Ste had tried and failed to improve the domestic balance. He needed to figure out what he was going to do and as soon as he got back from the next trip, he would try to address it… again.

Chapter 36

2001

It was a different day, in a different month, in a different year. It didn't matter what day it was. It never mattered what day it was, nor who was right and who was wrong. The sincerity of his apology made no difference either. His apology could have been one long piss-take or the sincerest of speeches. This time, it needed them both to be sincere. But Ste was the only one prepared to vocalise any kind of conciliatory noise. In the four years in which he had been part of this collective disaster with Greta, it was always him who said sorry.

Aside from his mum, his relationship with Greta was the only significant personal one he had ever had with a woman. In lighter moments with his male friends, they joked about the tribulations of their own relationships with women. His was different to the mostly exaggerated tales his friends told. Men and women are different and anyone who suggests otherwise is a fool. It's not about equality or entitlement. The differences between the sexes are intrinsically significant, and any normal logic could not be applied to understanding the differences and subsequent pinch points for relationship friction. Maybe he was being defeatist, but Ste was out of energy. He had no funny stories to tell; no tall tales of domestic strife. His pain was real and for him, there was no humorous spin to be told.

He sighed inside his soul; he didn't dare sigh out loud as it would only cause more confrontation. He had tried to walk away. He left the room to allow time to work its magic, enabling calmer heads to return. But his efforts were repelled by Greta blocking his exit. He wanted to go into the lounge, an escape that would give him a chance to spend his remaining time with Amy before he left for two weeks in the US. He gently asserted his way past, finally escaping the claustrophobic captivity of the kitchen and pulled his young daughter into his shaky arms. Ste had already forgotten what the row was about.

As he pulled her closer to him, all he felt was love; that special love every dad feels for a daughter. Everything else was a blur, and, as the immediate exhilaration faded, hopelessness returned. He didn't want Amy to see him like this and woe betide him if Greta walked in. She'd get a kick out of seeing the mess he was in. Greta wins again, in a game only she was playing. She'd taken pleasure in Ste's openness about how he struggled to cope with her. Since his mum's funeral, Ste had stopped vocalising his issues. He'd been honest in the early days and told her that they should never have been in a relationship. He felt trapped and Greta seemed to find sport in using his weaknesses to chip away at him. Amy was the solitary hold she had over him. But it was a vice-like grip which she maintained by setting out to win every argument in order to claim another victory that had no prize. There were no words to describe how exhausting she was.

Amy stuck her tongue out in the playful way three-year-olds do. But how long would it be before she would look at him differently when his relationship with her mum finally fell irrecoverably apart? All kids see their parents in the negative emotions of boredom, contempt, or disappointment. Ste wanted Amy to hold onto her innocent view of him. Her assessment of his imperfections would come one day. In the meantime, all he could do was carry on doing what he did. He brought home the money. Greta didn't care about the awards that came with his success or the reputation he carved out shaping the careers of the industry's top names. It meant nothing this side of his front door. But she did worship the mighty Pound, Dollar or soon-to-arrive Euro.

Life with Greta was a humourless, loveless, tedious existence. When at home, he fitted into their established routines and tiptoed around so as not to give Greta any opportunity to see his presence as a problem. Balloons burst when overfilled with air, and each time he had to leave, like a balloon, they always burst. Before leaving, Ste always attempted reconciliation in order to try and leave on good terms. But it never lasted. The only feelings he had on the road were for Amy. He didn't miss the domestic world and he certainly felt no loss for Greta when he travelled.

He was done. This time he meant it. The trips were increasingly intense, with no time for play. He had endless meetings with tour managers, the media contacts and bands desperate to get a piece of the musical pie. He couldn't perform at work whilst constantly performing his role in the lie that was his relationship.

He sat down with Amy to read Hairy Maclary for the tenth time that day. He just about held onto the composure required to pull off the voices he had worked out for each of the characters. Amy adored him.

After a few pages, he was saying the words from memory, but the words lacked the funny accents. Amy was onto him straight away.

"Do it properly, Daddy."

Ste was not good at hiding his mood, let alone from an astute three-year-old.

"Bottomley Potts, covered in spots and Hercules Morse, as big as a horse and Hairy Maclary, from Donaldson's Dairy."

Amy laughed as if hearing the words and the accents for the first time. She loved her Daddy and her laughter was infectious, Ste unable to resist joining her as if they were both being tickled.

He thought he had longer, but time had run away from him as his daydreaming was interrupted by the driver outside tooting his horn. Ste waved acknowledgement from the window, taking a moment alone with Amy.

The last bit was always the hardest. Having kissed Amy goodbye yet again, he would not walk away from Greta without at least trying to make peace. She was waiting in the kitchen; Ste knew that she knew he would come in with an apology. Ste knew that she knew he was built in a way that hated conflict and craved domestic peace, seemingly at any cost to his own self-worth. Therefore, he would always try and today was no different. He needed his head to be in a better place. He wouldn't be back for two weeks and leaving this way wasn't right.

"Greta, taxi's here. I'm off now."

This time, she didn't look up.

"Whatever that was about, I'm sorry for my part in it."

Normally 'sorry' would register with her; she would have looked up in recognition that she'd recorded another win.

But this time, she had no response and he had no more words. If she couldn't even look at him, he was out of ideas. And now, he was out of time.

Before he picked up his bags, he briefly considered ending things then and there. But there was no need. They both knew. So, rather than prolong the agony, he picked up his bags and left without another word. It was done. While they had tried to make the best of things, it had to be about keeping the breakup civil and grown-up. Hopes of love had long since disappeared. Any remaining hopes Ste held onto for kindness or compassion were gone.

Chapter 37

He squeezed his eyes shut when the door of the taxi closed. The first moment of relief had arrived, sweeping through his body like an adrenalin rush. It was a chance for Ste to get his head into the right place and disconnect. He had to focus on the future and that meant relegating what had just happened again to a remote part of his brain. What was done was done; and it would still be done when he got back.

There was no hope of making anything of the next few weeks on the road if he was carrying all that shit around with him. It was fun doing business in New York, but it was tough at any time of the year. In September, encased by the late summer stormy warmth, the real business got done. The crowds returned to give the city an annual rebirth after spending their summer months away from Manhattan. Whether coming back from Long Beach or The Hamptons, New Jersey or further afield, come the first weekend of September and Labor Day, the whites were put away for another year and the money was made.

This was a rare solo trip to set up the next six months' worth of plans with the East Coast players, including his most trusted compadre, Jarrod. Their relationship had launched with distrust but now it was a great one. They had quickly figured each other out, and their working relationship had flourished into a deeply significant friendship. Jarrod was still running the East Coast business and was always busy, but they made sure to carve out time for each other every time one of them was over. It was always the best part of every trip.

For a Sunday afternoon, the fifteen miles to Heathrow passed quickly. The taxi sped along the Euston Road out towards Paddington, before hitting the view of West London that the tourist buses never showed. From the A40, he gazed across the high-rise flats dominating the landscape; huge carbuncles on the skyline, housing thousands. As if London needed to feel tighter than it already did.

The view introduced a fear which swept over him. His impending break-up led to a sudden fear that he was about to lose the comforts he'd found after a decade in Islington. The family home near the canal would certainly be lost to the lawyers. He suspected Greta had already started the process. Her disinterest in conciliation was obvious. He would be cleaned out and those slum flats could be his new reality. Money be fucked. That wasn't important—his sanity was. Get your head back on it, Ste.

The security at Terminal Four was more manic than a typical Sunday. Things were getting stricter, but for the experienced traveller, Heathrow was still a straightforward airport to navigate through. The most important thing was not to get into a disagreement with anybody wearing a uniform because you can never win. Do as you are told, and you'd be through to the complimentary Sapphire and Tonics before too long.

Solo travelling was Ste's time to relax and catch up on lost sleep, but being left alone and free of work was rare. There were always people wanting to talk to him about things and plan the next 'to-dos' on the long list of things that were already planned to be done. He was in demand and sometimes colleagues and opportunists travelled with him just to steal his time. But not today. He was alone and, for this journey at least, he had a few hours to switch off and disengage from his dramas.

After a couple of looseners, the flight display screens changed to 'Boarding' and he went to his gate. Since the success of The Cormacks three years before, he had been all over the world. The US was his second home and the Americans went mad for the Rock Celtic sound. Ste was looking after a new group picked up by the fickle American press. It was great to have a new band, but there was a fatigue in starting the process again. How many times would he go through this process in his career? Was there a natural point at which you stop hanging around with the cool kids and join the ranks of yesterday's men? Do you even know it happens, or do you one day wake up and find you've been put out to seed, destined to promote 'Best of' albums until you professionally die?

The travel was gruelling even when he had time to rest on board. Suitcase living was a younger man's game. And he wasn't alone in being a reluctant globe trotter. Trudging towards the boarding ramp, he overheard one of his fellow business travellers confide in his companion, 'I'm not sure how many more times I can do this.' Glancing around, he didn't know who it was; it could be any of them. All the faces had the same look. Maybe it was no one, and he had simply mistaken his own inner voice for one of his fellow sweaty nightcaps. Was Terminal Four in fact London Bridge, and he was playing a character in a Twenty-First Century take of Elliot's Wasteland where 'each man fixed his eyes before his feet'?

The atmosphere weighed heavy, but a quiet flight and a nap would sort that. Without looking up, he handed his ticket to the stewardess on the door.

"Wow. Mr Stephen Lewis, I knew I'd see you again." As it did once before in Barbados, his heart skipped a beat. He recognised that gentle voice.

Chapter 38

He had looked for her on every flight he'd taken with BA in the three and a half years since they had last seen each other. The broad, familiar smile covered her young face. She still looked so naturally beautiful. The world seemed to temporarily stop as the memory of their last moment together made him shudder and the hairs on his arm jumped to attention. Isla was unmistakable. Unmissable. Unforgettable.

Ste watched her closely and she knew that her attempts to restore a professional interface were failing. She could not dull her enthusiasm at seeing him. It had been a long time.

"Mr Lewis, how good it is to see you again."

Ste instinctively knew that her smile was genuine, despite what had happened the last time they were together. There had been a lot of water under the bridge and he regretted letting her storm out of his room. Ste wasn't somebody who would spend time lamenting. His values stopped him from pursuing Isla at the time and despite the constant urge to do so, he didn't want to jeopardise the life he had chosen. And however painful it was, he didn't want to cross paths again only to stir things up and create pain for them both. He was glad he had chosen to do the right thing for his family, even if it meant leaving suddenly and obliterating the deep feelings that had taken hold of him.

She could have been the one, a woman who was so different from the groupies who tried it on at every gig and in every bar whether he was alone or not. Their lascivious, drooling faces would move closer as they tried to win his favour. Isla was different, uniquely interesting, kind and so attractive. She listened to him because she wanted to.

The Toots and Maytals reminded him of her, though they had never really listened to the band together. When he put them on and the sun shone, the song Pressure Drop always made him think about her. Every single time. Even when he was with Greta.

Having overcome the shock at the door, Ste smiled back at the woman who had stolen his heart even before their first kiss. Before fate had taken that away from him.

"Well, that's my peace and quiet done for." He was joking. Isla was on a short list of people he could have run into that he wanted to share his solo time with. Conscious that the queue was backing up behind him, he moved into the cabin still smiling.

"You will come and see me, won't you?"

"Of course, I'll be taking care of your area today. Seat 14A, Sir." She winked, and he remembered winking was one of the go-to flirtations he liked to think Isla reserved just for him.

And it wasn't long before she appeared at his seat.

"Champagne, Mr Lewis?'"

"Blimey, where did you spring from? Thought you were on door duty?"

"Sometimes I get to choose what I want to do. I'm no longer the new girl. Before I go off and do my thing, please tell me you're okay? Has everything worked out for you?"

"I'm okay, Isla. But if you want more detail, you're going to have to stop with the Mr Lewis stuff. He's my dad."

She grinned, quickly turning back to the rest of the passengers and the busiest time of the journey.

He sat back and took the first sip of the cheap bubbly BA provided for their business clientele. From the moment he had taken the call from Greta on that warm Barbadian morning, his world had been unrelenting. A constant of chaos and panic. He was under unrelenting pressure to put plans into action. He told his friends and family that there was someone called Greta on the scene. He had been bulldozed into being half of a couple. She was going to have his baby. Their 'love story' was nothing more than a 'Shall we keep it' conversation while Ste was both jetlagged and hungover following his night flight from Barbados. Not exactly Love's Young Dream. In contrast, he still remembered Isla leaving his suite as one of the saddest moments in his life.

He had done his best. He liked to think that Greta had as well. But he'd stuck to his rules of decency that were so integral to him, refusing to shift the direction of his moral compass despite it being far easier to do so. The useless guidance from many of his small group of well-meaning friends was unanimous; becoming a dad didn't have to mean Ste becoming one half of a loveless union.

Ste was a good parent and had tried his best to be a good partner to Greta. However, today had already become the point where the line had been drawn. Running into Isla had only reinforced that.

Chapter 39

Isla walked back into the galley, noticeably cheerier than when she'd boarded.

"You look perkier," whispered Sally, Chief Stewardess on the new 747. "I recognise that look. It's unmistakable. Someone just came on board who you know, didn't they?"

She had it all figured out already. Sally always had everything figured out. The mother hen providing more unnecessary parenting.

"It's someone I knew. Just briefly. Once upon a time."

Isla drifted off down the lane of memories that took her back three years. If he had not received that call, how would their lives be now? Would they be together now? She didn't even know if he was a parent and whether they'd kept the baby.

She had started seeing somebody a few months after returning from Barbados. Isla was young, beautiful and living a comfortable life, choosing her path as opposed to it being determined for her. With her folks continuing their tediously slow decline into inevitable madness, she had moved out to get away from their small world. The new development behind Watford Junction, while only seven miles away from her family home, seemed a world away from Hemel. Since moving out, things were better with her parents. Absence, heart, fonder, etc.

She had fallen into a routine of seeing her dad when she wasn't travelling, and it coincided with Watford playing at home. But since the much-loved manager, Graham Taylor, had left for a second time, her dad hadn't bothered to go with any sort of regularity. He didn't like change and although it had only been a few weeks, he'd already decided that he "*didn't care much for Vialli and all that Italian crap*". The distance between her and the family brought the perfect blend of isolation and familiarity.

Her boyfriend was local, but not too close, so they had to make an effort to see each other. It was a relaxed companionship and, as a result, her time away was never an issue for them. At her age, she felt too young to be tied to somebody because it was convenient. Isla thought that she was one of several people he was seeing and it didn't bother her. She was mature enough to reflect that her indifference spoke volumes about how she felt about him, which was far more relevant than what he thought about her. It wasn't just hearing the Toots that made her think of Ste; listening to the bands she knew he was involved in was just as much a trigger to initiate the memories. Checking passenger lists for his name was so much a habit that, after three years, she did it instinctively.

Lewis, Stephen

Tier: Gold – 44260900

But the name never came up.

The irony was that she was held up and late to board today, not leaving her enough time to go through the passenger list. This made his appearance a surprise for them both. She convinced herself the feelings she had disclosed to the sleeping man three years ago had evaporated. But still, she checked those lists and when she saw him today, she couldn't stop the feeling from coming back ten-fold.

Sally interrupted her daydreaming.

"You've got two nights away this time. Are you going to do anything about the bloke or just leave it to somebody else? He's gorgeous, Isla!"

"You may tap up the passengers up, Sally, but that's not me."

" Yes. Okay. There are no cases of people falling in love with passengers. Ever. You know Miranda, that posh lass from, oh where is she from, you know. Miranda? Up her own arse Miranda."

Sally struggled to clearly describe her, but Isla knew exactly who she meant and what was coming. This was another urban myth that she never bothered to entertain.

"I know who you mean. Tall, blonde Miranda. What about her?"

"That's the one. Well, she met someone on a trip back from Hong Kong and was engaged within a week. He was minted and old and got her a dream transfer from the plane right into his mansion. So, she married a passenger, and no one put her on a disciplinary."

Isla didn't want to get into this and set Sally straight. She had been friends with Miranda, and the truth was that she was in Hong Kong for the Rugby

Sevens with mates as part of the annual school reunion. The bloke was the brother of one of her friends, and she was not even working on the flight home. It was her holiday. A crap story all round and showed how this type of gossip morphed into fact by the third telling.

Isla watched Ste settle into his seat, staring peacefully out of the window, evidently deep in thought. He still had the same attractive charm and an easy calm that was at odds with the mania of his professional lifestyle. They'd only shared a few grains in life's hourglass, but she remembered his stories about how busy his life was. And that was then. No wonder people crashed and burned in an industry that was full of early deaths either through the pressure, or the age-old curse of creativity. Artists often died before their time and it was one of the things, Ste had told her, which underpinned why he was so attentive to his charges. Thinking about this stuff made her realise two things. She knew more about this business than she realised, and from staring at him, she could see that Ste was not okay.

Taking her jump seat next to the exit, Isla had a minute of peace. Ste was still staring out of the window, half-ignoring the attempts at conversation from the chap next to him. Once the plane was airborne, she wanted to get to him with the first round of drinks as quickly as she could, but Ste was moving through the cabin as soon as the seatbelt signs changed to allow movement. He was heading her way and Isla's heart raced. Had he been saving something to say and was this about to be a parody of that bit in The Wedding Singer where Adam Sandler starts playing guitar to Drew Barrymore? She caught Sally's eye. That woman was ready to pounce like a leopard stalking their prey given a half chance.

Isla braced herself as Ste closed in. She looked for his guitar, ready to scream "Yes" to whatever question he might ask.

"I just wanted to ask if I can move seats? I don't want a conversation with anyone today and I could do with not sitting next to somebody that will not stop talking until we reach JFK. I don't want to appear rude, so could you help me out, please?"

"Of course, Ste." She paused, instantly deflated by the functional, unexpected request. "Let me see what I can do."

He smiled back, grateful. He'd made his request and could have gone back to his seat, but he stayed, lurking around the galley. It was possible for her to move somebody up the cabin if there were seats available. But this flight was full and there was nothing she could do for him. After a few moments of trying, she delivered the bad news. Her heart had dropped when he said that he didn't want to speak to anybody, and she took it as a personal warning that he was settled with his partner and child—possibly even his wife by now—and to back off. Her tone was less cheery than before.

"I'm sorry, Ste. There's nothing available, but if you want to, when I've finished dishing out the goodies, you're welcome to come back up here and join me in the jump seats. I promise not to say a word if you don't want to talk. Or, we could catch up on what's happened the last few years. I won't have much time. Having to work kind of comes with the job title. But you'd be welcome to join me; your choice."

As she spoke, she glanced at his left hand. No ring. This encouraged her mouth to run faster, gibbering her way through every half-thought in her head. Passengers weren't supposed to sit in the steward's seats, but they often did. She hoped she hadn't come across as desperate, but given another minute, she would have invited him for dinner, suggested a location for their wedding and named their children.

There's no ring!

While much had changed in three years, when it came to her feelings for Ste, it was clear some things had stayed the same.

She now knew the US East Coast well. In New York, she sometimes went out to Long Beach or down through Jersey. She couldn't understand why her colleagues didn't want to explore further afield, unable to tear themselves away from the established locals where they'd let off steam each and every visit. But she wanted more. The trips to Washington were not as frequent as the busier hubs, but when she flew into the Capital, Isla would walk the loop from the White House to Capitol Hill, through the long park to the Lincoln Memorial before skipping over the Potomac River and around Arlington Cemetery. Rather than waste yet another day in yet another bar, she would spend it walking around some of the most famous resting places in the world. The American public continued to be the source of much of her amusement, especially those occupants of the tourist trams who couldn't get out and walk thirty metres to see the Kennedy grave, the historic focal point at the centre of the six-hundred-acre cemetery.

She didn't choose to go on the outings alone, and always encouraged her colleagues to join her. But their interest lay in drinking their per diems dry in a familiar, lively venue. It was great sometimes, but it was tedious when it happened every night. After a few months of joining in and being a team player, Isla chose daytime over nights and explored alone. New York held a poignancy for her and she always remembered her first visit and that one perfect evening with Ste.

Isla glanced over, taking pleasure in watching him drink the G&T that was already waiting for him at his seat. After three years, she remembered his favourite drink and knew that he would realise it was her who had put it there whilst he visited the facilities. Isla was acutely aware that she seemed unable to focus on anything else other than him. She just hoped that the journey would be kind enough to give them some proper time to reconnect.

Chapter 40

The cabin lights dimmed to encourage the calming of the masses, after which Isla waited a few minutes for a chance to let Ste know she had some spare time. With her break imminent, she hoped they could grab a few minutes and having caught his eye, Isla gestured him over. Ste moved past his neighbour, careful not to kick off more unrequited dialogue, before striding to the galley between First and Business. The plane was not moving smoothly and when Sally passed him, she fell into him. It all seemed a bit contrived, despite the bit of turbulence.

As he came through the closed curtain, a smiling Isla was already relaxing in her jump seat.

"So, is it appropriate that I ask for a hello hug? Or are you still mad at me? I wouldn't blame you if you were."

Isla was taken aback. She'd expected to get to the guts of things at some point, but not this early in the exchange.

"Of course you can, Ste. It's been a long time and it's so lovely to see you again. For the record, I was never mad. Just stunned and disappointed. I know you were too. But I was heartbroken. Maybe I will get around to forgiving you one day, but you'll have to work for it."

They embraced, feeling an immediate warmth from each other. Despite the three-year separation, there was no obvious nervousness.

"Your hair is longer," Ste pointed out.

"So is yours. Is that a grey I can see?"

"I refuse to comment. But you try not sleeping a full night at home in three years. Is this your normal route? I'd have thought I'd have seen you before now. It's not like I wasn't looking."

"You looked. And from that, I'm assuming you're now a dad."

"I still do the music. You might have seen me in the papers, or occasionally in the background on TV?"

He paused to pull a silly pose face.

"I'm in New York when I have to be, but I've been in Boston as well as the West Coast where things are busy. How come we've never crossed paths? I really did look for you."

"Well, no wonder I haven't seen you about. I never go further West than Chicago and have been doing the Caribbean up the coast to New York. I looked for you too, Ste. But here we are. I'm over here until Tuesday morning."

"Look, I am so sorry. Everything went mental that morning. My life ran away with me and I acted instinctively to do what I hoped was the right thing. I'm not sure I have ever been in control since. I wish I had stopped and talked before making decisions."

Ste was interrupted by the buzzer and Isla scanned the cabin for one of her colleagues to deal with it. Nobody was free, and despite being on a break, she was expected to respond to the call as laid out by the standards for onboard Business Class passengers.

Isla had hurried back to the galley, but Ste was already gone. The seatbelt signs were on and the mid-Atlantic turbulence was getting worse. It wouldn't last long, but it was just their luck that as soon as they had a minute together in the confined space of a mid-air tube, it was once again snatched from them.

Chapter 41

The turbulence turned into a long, violent storm. Ste gave up on the idea of getting back to the galley, as Isla was going to be busy with sick and nervous passengers for the rest of the flight. He turned on Cameron Crowe's 'Almost Famous'. There was no better recent film than this to pass the time, especially for a romantic and music aficionado such as Ste. He poured the very large G&T with four gin miniatures to one tonic that he'd swiped from the galley when nobody was looking. The unfulfilled love story of Penny Lane and William Miller unfolded to an unbelievable soundtrack of Led Zep, Elton John & The Who. It was appropriate and rang with echoes of his own situation. He was asleep by the time the bus rumbled through America, to the backdrop of Stillwater singing Tiny Dancer.

The thump onto American tarmac jolted him awake. As the passengers turned on their phones, the jostling for the doorway caused mayhem, much to the annoyance of the onboard crew. Groggy and still half asleep, Ste was caught in the dilemma of whether to join in and get to the front of the queue to win the race to the warm Border Force greeting or hang back and reconnect with Isla. He craned his neck but couldn't see her. The combination of the busy, the pissed and the excitable thronged around his favourite seat closest to the main exit. Standing where he was, he knew he would be pushed through the aircraft door whether he wanted to or not. Whatever happened next, he was going to find her even if he had to camp at JFK until her return leg on Tuesday morning.

The distance between the plane door and entry onto American soil was the longest short trip imaginable. In the years since he had first made the journey, things had got far worse. At least Ste knew the quickest way through it, and where he could sprint to beat the other passengers. Get stuck behind one of the flights landing from Asia at the same time and that was two hours of your life gone. Being first off the plane was worth the extra his Business Class exit seat cost, if only to protect his sanity.

After one final look for Isla amongst the hundreds of bobbing heads jostling towards the door, he sprinted up the extension ramp that linked door to terminal. There were no other planes disembarking, and, for a Sunday afternoon, JFK was quiet. There was still the unpredictable matter of the guards to negotiate, but Ste was well-rehearsed in how to deal with the stern, overweight, gun-toting bureaucrats. An American immigration hall was not the place to let on that they were anything other than the most important people.

"Good afternoon, Sir, what is the purpose of your trip to the US?"

Having made the mistake of saying, "*Sex, drugs and rock and roll,*' once before, Ste knew the score and chose the response that would get him through quickest.

The PR story did the trick, with the occasional follow up about the finer details. But by now, his travel history told the story in more detail than he needed to provide. They knew when he was booked to go home and where he stayed, even without his Customs Declaration form. They probably knew he'd had a shitty morning and was about to move out of the family home. Any delay meant they were checking for inconsistencies, or just fucking him around.

"So, who do you represent?" The follow-up question was not unexpected but felt like an imposition.

Careful not to show irritation, he offered a brief explanation about the band and who he was meeting; it was all routine, but he wasn't going to break his record time today. The tiny victory in his regular battle against '*The Man*' would wait for another day. Today was a draw, but the delay was enough that by the time he was stamped up and through the miserable focus of this '*Man*', he could see the cabin crew going through their processing lane, use of which was one of Ste's private fantasies. He looked for Isla through the massed huddle of her colleagues but didn't see her. With a sense of resignation, Ste walked out onto American soil. In front of him was the driver holding a placard with his name.

"Good afternoon, Sir. How was your flight? I assume you're staying at the Hilton?"

A polite nod would answer the question, but Ste was excellent at small talk and always chose polite conversation over silent indifference. A chat could liven the crawl into Manhattan and the throng of vehicles going into New York had turned the road to gridlock. But the driver wasn't interested in conversation and asked Ste if he minded the radio on. Aside from the US Open Tennis Final playing out around the corner at Flushing Meadow, the Yankees were playing the Red Sox at home. The fixture remains the Manchester United v Liverpool of baseball. With the Yankees closing in on another Divisional Championship and potentially another World Series, the driver was excited at the prospect of defeating their closest rivals. Ste didn't understand the rivalry, given that Boston was three hours north while the Mets in Queens were only ten miles away, and as the game petered out with another home win, Ste lost any grip on how far they'd travelled. To avoid domestic issues, he sent the arrival text to Greta; the driver cheered as the game was done. His Yankees had walloped the Red Sox and swept the series three-nil.

"There's even worse traffic ahead, buddy. Do you mind if I take a detour?"

"Whatever works best. It's your patch."

Ste was drained and didn't know whether he was tired or wrung out from the mental strain of his now-concluded relationship. Greta, of course, hadn't responded to his text. His mood didn't improve as the driver's attempts to exercise some local knowledge backfired, having ended up so far north that they ran into the exodus from Yankee Stadium. With his patience out, Ste felt uncharacteristically irritable and had an overwhelming craving for the solitude of his hotel room. Reasoning that his typical politeness was not helping, he temporarily became more American.

"Hey, pal, can you just get me to my hotel as quickly as possible? What are you thinking bringing us up here? Why are we up near Harlem? Do you think I don't know where we are?"

He immediately felt bad. He was not the sort of person who was generally rude to anyone, let alone someone driving him to a hotel.

His apologetic driver owned up to his mistake.

"Mr Lewis, Sir, I am really sorry. I didn't think it would be this bad. I'm doing my best. You're a very valued customer."

Ste felt worse the more his driver personalised the apology. It was his turn to apologise.

"I'm sorry, mate. Long day. I need my bed."

Chapter 42

Silence enveloped them for the rest of the journey into Manhattan. At least he wasn't going to run into more sports traffic as the Jets versus Colts game was finished; and despite being called New York, they resided over in New Jersey. After what felt like an eternity, the limousine pulled up outside his New York home away from home.

Typical. An executive minibus for cabin crew had pulled in ahead of Ste and was unloading. No amount of Hilton points was going to enable a queue jump ahead of this lot. Just another delay in a series of them. He should have been in his room ages ago. Calm through disengagement; evidence of agitation got you nowhere. Ste took a mindful breath in and prepared for another wait at the back of another queue. The joys of business travel. He was used to this. Close eyes, breathe and wait.

He tried his best to disengage from the orderly chaos around him. But soon enough, he recognised the sound and shape standing talking in front of him. Yes, it was her.

Sensing she was being stared at, Isla swung round, smiling as always, a little squiffy from the miniatures the crew continued to snaffle off the plane for consumption on the ride in. She showed no signs of surprise.

"You finally woke up, then. Shame you missed chatting with me. Have you forgotten how interesting I am?"

They both giggled like children. It was back on. Isla looked over to another queue where Sally was watching her every movement with an invasive interest.

"Thank you for being here." Ste made no effort to hide his excitement. "I thought I'd screwed up again and it would be another three years. I looked for you on board and in immigration. But you disappeared—how do you do that?"

He wouldn't need to tell her about his Plan B to locate her, which would end up with him stalking her at JFK.

"I was hiding from you, of course."

"You what?"

"As if. I'm pleased to see you, Ste, even if you and I are being watched. Don't look now. I mean it."

Ste instinctively looked around, and Isla burst out laughing. Men were useless.

"Actually, something way more glamorous came up. I had an intimate date with the blocked toilet I was in charge of. Anyhow, I guessed you'd be here. It's not like you ever stay anywhere other than Hiltons and I saw your immigration card when you were asleep."

She was a smart lady. And so gorgeous. There was no chance that he was going to blow it this time. He was enjoying the sport of this encounter.

"I saw you leave the plane but got here ahead of you. What happened?"

"Don't ask. The bloody driver and the Yankees. We ended up too far North, as though he was drawn to a homing device at Yankee Stadium. It's a miracle we got here at all."

"We do have a thing for meeting in hotel foyers. Although it's been a while, hasn't it? Did you want to catch up? We could meet for a drink."

"I was going to crash…" Ste noted an immediate evaporation of Isla's smile. He could play games, too. "but not now I know you want to hang out. Please say you're free and that you fancy some dinner?"

It had been an emotional day. Leaving Greta and his daughter was more difficult than usual. He knew it was going to be the last time he'd leave them as one family unit, but at least it had the potential of ending in a far better way than it had started.

"I take it you're working pretty much non-stop. I assume you're here working and I'm not interrupting another solo holiday, liaison, or a… family thing?"

She was digging, and Ste grinned at her lack of subtlety. The day had not given them the opportunity for Ste to answer the questions Isla asked, and he wanted to get cleared up. It had been forty-two months. They had both totted them up on the drive in.

Ste didn't want to go into the details of his private life whilst standing in a hotel lobby being watched by the intrusive stares of Isla's colleagues. He had no concern about what he would say. Always the truth. But there was a time and a place.

"You're right, just back-to-back work starting tomorrow morning. But in the words of Bob Segar, '*We've got Tonight.*'"

Isla almost spat out her reaction to the mention of one of her favourite songs.

"That song. If you're not thinking about 'The Wonder Years', I will lose all respect and you can forget dinner. From the one where Kevin climbs on Winnie Cooper's roof after the car crash and stares at her. It's a wonderful bit of telly. Can you imagine a more beautiful song to play over that piece of TV?"

Of course, Ste knew plenty of other songs that would make that scene special, but he nodded in agreement.

"Isn't it a brilliant scene?"

"I watched The Wonder Years every week. Any reasonable person now in their 20s watched that. I don't think I could have any respect for anyone who didn't. What a great song. What a romance."

"Did you know, in 1983, Kenny Rogers covered that song with Sheena Easton and it went…."

Isla interrupted his geeky download with a loud sigh.

"Not now, Ste. Save it for the date. We have to find something to talk about. See you in twenty minutes?"

They smiled. It had started again.

Chapter 43

Normally, he had the same feeling when he checked into a room. They all looked the same; same views, coffee and disappointing menu choices. Blankets in the cupboard, toiletries in the bathroom and towel configurations hung uniformly over the heated rails, rounded off with a folded toilet roll triangle.

His fatigue was to be expected after years of patronising the Hilton chain around the world. The rewards scheme was like a trap that snared you with the upgrades and access to the free stuff in the lounges. Today, he felt a different vibe. Ste barely gave the room a glance as he threw his bags on the bed, undressed, and dipped in and out of the shower at a speed that meant he barely needed a towel. Three minutes later, he was ready to go. He didn't want to be early like a sad sap, so sat on the edge of his bed working out how long twenty minutes was. He was ready in less than ten.

Checking his phone again, there was nothing from Greta, but there were, as always, enough messages from work to keep him busy. His new band were in touch, and there were two messages from JJ, the lead singer of 'Son of No Town' who were the current 'Next Best Thing.' He was checking in, which was nice of him, but self-serving. He wanted to know everything, and a day didn't go by without communication between them. He sent a reply to confirm arrival, but nothing else. He had only one plan tonight. He was spending the evening with Isla and connecting again. He remembered that just before 'The Call', he was going to kiss her. It was a long time to wait for a kiss.

Chapter 44

Normally, she had the same feeling when she checked into a room. They all looked the same. The same views, coffee and disappointing menu choices. The bed was always to spec, along with the mattress, duvet and pillows that offered no surprises. They used one brand of toiletry miniatures that littered the bathroom, under the gaze of the similarly configured towels and pointlessly triangulated toilet roll.

But today, Isla felt a different vibe running into the room. She chucked her bag on the bed before rushing through the wash and brush up far quicker than she'd normally entertain. She was ready in ten minutes, looking around the room remembering the last time they had been in a hotel room together when they had nearly kissed and she had wanted to give herself to the darling man who made her smile and played such great music. The groundwork had been quickly laid for a lot more. But 'The Call' came and Isla was left heartbroken for the first and, so far, only time. Isla had never felt anything that powerful for any other man.

She stepped into the lift and had pressed 'One' before she noticed that the button had been pressed by the other person in there. Her gaze moved slowly upwards, eventually landing on Ste whose own nervous pacing had stopped as she entered the small space they now nervously co-inhabited. The doors closed and they smiled, taking a moment to embrace, Ste stooping into the hug with his smaller companion. She moved away first as the lift slowed to its journey's end, not wanting her nosey colleagues jumping to a gossiping conclusion. This thing with Ste was something that was between them. Nobody else. If it was a thing. It had been a long time.

"So, where do we go? At least this time you can drink."

"To be honest, Ste, I fancy a walk more than boozing. I think we need to get everything out there, so we don't have any more surprises."

"I owe you some answers before we hit New York with you as a legal grown-up. And I want to know what's going on in your world. I think yours will be less complicated, so how about you go first."

"Ste, please. This isn't something I want to rush through. Last time we met up, we were on the point of taking things much further and I know I'm not misreading things by saying if you hadn't got that call, we might have had a run at things together. We were about to kiss, Ste. Spend the day on a boat together. It doesn't get much more romantic than that. Look, I understand why you dropped everything to run back to England, but I think you owe me some words of explanation."

He understood that this had to be a grown-up conversation. His natural attempts to find a more humorous path through a delicate conversation would have to wait.

"You're right. I'm sorry, Isla. I was trying to keep it light."

"Let's find somewhere quiet, away from this hotel but not in the Village?"

"How about going to that boathouse by the water? I've walked past it so many times and only ordered a drink. In the meantime, you can tell me about your latest band."

Ste held Isla's hand as they took the winding paths through Central Park which meandered up to the Loeb Boathouse. He indulgently disappeared into his evocative descriptions of all the irrelevant bits in his life, taking as long as he could to delay the personal stuff until they were settled with a drink. He wanted to tell her everything but didn't know how his news would land. At least this way, when he finally spilled his guts, if she'd had enough of him and didn't want to stick around, this walk would be the memory he'd keep when recalling his last few minutes of happiness with her.

Isla might have a partner, after all. Following their three-year hiatus, it was unlikely they'd meet by chance and both of them be in a position to rekindle their spark, regardless of how excited he was and the affectionate ease with which she held his hand. Ste suddenly realised that she was holding his hand. This wasn't somebody who was yearning for somebody else.

The restaurant was closing in an hour, so they slipped into a table and ordered a drink. The waiting was over. D-Day was here, and it was time for the chat. Isla was first out of the blocks.

139

"I've got plenty to tell you. But given how things finished, I think the onus should be on you, Ste. Do you want to start?"

"Fair enough. First of all, Isla, I'm sorry."

"For what?"

"Well, truth be told, I'm not really sure. But I feel like sorry is appropriate in this case. And you're right. If I had not taken the call from Greta, we would have spent an incredible day together; and I've always looked back on that moment and felt I lost out on what could have been a life-changing day for you and me. You don't get many of those in a lifetime and to let you go was tragic. We always click; we've done it again today. Being with you is meaningful. And memorable."

There was a silent acknowledgement of the irony. For them both, that day had been life changing. But in a totally different way.

"And Greta. She's your wife, partner, your what?"

"Hard to say, really. We're certainly not married, and she falls short of the standards you'd expect of a partner."

"You're not making this easy. What about the baby? I presume you're a father?"

"You want me to give you the potted history?"

Isla nodded. Ste explained what had happened back from before they had met up in Barbados to the present day, how there had been nothing between Greta and him, so much so that he had no real recollection of there being a relationship that warranted a mention. Certainly, nothing he was cheating on by spending his time with her, firstly in New York and then Barbados. He felt no guilt about getting close to Isla.

"And now?" she had the history. "What about the present, Ste?"

"And now, we are well into the process of breaking up. Amy is the only thing which makes it complicated."

"So, you're broken up, or not broken up? It is binary. One or the other."

"If you asked Greta, she'd say we are broken. And that is how I feel. But I haven't had a chance to pack up and leave the home, or have that final conversation despite the many conversations on the subject. You know that the woman didn't even come to my mum's funeral! Who doesn't come to a family funeral? But even before I saw you earlier today, I had decided that when I get back to England, I would not be walking back into a relationship with her. So, as it stands, I guess we are in the process of breaking up, which technically means…"

"Look, I get it, Ste. You're breaking up, in the process of starting to separate and there are a bunch of things you need to take care of. But to be clear, Ste, you still live in the same house as the mother of your daughter. That's still quite a big deal."

"I'm not going back, Isla. I've promised myself and am promising you. And that decision is in no way related to you. Before I saw you today, I'd already made that decision—seeing you has just enforced it for me. I love my daughter; that won't change. But what little life I had with Greta… well, that's truly over. And now that I've laid myself bare, what about you?"

"My story is nowhere near as dramatic as having a three-year-old daughter. I'm old enough to drink in America. For the last three years I've been enjoying life. I'm working my way up, but promotions don't come as quickly as I'd like. And I'm fitting in guilt trips to see my parents when I must. It's not very Rock and Roll."

"So, you've not had a reason to run back to England because you've been impregnated by someone you barely know, stuck at the relationship because it seemed like the morally correct thing to do, and three years on, you're on the verge of falling apart because you've given it everything and it still isn't enough?"

"Nope. And in case you were in any doubt, I would have come to your mum's funeral even if I was just your friend. Fancy another drink?"

"Yes, but not here. They're closing soon and I want to walk some more. This is not how I saw the conversation going. I feel depressed by it all, if I'm honest." Ste slumped back in his chair, deflated by the narration of his own reality.

"How did you see it going? I'm okay with everything you've told me, but which part of the truth was likely to land differently?"

"I don't know. But I'm glad it is out there. I haven't confided in anybody. My friends see me as holding life together, but they really have no idea. Mainly because I'm embarrassed by myself and this ridiculous situation that I've made every effort to make good."

"No wonder you're on the verge of a breakdown – it's a wonder your boss hasn't sent you to Barbados again. You dear man. This is normal stuff these days. You've done the right thing, and you're a good person. You're a bloody good bloke, Ste. You did what you had to do, stuck at it, and gave it your best shot. It hasn't worked and I assume you've been faithful and loyal. You didn't have to tell me what was going on in Barbados; you could have shagged me rotten and let me fly off none the wiser before doing the honourable thing. You chose not to. That's a really attractive quality, Ste. Now, pay the bill and I'll be back in a minute. Your choice where we go next."

Isla went to freshen up, unsure whether to laugh or chastise herself at introducing shagging into the conversation. Ste settled the extortionate bill for two hot drinks before they walked towards the skyscrapers where there were bars more suited to their returning optimism. Irish Bars in New York were open late, and many didn't close at all. They found one and took stools at the quieter end of the bar.

"Isla, please put me out of my misery. You know everything. Where does that now leave us? Is there any chance of an us? What happens next?"

"Forget everything and look at this through the eyes of somebody who isn't involved. You aren't ready to jump into anything until you've sorted your life out. You need to sort out your domestic shit. In the meantime, we can hang out and slowly figure out where we go once you're free. I've no problem with that at all."

"Let me get this straight. I need to play this back and there's no point doing it on my own. What you are saying is correct, I'm trying to sort out my domestic life."

"Yes, you are."

"And whilst I do so, we can hang out."

"If you want to, yes we can."

"And once I sort myself out, we can look at moving forward and potentially starting something together?"

"That's pretty much captured what I was saying."

"Does the hanging out extend to a kiss?"

"Not officially. But I think I owe you one, so maybe just this once."

Not hesitating for a second in case something scuppered him like a ringing phone, Ste leaned in. His hand wrapped around the back of her head and his fingers caressed the hair draped over her shoulders. After four years of waiting, they finally kissed.

Isla felt the long-overdue embrace in her core. It seemed to last a lifetime and would have lasted for longer were it not for the intrusive piss-taking applause coming from a bunch of drunk Yankees fans at the other end of the bar.

"That was nice. You'd have had something even better three years ago if you hadn't fallen asleep."

"What do you mean?"

Isla filled him in on what almost happened during their previous night together.

"I fell asleep while you were saying that you wanted me?"

"Well, I did say that you might have shagged me rotten. But don't get carried away, Ste. You're older than you were, and I'm now well out of your league. You've still got a lot of work to do."

It wasn't going to happen tonight. But they knew things were going to be alright. This was going to happen.

They devoured their calamari and buffalo wings as the bar emptied. Although this was a drinking den, the Blaggard's Pub was not going to get any busier on the first Sunday night after Labor Day. New York was ready for the working week and things had thinned out. Although they had the freedom of the city, it was late and the five-hour time difference was now kicking in. Despite being desperate to stay out, their bodies were screaming for sleep so they set off on the short walk back to the hotel.

"If the lobby bar is still full of my colleagues, you'll understand if I can't be arsed answering questions. Especially questions which I don't know the answers to myself. I want this to mean more, Ste, however, until the situation with Greta is sorted, you and I can't be anything more than this."

"And what is this?"

"We are everything, except Bedroom People."

"Hey, I have a Suite. Can we be Suite People?"

Isla smiled, accustomed by now to Ste making a joke wherever possible. But she clearly needed to be understood.

"Ste. Sort your shit out and then we can be whatever people we want us to be. I'm not charging into this under a cloud, and I will not be the woman who broke up your family. It's not right. You wouldn't want it the other way. I know you well enough to know that."

"You're right, Isla. Frustratingly accurate. How do you know me like this?"

"Because you've had my attention for a really long time, Ste. It's just a shame it's taken us so long to get to today. But I'll be here when you're sorted. Unless you screw it up again, in which case, it will be a lucky escape for me."

Isla saw her colleagues in the reception bar.

"This is where we go our separate ways, is that okay?"

"You go first, Isla. Have a nice night and call me tomorrow. Here's my new card with my US and UK numbers. My e-mail is on there, and the agency website which takes messages. Please don't lose it this time."

Isla moved forwards and landed the last kiss of the evening onto Ste's cheek. Although he wanted more, Ste happily went off to his suite, alone, but very happy.

Before going to sleep, he received a text message from an unknown number.

'*Thanks for tonight. See you tomorrow. This is Isla, by the way. You're going to need this number xx*'

Chapter 45

Isla wanted to stay close to the hotel so she didn't miss a minute with Ste once he finished work. He'd responded to her text straight away but at seventy-five pence a text, she wasn't well-heeled enough to be sending too many affectionate prompts by phone. Regardless of money, she knew Ste would be consumed with his own business and she wasn't ready to play the role of the fawning woman waiting for her man to find time for her.

Last night had ended up being a late one as Sally pulled rank and kept her at the bar long into the night. She wanted the scoop about why Isla was so happy and who the bloke was. It wasn't until Isla got back to the privacy of her bedroom well into the early hours that she finally allowed her emotions out, jumping onto the bed, banging her arms and legs like a child having a tantrum. But instead of the despair felt the previous time she had walked away from Ste, this time, it was in rapturous celebration.

Isla had one of the new Creative Labs MP3 players which could store hundreds of tunes. She'd developed a far greater interest in music and had a playlist ready for any mood. As she looked out of the sixth-floor window, across the New York night sky to the skyscrapers around Wall Street, she plugged her headphones in and put on the song that had been nagging at her all night.

'*Ay Ay Ay, Ay Ay Ay.. Them a-tell me, you huggin' up a big monkey man*'

Good old Toots Hibbert. These familiar sounds of the Caribbean followed her around the world, but tonight she was shattered and anything more than one song was wasted on her tired soul. Some hours later, she awoke in the chair she'd sat down in. Despite being in her clothes and sitting upright, she'd ended up sleeping far longer than usual for a first night away. Keen to pretend she wasn't going to spend the day waiting for Ste to come back, she made plans to hide away for the day, somewhere quiet, where she would not be disturbed by the world.

The Quad Cinema showed films Isla wouldn't ordinarily get to see. It was dark in there and nobody would bother her, giving her both the time to rest and unapologetically kill the day, with the added bonus of looking cultured as opposed to appearing to be a saddo with nothing to do. It was mid-afternoon when she came out, squinting at the sunlight enveloping her. While she was dozing through the film, Ste had messaged. Isla was glad of the delay in receiving the message, otherwise, she'd have responded instantly.

'*Hey Isla – 5 OK? Hotel Bar? xx*'

'*Absolutely. CU then x*' – she didn't obsess about how many kisses to leave. This was straightforward.

By the look of the darkening skies, one of New York's flash storms was approaching. She was excited and wanted to take it easy with a long bath and a glass of wine, before ambling down to the bar in time for five. She was ready by four.

She arrived in the bar just in time to see Ste come sliding across the foyer like an ice skater. He was right on cue for her to order their first drink but soaked from the rainstorm and looked like an extra from a cheesy eighties pop video. He started to pant his apologies.

"Couldn't get a cab. Had to run in the pissing rain."

He leant against the bar, exhausted. A hot, steaming, bedraggled mess. Sally might change her mind if she saw him now.

"Need to get changed. Do you mind….. waiting? So sorry."

He continued to pant out his few words whilst trying to catch his breath after his long run through the Manhattan rush hour. Grabbing a jug of water from the edge of the bar, he poured a long glass and downed it in one. Given her colleagues were likely to appear at any time, Isla saw his bedraggled state as a feeble excuse to relocate. Rather than order down here, Isla offered to come with and keep him company while he got ready. In his room. Once again.

The sky had now cleared, and Isla took her seat in the window while Ste made use of the facilities.

"It's really unfair, you getting these good rooms all the time."

She gave up on conversation because Ste couldn't hear her. There was nothing to do but scan Manhattan Island, the sun having started its slow descent in the West.

As he emerged from his shower wrapped in just a towel, it would have been considered polite for Isla to look away. But she'd seen enough of New York from this angle and she cheekily follow her base instincts and ogled the hell out of him. Although she'd never seen him topless, there had been many times she had imagined it and quickly gave up any pretence that she was not looking. Sitting back to take in the full view of Ste picking up his clothes with one hand and holding the towel around his waist with the other, she was making a huge effort not to jump on him.

To hell with the rules! Stop it, Isla – all good things.

Isla could see Ste noticing her watching his simple efforts to retain his dignity. The humour of the situation aside, she was relieved that there were no ghastly tattoos of permanent dedication to Greta or any of his bands. He didn't hurry to look up from the towel-drying of his hair, but when he did look towards Isla, she didn't look away. Instead, she moved towards his partially covered body and kissed him with passion. Careful to not make a lovely situation awkward, she turned back to the outside view. It was a beautiful evening, with the city now clear of the earlier stormy haze.

"We've done enough serious for now, haven't we, Ste? Can we go and have fun on our first date tonight? Let's go back to the Village and I'll show you why I like karaoke!"

"Sounds great. What are you going to sing? And what is this 'first date' business? Does the past not count anymore?"

"I've been thinking about it and am undecided, so let's treat it like a first date. Let's just say that the past is practice. As for the singing, just wait and see. But I need to eat something soon and then we'll see if you want to sign Hertfordshire's hottest new female singer."

"Wicked Willy's it is then. Got to tell you though, karaoke is anti-music. And before you start shouting at me, a lot of people I spend time with love to show off. Most of them are God-awful, bearable at best, but they believe that they could have made it and it's normal for me to be still watching the massacre of great songs at two or three in the morning. As a result, I'm no stranger to it and can belt out my own version of Lost Weekend or Boys Don't Cry. If I'm forced to, that is."

"Forced to? You can't be forced to sing karaoke. Don't kid me, Lewis - You love it."

In no time they were walking down Bleeker St after a four-year break.

"Did you speak to Amy today?"

"Absolutely. Well, kind of. She's too young to have much conversation, but I try to speak to her every day. I check in just to tell her I love her. It's the least I can do when I'm away so much."

Isla was really asking whether he had spoken to Greta.

"Greta didn't even say hello. She passed the phone to Amy and walked away. There was no point in forcing a conversation. But, Isla, you have my word that the moment I am home, this gets sorted."

"I trust you, Ste."

With the entertainment, if that was the right word, not starting until eight-thirty, they wandered back to the same restaurant where their friendship had started years before.

"It's nice to be back here, considering everything. I think you're right - the past was just a bit of practice and this really is our start!"

They both nodded in violent agreement.

Like the first time, when they had eaten in the fabulous Italian, the ease of their chatter gave the impression that they had known each other forever and this was another of numerous meetings across many years. Ste opened his heart about Amy. He recounted her bedtime stories and the voices that went with them.

His devotion to his little girl was obvious. Ste didn't do anything by halves and his parental bona fides were clear from the dedicated, kind and affectionate way he spoke about his daughter. He was even kind in his description of Greta, even though she sounded like a nightmare. A nice touch.

Isla was itching to sing, so they went back to the half-empty karaoke bar full of students and tourists, all waiting for their turn to show off. Technical problems were holding things up, and with a start time becoming more and more vague, the irritated audience had already started to leave in search of an alternate venue. These problems weren't going to be resolved tonight. Ste could sense Isla's disappointment. She wasn't good at hiding her emotions. She had drunk enough alcohol that her confidence level was just right to knock out her songs uninhibited by suppressed nerves. Against all his better music-loving instincts, he suggested they give up in 'Willy's' and move on somewhere different.

"This is New York. We'll find a place in no time and you can finally show me what you've got."

They walked hand in hand towards Midtown Manhattan and the mass of bars that lined the busy streets. It was nearly ten o'clock and the clouds above the city were massing together in advance of another late summer storm. As the first spots of rain fell, they could both see that the weather was winning in their battle to find an active karaoke bar. They'd drawn a blank.

With Isla's shuttle arriving at five in the morning and Ste due downtown to meet with Jarrod nice and early, time had beaten them. For now. They stood under the canopy covering the entrance of one of the nearby buildings and held each other tight. Ste said he wished he could phone up Greta right now and end the relationship. But that would be a spineless, awful way to do things. Isla wished Ste would phone Greta right away and finish whatever it was he was ending. But she knew it was not the mark Ste left on things. She admired him for doing the right thing. He could have carried out a quick execution of the obstacle so that they could progress things to the bedroom. Instead, they just kissed and after a squeeze of her hand, Ste hailed a taxi.

The rain was falling hard now and wasn't stopping anytime soon, slowing the traffic to a crawl. They chatted about the days between now and when they would meet again, which translated into a manic chat about everything Ste needed to do over the next few days, while Isla focused on seeing her parents on Wednesday, reminding herself in the process about the present for her mum at JFK.

They wandered into the foyer, instinctively heading towards the bar for one last drink. It was busy. None of Isla's colleagues were in the bar. Aside from the alcohol curfew all flight staff had to honour, they had to be ready for a long day's work in just seven hours.

"One final drink in the bar? Or should we raid the minibar in my room?"

Ste was frantically clutching at straws to extend the night. While neither of them wanted the evening to end, they were both knackered and it was time to play at being grown-ups. For now, they couldn't just be the headstrong kids who'd fallen into affectionate lust with each other.

"I think we know what we want, but we need to call it a night. Walk me up? If I drink any more, I'll be in trouble tomorrow."

Ste smiled. Another trip to his bedroom without a happy ending. But that was okay. It wouldn't be this way for long. They'd already arranged their next date for when they were both next in London. Monday the twenty-fourth for three whole days.

"I promise you, Isla, by the time we see each other again, I will have sorted my life out. Can I take you to dinner as soon as you've enough energy to enjoy it? I want to see a lot more of you. You're an incredible woman and I feel things when I am with you that I have never experienced before. I'm so excited."

She threw herself into Ste's arms and held him. He landed a final kiss on her and they said goodnight.

She couldn't go straight to bed. The pre-flight routine where she sorted her stuff for the journey home had to be done before she went to sleep, just in case she overslept. That shuttle bus would not wait for her and there were serious consequences if someone missed it. Having packed and tidied up, she instantly flopped onto the bed with the grandest of smiles. She lay there, her arms wrapped around her neck, imagining they were his. Imagining he was there. There was now a calm about her feelings towards Ste. She was confident that they had a future. Within moments, she was asleep.

Chapter 46

The four-thirty alarm call intruded the way alarm calls at that time of the morning typically do. It was a total violation of the senses, and without a coffee in front of her, Isla would not be able to engage with the world. Last night wasn't the drunken singalong event that she'd wanted, but what an evening she had had; and yet again, what a guy Ste was. She missed his company already. They had talked, laughed constantly and they ate well. It was all very grown-up, and different from her substandard experiences with the men she dated in England.

Dare she phone in sick, consign herself to her hotel room pretending she was too ill to travel, just to stay for an extra bit of time with him? Of course not. That would be both silly and needy, and given their history, would inevitably backfire. She'd see him soon enough. But it was so tempting!

She quickly pulled herself together and made for the door, immediately running into a familiar face in the corridor outside.

"Morning, Isla. Not hiding anyone in your room, are you? You've been AWOL on this trip." Sally never missed a trick to poke her nose in.

"Morning, Sally. I've been very well behaved. Nothing my flight Mum needs to worry about – you're welcome to poke your head in and check."

Neither of them was chatty given the early hour; and other than their colleagues, no one else was around reception. The empty road out towards the airport reflected that it was too early for reasonable people to be up.

Terminal Seven was typically busy, a twenty-four-hour hub of energy and familiar territory for the team. They all knew how to navigate to airside the quickest way, avoiding the crowds at every pinch point. It was a full flight and Isla instinctively examined the passenger list, before remembering the name she blearily checked for was tucked up in bed back in Manhattan.

She yawned. Another long day at work and another trip back home was regrettably underway.

Chapter 47

Since their first meeting at the *wrong* Hilton four years ago, Ste and Jarrod continued to meet regularly for breakfast. After the success of their first venture, and with full understanding that Jarrod was still coming in from Staten Island, it was no hassle for Ste to get up and go to the south of Manhattan. It was now a tradition, and he either walked or took the Broadway-Seventh Avenue Metro to Cortlandt Street. Typically, he was up early, still excited from his date with Isla. With time on his hands, he walked the familiar route through what was the clearest morning he'd ever experienced in New York. Americans are not fans of walking anywhere, but in New York, where public transport is a hot, cramped, and smelly experience, the streets are full of people walking their way around the compact island.

A year before, he had attended a dinner meeting a few miles over the Hudson River, out by Woodcliff Lakes. Deciding to stay the night outside the city, he'd walked back to the hotel after dinner, hoping for a view of America that his non-stop tour of the cities would not give. Although it was only a mile, he quickly wished he'd got a cab as a police car pulled over and he was aggressively interrogated about why he was walking. Not where he was walking to, or his reason for going there. Just why he was walking in the first place when there were plenty of transportation options available. It was assumed that he was either a criminal, a vagrant or mentally unwell. Ste was required to produce his hotel documentation and passport to convince the disbelieving gun-wielding officer that he was neither homeless nor mad. He just fancied a walk.

There was a spring in his step this morning. It was stunningly beautiful, the clear blue sky and late summer warmth proving a stark contrast to the many dull and misty mornings that had greeted Ste on many of the previous times he'd taken this familiar four-mile wander through the city. The perfection of the morning seemed to make everything more proximate than usual. Ste drank in the September sunshine, allowing his neck to fall backwards so that the rays could hit his face each time he passed between the gaps in the tall buildings. He felt alive and present, quickly losing all track of time, only snapping back to reality as his phone beeped just as he approached the hotel. His face lit up once more. It was a text from Isla.

'Morning – are you up? You're worth the 75p to find out. At JFK waiting for plane. I miss you. x'

A smile covered his entire face.

'Looking forward to us being together again. You're the bomb.'

Damn. He hadn't put a kiss.

'I forgot the X. Forgive me. XX'

He put the phone back in his pocket just as Jarrod rose, his arms extended to engulf each other in the sort of tight bear hug reserved only for the very dearest of people.

"You know, if you always get here early, we could meet closer to me in future. Then I don't have to leave so bloody early."

"But then, my odd English friend, we would not get to honour this great tradition. And this way I get to bug you every time you come over here doing an American out of a job."

After four years of working together, theirs was a fabulous friendship. Jarrod loved his trips to London, but it was on the East Coast that they mostly got to hang out, working with the media, promoters and the groups of people essential to turning their unknown British acts into American sensations. Between them, they knew what they were doing, and their partnership was one of the most revered in the industry. They were a truly great team.

"But the other reason we had to meet here today is that I've got to meet someone at eight-thirty and I can't be in two places at the same time."

"Cheating on me, Jarrod?"

"Of course. I cheat on all my women."

Ste laughed. They were both decent, honest men.

"Seriously, this investor guy is a whale. He sold his theatre a year ago and is looking to put a load into something cool. I'm meeting him for breakfast at the Windows on the World restaurant to see if we can't help him find a home for the money."

"Thought you didn't like heights? It's a hundred and six floors up."

"Needs must. He's from out of town and wants to see the place. I'm rolling out the big guns and taking one for the team. Vertigo. Ha, it's all in the mind. At least, I hope it is. If I puke on his shoes, it will be a short-lived business association."

"So how long have I got you for, old friend?"

"Less than an hour right now, so let's get to it. Remind me why you're here again?"

Jarrod ran through the plan for the next ten days. There were no surprises. They were a well-oiled machine. Tina was right about Jarrod from the word go but had been experienced enough to not undermine them. She left them to figure out how to work together. When Jarrod needed to go, everything was in place and, after a brief hug, they arranged to re-group at the office later in the morning. Ste hadn't finished his breakfast, staying where he was to allow the waitress one further opportunity to refuel his coffee. He'd steal these five minutes for himself just before his day went crazy.

That five minutes became three. Tina was calling to disturb his peace. She checked in most mornings and today she was struggling with a different band in London. She needed his advice and as her right-hand man, Ste would always set her at ease. The trust between them was absolute. It had to be, especially given how little time they spent together.

"I can't get them to think about things differently." She was frustrated by the band of experienced musicians who should have more trust in the woman who made them a fortune.

Ste offered an ear and advice which she wouldn't take because Tina knew what to do. They were interrupted by a waitress with the bill.

"Tina, I need to go to the office. I'm getting the Metro. I'll call you when I'm there, okay?"

When Ste got onto the street, somebody was screaming. His call to Tina was still connected and she was still speaking; but Ste focused upwards before fumbling to hang up the call.

Chapter 48

There is always a witness to history.

At eight-forty-six in the morning of September the eleventh, two-thousand-and-one, Ste was one of those witnesses. The date and time were forever tattooed onto his soul and would inevitably become as significant to the history books as the eleventh hour of the eleventh day of the eleventh month which had ended World War One eighty-three years before.

The screaming woman was transfixed by movement through the sky. People scream all the time throughout New York. But as more eyes were drawn skywards, the plane they were all watching crashed straight into the top of the building next to where he was standing. It was the same building that Ste presumed Jarrod had gone into for his meeting only a few minutes before. The restaurant was in line with the plane crash. Ste knew immediately what it meant.

The loudest explosion he had ever heard followed. The tower shook, prompting a mass of papers and glass to shoot through the windows like bullets, before falling to the ground, covering the whole area around him in the building's debris.

The screams multiplied as more people saw the devastation. Another terrific noise engulfed them. It seemed that every alarm in the area simultaneously went off, but even that failed to drown out the constant sound of screaming coming from the witnesses to the unfolding tragedy. The crowds grew, joined by people running out of the surrounding Towers, desperate to see what was happening whilst they ran for safety. The flames at the top of the building had quickly taken hold. Thick smoke billowed upwards, but with a swirling wind, it seemed to be collecting up the debris, wrapping around the tower before dumping the glass, brick and hundreds of thousands of papers collected from the hundred or so floors on their way down to earth.

The ground floor windows were suddenly blown out. All this happened in an instant, although, to the watching crowds, it seemed to take forever.

Ste's instinct was to run, but he was rooted to the spot in shock. His mind suddenly turned to panic. What about Jarrod and Isla? She was flying right now. Was that her plane? He tried to call Jarrod but there was no network connection, not just to Jarrod's phone, but a connection to anything. His next instinct was to run towards the Tower to see if he could help. The first fire crews had started to arrive, an unbelievably fast response to the unfolding chaos. They took control, demanding people leave the area.

He offered his services to a firefighter but was told to, 'Go. NOW.' Ste felt safe enough where he was, but he had no experience in a situation like this. There was no way he could leave, not when his friend was likely to be stranded in that building. People were bleeding, covered in cuts from the falling debris. Others emerged from the building, choking on the thick, grey dust that was falling like rain, enveloping all of those in its path. Dust and smoke started to cover everything.

He learnt later that it was just seventeen minutes later, but Ste's normal sense of time had evaporated as the world changed in front of his eyes. Just seventeen minutes before he heard the same loud noise above him for a second time. Then the same scream from a different woman. As he had seventeen minutes before, Ste looked at the sky. It was as if time was playing tricks with his mind. Another plane went straight into the second tower in the same way the first tower had been hit. It must be deliberate. He thought about Isla. The odds of it being her plane had just doubled. People started to run again, terrorised by what was unfolding. The force of the panicked crowd pushed him along the road. He had to move or he would have been crushed as everyone started fleeing the scene, fearful for their own lives. An exceptional few who had managed to get a mobile signal, screamed hysterically into their phones, while others screamed hysterically at their phone's refusal to connect. Ste tried once more to make the necessary calls; firstly, to Jarrod, followed immediately by Isla. Lastly Tina. He couldn't connect to anybody. He was cut off with no idea what to do.

It was just after nine o'clock and the world had truly changed forever.

Chapter 49

They had been all set to leave in what had been an uneventful morning. The easy-going calm of the early flight back to London was panning out to be a typical trip on a typical day. Day flights were a much quieter experience, as the passengers had to get up early to make the flight which always made them better behaved. The frenetic atmosphere of the evening flight boarding, where the travellers were often boozed up, grumpy and full of their own egos, was rarely present on the day flight.

Boarding was quickly complete and the doors were closed. The sequence for rolling back was underway when the plane suddenly stopped without warning. Delays were typical, but there was no explanation for this one, however, it was clear that this plane was no longer leaving the gate. Within moments, the staff were alerted that Air Traffic Control had grounded everything out of JFK, effective immediately. Passengers switched their mobiles on and ringing instantly filled the plane. A passenger gasped loud enough for everybody in the Economy Cabin to hear. Everyone turned to see where the distressed noise had come from as the cry grew louder, before the passenger stood and ran to the front of the cabin. Sally appeared from Business to find the source of the commotion, suddenly finding herself holding a hysterically inconsolable man.

The passengers moved out of his way so he could be seated and calmed. The Captain announced the plane was to be emptied. They were going back into the terminal to await instruction. The relocated passengers and crew were all unaware that they were now statistics in a story that silenced the world. TV screens ran live reports from Manhattan. Something horrendous had happened at the World Trade Centre. It was near where Ste was supposed to be having breakfast. And while everybody focused on the crying passenger, Isla repeatedly tried to ring Ste's. Although she was lucky enough to have a signal, as far as Isla knew, Ste was at the scene and was now missing.

Chapter 50

Ste helped direct the people who most needed help. He supported those from nearby buildings who were handing out water, thrusting bottles into the hands of the desperate souls who staggered by. They were like ghosts, discoloured by the debris which continued to rain down from above. And these were the lucky ones. Others stumbled past wearing another, equally distinctive colour; the colour of their own blood.

When the bottles started running low, they limited the offers to essential sips for the desperate, doing whatever they could to support as many of the needy as possible. The souls who had already given up hope of being rescued from the upper floors chose their own way out of this disaster. Like birds shot on the wing, they fell from the heights in a brave act of taking control when they knew that their perishing was both inevitable and imminent. They threw whatever they could to break the remaining glass. The clear air was their only way out of hell. Some panicked before falling, failing to fully commit to their final act, left to hang for a short time from the ledges that represented a no-man's-land between life and death.

Ste heard a rumbling sound. It was getting closer. He looked up at the North Tower. The noise manifested into a vision that was to become iconic - and it was right in front of him. He was transfixed as the tower collapsed into itself. Manhattan shook and the surrounding water level rose. The implosion was so neat in its collapse that it looked as though it had been detonated from within.

Everyone ran. Even the emergency authorities had to abandon both the acts of rescue and their initial attempts to triage the sick from the dead.

Ste continued to run. Like everyone around him, he would have been consumed by the falling building, joining the casualty numbers, had he not moved. Everybody headed in the same direction, fleeing the disaster consuming the city. As the tower crashed to the ground, the debris rained down like a meteor storm. A cloud of dust chased the closest pedestrians. Ste couldn't outrun it. He dived under an abandoned van in time to avoid being taken by the marauding grey cloud which followed those still running. An elderly man fell next to the van and Ste dragged him underneath, covering the man's face with his jacket.

"Thank you."

The man exhaled and Ste held the man's head in his hands, helping him sip the last bit of water in his bottle. He used some to clear dust from the man's eyes. They were both still alive, for now. Ste risked looking out and was horrified by the scene that they were caught in. The ground was completely painted with a thick grey powder, similar to that which covered the ghosts who had emerged from the Towers. Only now, it had caked everything in the vicinity. The street took on the appearance of a post-apocalyptic horror film. This was not the New York he had grown to love over the last four years. The footsteps made by those who could walk looked like tracks in snow. It was not winter, and this wasn't snow. It was September 2001 and New York was now a city that mirrored the classic images of Hell.

Chapter 51

He waited for the dust to settle—but it didn't. Fighting the suffocating smog, he helped the stranger to his feet and wrapped the man's arms around his neck. He moved them as far away from the devastation as he could. Anywhere would be safer than here. Aside from the emergency services who were struggling to see each other through the dust bomb, there was no movement. They found a deli. It was empty of staff and customers, but a fire crew had taken refuge from the cloud and were quickly taking on water. The man Ste was supporting had sagged after running for his life and was now no longer capable of walking. With the help of the firemen, Ste propped him against an inside wall and went to the fridge for water. There wasn't any, so he took a bottle of Gatorade to the man who Ste knew it was now his responsibility to keep alive. The firemen ran outside in response to a whistle. Regrouping with their team in the street, they went back towards what remained of the Towers. The two men were alone. Ste dabbed the face of his charge with tap water, desperately encouraging him to drink something. Where there had been movement before, now there was none. Where there had been breath, Ste felt nothing. There was no sound. Instinct kicked in. Ste tried to bring him back using basic CPR training.

He continued to try, but the man was unresponsive. His attempts to call 9-1-1 all failed, as there was no network. He tried again and again. 9-1-1. 9-1-1. *Today's date. How ironic.*

But the fight for this poor soul was now over. All efforts to raise help and use his basic medical knowledge to bring this bloke back had failed. There was nothing Ste could now do. The stranger was gone.

There were no medics. There was nobody else and Ste sat alone with the man's body close enough that he could hold his cold hand. A final act of compassion. Not knowing the stranger's name, he reached into the man's pocket for an ID, finding a work badge. He'd assumed that the man was a white guy, so covered in dust that Ste had no reason to assume he was anything else. But Irfan Shahid now looked nothing like the Arab man in the photograph. Ste closed Irfan's eyes and said a prayer over his body. It didn't seem to matter what God he prayed to, but it felt like the appropriate thing to do.

He looked behind the counter for any means with which to communicate with the outside world. Although the deli telephone was on the floor, it had a dial tone so he once more tried the same set of numbers. The network might be working by now and just maybe he'd find Jarrod. Nothing. Then Isla. Nothing. He phoned Greta at home in London. He had a ringtone, but the line rang out and went to the answerphone. He hung up. Picking up a pad and a pen that an hour earlier had been used by the staff to take breakfast orders, Ste wrote a note to leave with Irfan. He struggled for the right words, and for the first time in the ninety minutes of chaos, he cried. It was intense and uncontrollable, the sort of tearful fit that makes a body shake. He lay alone on the floor, once again holding the hand of the stranger who had spent his last moments on earth hoping Ste would save him. He calmed to a point where he could now focus clearly on the pen in his hand. The tears would stop long enough that he could write what he needed to. He couldn't leave until that was done.

'To whoever finds this message: My name is Stephen Lewis. I tried to help Mr Irfan Shahid but could not save him. I was with him at the end. The last thing I can do for him is let his loved ones know that he wasn't alone. Please contact me if you want to. I am so sorry I could not do more.'

He left his details, before putting the note into Irfan's inside pocket along with his work pass. He wiped his face and started to walk into the newly devastated world beyond the door.

As he reached the hastily erected perimeter, Ste turned to look at the mess he had come through. He heard the rumbling noise; he recognised it from earlier though it wasn't as deafening at this distance. This was the moment the South Tower fell. It imploded in the same way and followed its northern sister to the ground. A new wave of terrified people came towards Ste from the wreckage. Some were hanging onto the outside of retreating emergency vehicles, shouting encouragement to the people on foot that they should run faster to escape the next cloud. The progress through the crowds was slow enough that a few of the stronger and more able men held their hands down to pull people in need from the ground to the back of the fire engine. Whether suited, in uniform or just in casual clothes, whether black or white or any colour underneath, everybody looked the same. They were all coated in a mess of filthy powder. Even the media crews were covered in the same dust as the tragic victims on whom they were reporting.

Some were lucky enough to have water, others were picked up by medics who attached oxygen masks to their faces. Bags of rubbish on the street were covered in dust, making them difficult to distinguish from the many victims Ste had seen. People screamed. People cried. And some people fell to their knees amongst the filth and prayed.

His phone beeped. He had walked into a signal zone that allowed enough connection for his phone to fill with messages. Everybody in the world knew someone in New York City, and these messages were fortunate enough to have successfully fought their way through the overloaded system. He looked for a message from Jarrod. There was nothing. Nobody on the hundred and sixth floor could have survived. There was nothing from Isla and none of the other messages mattered. He tried to connect again to Jarrod. Nothing. He sent a simple, message.

'RUOK?'

He received a sending error. The network had crashed again.

He didn't know where to go or what to do. He was filthy. His lungs were full of dust and his breathing was tight and painful. Once more, he stopped to cough with the intensity of a seriously sick man. He continued to walk in the direction the emergency traffic was heading, somehow reaching the Hudson River where a large crowd was gathered.

People pointed at him and some offered support. He stumbled to the water's edge. If there was a point where he could, Ste would have jumped into the cold, dirty water just to wash the dust off. And in that moment of anguish—despite an unknown number of strangers losing their lives—he didn't care whether he lived or died. Ste kept walking. He stopped at the first public toilets he came to and cleaned up as much as he could. With his body cleaner, his head started to feel a little clearer. Although he was still walking, he didn't have a plan, so sat on an unoccupied bench and stared over the water to Hoboken. He could make out the huge crowd of people on the far riverbank and watched it grow. The dust cloud billowed over the landscape like expanding foam, continuing to circle Lower Manhattan and beyond. With each glance, he saw Jarrod and Irfan. He saw two planes. He saw it all, playing like a film in his head.

Some people tried to engage with his emotionless shell. He stared over the mayhem on the water as the mass evacuation of New York took hold. Most people kept a respectful distance from a man in such obvious grief—in a city full of similarly damaged souls. They had a raw, visceral view into an intensely private matter. The ones who approached him were kind; they wanted to give support. Every human dot on the landscape was writing its part in the unfolding page of history.

He had seen far too much to digest and had no response to any of the strangers offering help and kind words. How could he describe being with Irfan at the moment of his death? And there was still nothing from Jarrod. Ste would do anything for his next words to be with his friend. Whenever his gaze over the river filled with evacuation vessels was broken, Ste would once again try, and consistently fail, to connect to the phone numbers.

The shock of what he had witnessed just did not want to dissipate. And he did not know how to make the pain stop.

Chapter 52

His phone had long since died. Light had started to give way to dark. He'd been motionless for over six hours, maybe more. He stretched his legs and the part of his brain that was coming back to life told him that he should move. He stood and felt like a drunk waking from a booze-induced coma. He followed his instinct to head alongside the Hudson. Rather than being an intelligent, logical decision, it was because that was the direction where the heaviest cloud of dust was not sat. He got to the cruise points north of the Lincoln Tunnel and knew he was near the hotel. Sirens in the distance were prolific, mirroring the sounds of screeches and screams and the impassioned cries for help that he heard throughout the nightmare. He couldn't shift the screaming. The deathlike fanfare was living in his head and on constant replay. He related specific screams to specific faces in the sea of strangers. Every noise made him jump, and still, he replayed every second of the trauma. If this was the cost of living, he would rather have been dead.

At Little Brazil, and its connection to Sixth, the simple job of crossing the road was too much. He sat on the kerb, covered in dust, and waited for everything to stop. Although he had been spared, he was now sat fully prepared to die.

Passers-by offered help but he shut down. He couldn't acknowledge their offers of assistance, occasionally not even registering their presence. Time moved on without him. Looking up, he could see his New York home a few blocks North. In a moment of clarity and with an energy that had been missing for hours, he stood and walked towards the building. He had momentarily found his purpose and walked fast for fear that he wouldn't make it to his room if he stopped. It had been many hours since he had left Irfan's lifeless body, and an hour or so more since his friend left their breakfast for the North Tower. Finally, he stumbled through the glass entrance to his hotel.

One of the concierge staff was immediately at his side.

"Mr Lewis. Mr Lewis. We have been so worried about you. Can I help you, please? Some water; food? Please, Mr Lewis. Are you okay?"

Ste didn't recognise the young chap who addressed him so intently. But he was grateful for the supporting arm that now held onto him. But this first human touch he'd felt since leaving Irfan was suddenly too much, and having tried to hold himself together until now, he finally collapsed onto his knees in the centre of the packed foyer. Everyone stopped, stunned into silence, understandably nosing into this stranger's grief. Another staff member appeared with a bottle of water and they unsuccessfully tried to help him into a nearby seat. From the growing crowd emerged another face, this one more familiar.

"You're Isla's friend, aren't you?" It was Sally.

Ste stared at her. "Yes, I am. What are you doing here? Is she okay?"

Sally put a comforting hand on his arm, quietly reassuring him that Isla was fine, before kindly standing the attentive staff down. She would look after Ste from here. The Duty Manager appeared. He was carrying a large bundle of papers.

"Mr Lewis, Sir. I am so sorry and if I can help in any way, please ask. Sir, I have several urgent messages for you. We were so concerned for you. Can I give these to you?"

"Give them to me, please." Sally took them. "I've got it from here."

Ste had no real idea who Sally was or why she was helping him. He was struggling to recall who anyone was, but her presence was reassuring. She took the papers and led him away. As they approached the room, he could see someone sitting outside his room.

"She's been switching between here and reception for hours just waiting for you," Sally whispered into his ear, "worried sick."

The woman ran straight to him. She'd had hours of not knowing if he was dead or alive. She went to jump into him, but as she got closer, she saw his wretchedness and burst into tears. A combination of joy and despair erupted in the long corridor.

Sally gave the bundle of papers to Isla and left them alone.

Chapter 53

Although he hadn't eaten since breakfast and had only taken on mouthfuls of water since he emerged from his temporary residence in Hell, Ste was not hungry or aware of being thirsty. Isla had so many questions, but she was too relieved to push too hard. She wanted to comfort him through the night. In the luxurious surroundings of his suite, Ste was confused why Isla was in New York but couldn't form the words to ask what had happened to her. His shock was deep and he seemed unable to make a coherent sentence.

She suggested that he shower. Aside from removing the dirt from his body, perhaps the stench of death could be tempered by getting rid of both the grime and the clothes he wore; the first line drawn in expelling the horror. Isla didn't know how close Ste had been to the disaster, but Ste knew it would take more than a long wash and a change of clothes to help him out of the desperate pit he was in.

He emerged from the shower in a hotel robe, noticing Isla in the window with her stare fixed on where the Towers had stood until earlier that day, a space now replaced by a powerfully lit emptiness.

Things had to be addressed.

"Ste, I don't know what to say to you right now, but there are some calls you need to make. I hope you don't mind, but I looked through these messages and there are some important people who don't know if you're alive."

Without addressing the question, he looked at Isla to start the process by addressing his own basic question. "Isla, how come you're here? You're supposed to be back home!"

She gave an account of her day, starting with the plane being unloaded. Ste didn't need details and quickly switched off. He understood the basics and had no room to take onboard anything beyond the simple facts.

He reached into his jacket and found his dead phone. Isla put it on charge for him and handed him the messages and suggested he go through them.

Ste's eyes were blank.

"It's okay, darling. You make the calls you need to, and I will do the ones you don't want to. I'll say I work for the company. Come on, darling, doing something will help you process. Does that work?"

Ste nodded. He had to get a grip and call his dad, Tina and then Greta. But what could he say about Jarrod? He burst into tears. Isla reached over and held him. The calls could wait another few minutes.

He lay on her lap and Isla stroked his hair allowing the silence to dominate the room. Unusually, but appropriately, there was no music; just a unique silence, interrupted by the quiet sobs and emotional shivering Ste continued to experience with every flashback.

After a while, Isla tried again.

"Ste, these calls?"

"I can't."

"Okay. Shall I do them all?"

"Would you?"

"If you tell me what to say."

He looked at the message cards and walked Isla through who needed to be contacted.

"I think I should call my dad. He should hear it from me. Can you give me a minute?"

"Of course. Do you want me to go for a walk?"

"No, you're not going out there. I can't lose you as well. I won't lose you again, Isla. Please could you stay?"

"Of course, my darling. For as long as you want. Now make the calls."

She'd called him darling. Ste's frantic mind was in a different place. Isla went over to the window and sat out of earshot, giving him the space he needed to make the calls.

Ste dialled his dad first. Today was already tomorrow in England, but he was still awake, answering after a single ring. The whole world was fixed on the twenty-four-hour news cycle and it fell to Sky to pump the British version of events into his father's living room. Ste's Dad had a vested interest in every new scrap of information that came from the southern tip of Manhattan.

"Stephen? My boy!"

"Yes, Dad. It's me."

After a moment when only sobbing came down the line, his Dad managed to speak.

"Son? Thank God. Are you okay?" His relief was hard to fathom among the sobs, but Ste was glad to have called home.

"Dad, I love you. I can't talk, but I am safe and I've just got back to the hotel. I love you so much." Aside from the tears that they had shed together when his mum was lost to the world, Ste hadn't cried in front of his dad since he broke his arm in a Junior football match.

"It's okay, son. I love you. Let it out. You know your Mum was looking out for you today. Can you tell me how you are?"

"I'm safe, at the hotel. I promise to call you when I can. But my friend is missing Dad. I watched him leave and go towards the…." He broke down, dropping the phone on the bed. Isla saw what had happened and rushed into the room to help.

"Hi, Mr Lewis. This is Isla. I work with Stephen. I'll make sure he calls you back tomorrow if that's okay. He's in a state and has literally just got back to the hotel. But he is safe, and I am doing whatever it takes to look after him."

"Thank you, Isla, is it? Please take care of my boy."

From the carpet, Ste called out a goodbye, his tears drowned out by his father's explosion of relief.

Isla took charge.

"I really think you need to call Greta, then Tina." She handed him three messages from the mother of his daughter. "You know I can't make this call."

"Isla, I've nothing to say to her. I tried to call earlier, and it even connected, but I didn't know what to say. Can you call her for me and just tell her I'm safe?"

This was not what Isla had expected. Handling calls to friends and colleagues wasn't a problem. Even taking to his dad was okay, but talking to the woman she had hoped to replace seemed a step too far.

"If you are sure, I can try."

"Are you okay doing this?"

Ste acknowledge it wasn't easy for Isla either. But his mind wasn't capable of computing.

"For you, darling, anything."

Like his dad, Greta picked up on the first ring.

"Ste?"

"Hi, sorry to call so late; my name is Isla….."

Greta interrupted her immediately.

"He's dead, isn't he? That's why you're phoning. He's dead. I knew it. Oh Fucking Hell. Not Ste."

"No, Greta. It's okay. Ste is safe. He has been located and wanted to let you and Amy know straight away that he was alive."

"I need to talk to him. Can you put him on?"

"I'm sorry. I just work with Ste and make the calls he tells me to. He isn't available at the moment but wanted me to call straight away."

Ste could hear Greta's request from his position on the carpet. He put his hand out to take the call. She passed the phone to him and took her seat, once again out of earshot. Privacy was not requested, but it was required.

"Hello."

Even from a distance, Isla could hear Greta's tears. Now was not the time for her to indulge the insecurities she held about the relationship between Ste and Greta which still never seemed to end.

After a respectable amount of time, she started to re-engage with the room. Ste was still on the phone and talking more freely, finally speaking in coherent sentences. Even though it was the middle of the night back in England, he was talking to Amy.

"Schnitzel von….." he was doing the voices. He was smiling. And he was not talking to Greta.

Ste sensed Isla standing in the doorway and faced her as if to prove his more upbeat status. But he was about to lose it. His chin was full of the deep potholes that came before the tears. How he was managing to speak to his daughter without falling apart seemed miraculous.

"I love you, Amy." He paused, waiting for the little girl to respond. The moment she sent her love, he put the phone down, emotionally crushed by being Dad. He pushed out the wail he had been holding onto throughout his chat, burying himself in a pillow as his body tensed and shivered. The adrenalin that had propped him up all day was finally seeping away.

After a time, Isla asked how the conversation with Greta had gone. It wasn't the time to address '*Them*', but at this tragic time, neither of them wanted it to be anyone other than Isla who Ste turned to, to lie on the bed and be unapologetically comforted. Given what had gone on, all bets regarding the order of events for them to go to bed were off in Isla's mind. But Ste couldn't cope.

She went to comfort him as before, but as she lay her hand on his head, Ste tensed and didn't move towards her.

"Can I do anything, Darling?"

Although he didn't respond, Isla knew she must persist. It wasn't fair on all the people who were clearly frantic with worry.

"I don't want to do anything you don't want me to, but these people need telling you're safe."

He grunted an acknowledgement. He knew he had to deal with things. His crushed feelings would wait. But he was crying uncontrollably at the dark visions playing in his head. Four miles south, visible from the suite, they could see the rescue lights illuminating the cloud that would not disperse. Isla moved closer and Ste was more accepting. He moved his head towards her, and she stroked his hair as a parent would comfort a distressed child.

"Do you want me to return these calls for you, Ste?"

He nodded, glad that she was taking over. She picked up the messages and separated them as best she could. Ste was popular. There were at least fifty messages to sort through and she put them as best she could into some order of importance. No wonder the staff found him the moment he reappeared.

Chapter 54

One name stood out, given the number of times it appeared. It was from 'Star'. And the name Jarrod appeared on the message.

"I think this is a call you need to make yourself. It's from someone called Star." Isla knew instinctively that this was significant. A sense of panic immediately overcame the room. Ste seemed almost paralysed.

"Star. She's Jarrod's wife. Pass them here, please."

The sudden urgency led to Isla clumsily fumbling with the pile of papers, immediately agitating Ste.

"Now, Isla."

His tone had changed from a broken man to somebody with an urgent job to do. The adrenalin had returned, paralysis dissipated, as he knew he must speak to his friend's wife. The least he could do was pull himself together.

The telephone rang and Ste huffed in irritation. "Can you just get rid of them? I don't want to speak to anybody except Star. Get them off the phone, please."

"Hello." She mouthed the name Star and Ste jumped forward and grabbed the receiver from her.

"Star. This is Ste, I have just got back and was about to ring you."

Her tears disguised what Star was trying to say, to the point that Ste could not understand a word. But he knew instinctively what she was trying to communicate. He waited for her to calm before he felt able to tell her what he knew.

'Star, I don't know what to say. I've been trying Jarrod all day. We were together. We were there just before it happened, and he went to another breakfast meeting with an investor. It was in the Tower, the North Tower. The one that was hit first. I don't know if he made it to the restaurant. You know how things change all the time with him and what's he's like. He may not have even gone into the building and gone to Starbucks instead.'

It was at this point that Ste lost it. The optimism that Jarrod had not been in the Tower was enough for the tears to return. He let the phone loose from his grasp and Isla picked up.

'Hi there, Star. This is Isla, a friend of Ste's.'

Star wasn't listening. She was in as wretched a state as Ste. The confirmation from Ste that he was not with Jarrod was all that Star needed to know that her husband was gone. Isla couldn't do anything to help. Ste took the phone again and they cried together. The emotion of the moment was too much, even for a bystander as she was. Nothing could prepare somebody for now. There were no words. But no words were needed.

Star was first to regain her composure, explaining how she was heading over from Staten Island to search for her husband. He might have escaped the building and was lying somewhere concussed. Surely, they had to try. It hadn't crossed Ste's mind to search. His confused wander towards the hotel had been enough of a struggle. But with the suggestion now out there that there was a hope, however slender, he said that they would look. However pointless the search, it had to be better than doing nothing. If Jarrod had escaped, he would have contacted them – but there were so few working phones; this offered some hope. If he was knocked out, he would have been taken to hospital and they'd have his ID. Any other scenario made no sense. The news channels were telling people to stay away. The tunnels and bridges were closed, and the ferries were only taking people off Manhattan as the evacuation of half a million people continued. Entry to the island was limited to those officially supporting the rescue efforts.

Ste broke the silence. 'Star, please stay where you are for tonight. Stay by the phone and wait for news. That's all we can do for now. I will go to the office and check. I'll go to every bar I know Jarrod likes and every restaurant he could be at. And I will check anywhere else I can think of. Leave it with me and tell me if you think I'm missing somewhere he might be. Isla and I will do everything we can to find him.'

Isla nodded back, quietly crying. Ste was glad to see that she was happy to be included. Although he was trying to do something, instinctively, Ste knew that it was useless and a waste of their time; but it was, at least, something.

Ste jumped up, and with a renewed sense of purpose, pulled on clean clothes and downed a long swig of water.

"What about the other calls, Ste? People still need to know you're safe."

"Right. Good point. Okay. I'll call Tina and she can deal with them."

He immediately called Tina, giving her the details she needed from him to fill in the gaps. He finished by giving his boss the numbers of people who needed contacting. Only then could they get on with the search. It was Isla's idea to print posters detailing Jarrod's missing status and contact information. But the Business Lounge was packed - too many people in the hotel had the same idea, so Ste suggested they head to his office. They could do the printing there.

It wasn't late, although neither of them had registered what time it was. All time had suddenly been rendered meaningless. Isla had a message confirming that flights were grounded for at least twenty-four hours and she should stay put.

"How did you get a room in the hotel?"

"The new crew coming in later aren't now, so we took their rooms. I don't know for how long, but I can't see us going anywhere for a while. The skies are totally shut."

At the office, a couple of the team were still at their desks. Ste's arrival was greeted with an explosion of relief. It had been twelve hours since anybody had heard from Jarrod, and no one in the office had heard from Ste all day. It hadn't occurred to him that he'd been a cause for their concern. But his team had been trying to get hold of both of their missing colleagues since the initial news of a plane striking the North Tower broke. Jarrod and Ste were also their friends and apart from comfort breaks, they had not moved from their desks, frantically searching by calling everyone they knew to find out what might have happened to them both. Although Tina had phoned ahead to assure them that Ste was alive, his presence in the office still came as a welcome piece of good news; a validation that it was true. Ste looked at the two piles of papers on one of the desks. They were the posters one of the team had already made up, one pile for Jarrod and another one with his face on it. Ste gasped, bending his knees to steady himself as he realised how close he had come to becoming a statistic in this horror show.

Ste tried to make light of his own WANTED poster, joking about the picture they'd used.

"No one needs to see this picture. I look like a deviant. They'll be slapping me with an exclusion notice from the local schools if this gets out."

But when it came to the other pile of papers, he picked some of them up and ushered all the team into a circle where they could hold each other close. The emotion of the last few hours fed into an energy and nobody spoke until Jackie, the PA who had known Jarrod since their office had opened more than five years before, asked for a moment's prayer.

They held hands and begged for God's help. The possessors of faith and no faith paused as one, united in hoping good came from bad, God or no God. They broke from the huddle, divided the papers and agreed who would go where. Ste and Isla headed to the Village, while Jarrod's deputy, Devon, went as far south as he could get before heading back north. Ste asked Jackie to call Star and let her know what was going on, but to stay in the office and field everything that came in from their base camp. She should call Tina to involve her. He knew she would now be through his call list and frantic for news on Jarrod, who like all her closest staff, was as much her friend as her colleague.

The office was littered with promotional bottles and packets of sweets that acted as crappy giveaways to visitors. Filling as many bottles with water as they could carry in one of the rucksacks lying around, Devon, Isla and Ste set off in search of news. However hopeless a task, they had to try.

Chapter 55

The streets of Midtown were not busy. Anybody who could leave the island had left. And everybody left seemed to be hiding indoors, glued to the rolling news coverage which, for now, was fixed on their devastated city. The bars were closed. The never-dormant city had been shocked to sleep. They attached posters onto lampposts and the makeshift noticeboards appearing wherever there was space. Hundreds of similar posters begged for information about husbands, wives, brothers, sisters, sons, daughters and friends. Everybody walking the streets was searching for somebody, undertaking the same optimistic search with the same weariness associated with their collective despair and grief. On a TV inside a shop window, a headline said that one person had been pulled from the rubble. One. Just one. From all those thousands trapped. Ste cursed the hopelessness of the search for his dear friend.

He knew Isla was trying to stay strong; she wanted to be his rock, but she said she was concerned for him. He couldn't speak in sentences and hadn't talked about how he felt, or even what had happened. He told her he had seen things from very close quarters and left it at that, robotically sticking to the task of pressing on through the streets, poster by poster, wall by wall, block by block and beyond.

The phone network sporadically pinged into life as the night sky brightened, slowly introducing a new dawn. Messages randomly started appearing on everyone's phones as the network demand slowed, with a combination of loved ones making sure they were still okay and the random people who were dipping in just to be nosey. They replied to the ones that they needed to and ignored the rest. Tina promised to put something on their website informing the hundreds of well-wishers who were contacting the record company that Ste was safe and well. She would also put out an appeal for information on Jarrod. It was all that they could do.

Isla took Ste's hand and tried to look into his eyes. They had been walking all night and had come full circle towards the office. She was tired and knew Ste was likely to be no more energised than her.

"Shall we check in with Jackie? And try for some sleep?"

"You can. I'm going to keep looking." Ste still couldn't make meaningful eye contact. He was shattered and still trying to disguise the haunted feeling he knew he gave off every time he focused on anything for too long. Everything he saw reminded him of the previous morning. Everything. They walked the two blocks to the office where Jackie was still at her desk, fielding calls from all over the world.

"Jackie, please go home. If you can't get home, can I find you a room in my hotel?" Ste had agreed to the trip to the office but was itching to get back out on the streets.

"I have a room you can use," Isla helpfully chipped in.

"I'm okay here. I'm not going anywhere until we know something, and I can grab a nap if I need to."

She pointed at Jarrod's office where there was a sofa bed for the times when it was either too late for one of them to get home, or where Jarrod was in no state to try. Ste knew he couldn't convince her to leave the office and gave up just as Devon reappeared, out of both posters and energy, too tired to continue for now.

Devon had made it as far south as he was allowed, before being turned back. He was shocked, having got so near to the rescue efforts that Ste could see from their exchanged glances that he now had his own haunted visions to address. They had both seen a vision of Hell which could not be put into words.

Devon only managed to murmur '*Night*,' before lying down on the sofa bed. Jackie would have to wait if she wanted it.

The three of them held each other once again, as Jackie muttered another prayer before the English contingent made their way back to the hotel in silence. With Devon now asleep, Jackie on her last legs and Isla openly exhausted, Ste took little persuasion to give up the search for now and get some sleep. He was once again greeted by hotel staff who passed him another set of messages, while Isla had a note from BA giving a holding update. They weren't going anywhere for another day at least, but there was a team meeting at nine am, just two hours away. She left a note with reception for Sally to make her excuses, explaining her absence. They had been up for over twenty-four hours and had spent much of the last twelve out searching. They desperately needed sleep.

"Ste, do you want me to come with you, or shall I go back to my own room?" Ste smiled and took her hand as they made their way to his suite.

He opened the door and walked into his room. The move from night to dawn was complete and he slumped into a chair by the window. To the South, the dust cloud blotted the sky. The floodlights at what had now been renamed '*Ground Zero*' had been replaced by sunlight, and Ste was transfixed by the new landscape.

"Can I get you anything, Darling? You haven't eaten." Ste's emotional state was fragile, but he continued to give away nothing about his inner hell.

He shook his head, fixed on the absence of the two great landmarks that he had seen every time he'd ever looked out of a plane arriving at JFK. Isla gave up on conversation and lay on the huge bed. Although not intending to, within a moment, she was asleep. Ste looked over her, briefly acknowledging that if somebody was in his room tonight, he wanted it to be her. Much as he would happily share his bed with Isla tonight, he would do anything to share the room with his dear friend at the expense of any woman, just because it would mean that Jarrod was alive. The thought of never seeing him again provoked tears. He pulled two JD miniatures out of the minibar, pouring them into a glass before downing it straight. He closed his eyes but only saw images of Jarrod walking away from their breakfast, followed by the lifeless body of Irfan.

He had a nagging tune in his head and stumbled through his music memories to properly identify it.

'*This is our last goodbye….. This is our last embrace….. And the memories offer signs that it's over.*' He had typically staggered into an appropriate Jeff Buckley lament.

For now, only the minibar held the answers.

Chapter 56

Isla awoke, all alone in the room. Her phone displayed a new text message. It was from Ste.

'*Gone out to look again.*'

He'd left a handwritten note saying the same. Reassured that he was communicating and covering the relevant bases, she checked the other messages on her phone from friends in England asking if she was okay. She was far from okay. And judging by the tidiness of the bed and the number of miniatures next to his chair, Ste was still in a bad way. He clearly hadn't come to bed, but the minibar was empty of drink, although the chocolatey snacks were untouched. She could only imagine the state he was in. She tried his mobile but it went to voicemail, either because it was out of charge, the network was down, or more concerningly, he had turned it off. She went to her room to wash and dress for whatever today had in store. Much as she wanted to be there for him, she briefly considered the inconvenient truth that Ste no longer wanted the sort of support she could offer.

In the absence of any other ideas, or direction from Ste, Isla went back to his office. Jackie was still there. She had not moved since yesterday morning. Devon had been out on another fruitless trip but came back when it was clear that his efforts were useless. As individuals, they had already acknowledged that Jarrod was gone. Isla told them Ste was missing again. Jackie hadn't seen him, and they both seemed to be out of all ideas. The girls exchanged numbers and Isla returned to the hotel. It was the best place to wait. Jackie was falling asleep and gave in. It was time to go home. So, after locking up the cluttered office space that now desperately needed tidying, they left together. There was nothing more to do here.

Isla tried Ste's phone again. Nothing. Her concern grew. She couldn't support somebody who wasn't there. She felt immersed in the collective pain of the city, but selfishly, she was becoming concerned that her embryonic relationship with Ste was in trouble yet again. For a while, she was useful, willing to act out the role of the supportive shoulder that a loving partner provides. But since their fruitless search around New York had ended earlier that morning, she seemed suddenly redundant.

At the hotel, her team were typically in the bar. Most of them were seasoned visitors to New York and some had friendships with people who were in the Towers. With a significant number of Brits missing or confirmed dead, most of the cabin crew knew one or more of these regular passengers. They had all built up familiar relationships with many of them over the years. And now, their faces were the ones filling the television screens.

Isla slipped into the chair next to Sally. She couldn't put into words what had happened with Ste. There had been no joy in their reunion since Ste re-appeared yesterday and she knew he was alive, if not well.

The unbroken CNN coverage dominating the main screen ran video of the Towers collapsing. They showed some new footage of survivors. Isla looked at the TV and the footage that panned the crowds running away from the approaching dust cloud as it consumed everything. They couldn't outrun it. Everybody looked the same and it was difficult to see any identifying features. They were a mass of limbs covered in the dust that Armageddon dropped upon them.

The footage then cut to a live broadcast by the Hudson River. An excitable presenter revealed more details of the day before. Isla was drawn to the images of the two people sitting behind the correspondent. It took her a second to be sure, but there, sitting next to an older woman, she saw Ste. She recognised the place from the landmarks she regularly passed on her morning runs. She instantly got up and ran from the bar, jumping into the nearest taxi.

"Pier Sixty-Four, quickly."

She was there within minutes. Most of the city had taken the day off and the suburbs closest to Ground Zero were cordoned off so the normally hectic roads were quiet. When she got there, the broadcast was finished and much of the crowd had dispersed, their macabre interest moved onto the next sensation. Ste was still in the same seat with the older lady next to him.

Isla wanted to keep her appearance low key and wandered over towards him. He saw her coming before she had time to speak. Although she couldn't make out who the woman was, the lady was in tears. Ste looked furious that the private moment was interrupted. He got up to meet Isla and his face was set and angry. Isla clearly wasn't welcome and felt as though she was gate-crashing. She'd really screwed this up.

"Isla, what the hell?"

"I'm so sorry, Ste. I know I've messed this up. I saw you on the news and wanted to know you were okay. Are you?"

"No, of course I'm not. But that doesn't make this okay. I'm a grown man and don't need some woman I barely know following me around. I need to have time on my own. I will explain later; I haven't got time for this. Please go. Now."

Isla felt awful. She had walked into something private and wasn't welcome. She was horrified with the way Ste had spoken to her. He had never treated her with anything less than loving respect, but this was somebody she didn't recognise. She ran back along the river path towards the hotel.

Chapter 57

Ste returned to the bench where the lady was still crying.

"I'm sorry about that. My friend is worried about me and I should have been kinder. But I'm angry. People who weren't there have no idea, and they offer meaningless platitudes when they haven't got a clue what I'm going through. Mrs Shahid, I wish I could have saved your husband."

"Mr Lewis, don't be too harsh on your friend. Thank you for trying and I know it was God's plan that he was not alone when he left us. You are a good man, Sir. May love travel with you. Now, I think you have someone else you need to talk to. After speaking to you, I can now find peace."

They embraced—friends for a reason—before going their separate ways. Ste went to the office, but it was locked. New York was shut down and he assumed that both Jackie and Devon had finally gone home. Knowing where he needed to be, he headed back towards the hotel.

Isla was in the bar with Sally. Ste knew he should go over, but before he had the chance, she came towards him.

"I'm sorry, Ste. I panicked. I saw you. I came. I don't know how to help you."

"Isla, you don't need to apologise. I'm not going to explain right now; I need to sleep. I'll call you later."

Ste went in one lift while Isla waited, alone and broken. Another lift arrived and she went to her room. This was not good. Her man was in crisis. She fell into bed, pulling her legs into her body. Her grieving was interrupted by a knock at the door. Ste? He did want to talk! Isla jumped up, rushing to open the door to let him in.

It was Sally; a welcome face, but not the one she was expecting or hoping to see.

"Okay, what's the problem that you don't want to talk about?" She walked in without invitation, handing Isla the drink she had left on the bar.

"I don't know what to do. He has stopped talking. He's all broken and removed himself. Rather than turning to me for comfort, I seem to be in his way."

"You don't always need words to express yourself, Isla. You can stick with this, but you need to remember the rules of love. It takes two. And if you have the chance to get out, consider taking it before it gets worse." Sally was making more sense than Isla had figured out for herself.

"Isla, you don't know what happened, but there's clear evidence that something awful happened to him and he's fucked up by it. That's not your fault; it's not his fault. But he might be a different man coming out of this."

Sally was careful not to lay blame. Neither of them was at fault.

"You can't help who you fall in love with, but without the love and romance, it can't work. Something built on this kind of shit will struggle to survive. The little you told me about his last relationship should tell you that."

Isla hadn't given Greta a thought in comparison to her relationship with Ste.

"It's more than that. I can support us through what's happening now, and we can get back to romance when he is better. I have to try, Sally."

Isla pushed hope into the conversation, clutching at straws. In her heart, she knew she had to try.

"What if he can't be pulled from the rubble? You're too young for this, Isla. You've a whole life in front of you. It's tragic. You've landed where you are, but the man you've fallen for is fucked up. But he is fucked up, Isla, and if you don't want it to pull you down as well, you need to put some distance between you both. Just for now. Give him the space to know what he wants to do next. If he wants you, he'll come for you. But darling, don't be too available. Let him grieve and work it out for himself when the time's right."

Sally appeared far more helpful than Isla had expected. Now alone, the daytime light outside was a stark contrast to the darkness Isla had suddenly wrapped herself in.

Chapter 58

Ste phoned his Dad to reassure him and the wider family that he was fine. He wanted to hear him speak without being bombarded by questions. He could rely on his old man. Ste just wasn't willing to relive the details of his horror.

Glad he had made the effort to call, he had to update Tina on their fruitless search for Jarrod and the conversations with Star. Despite the searches the team had made, there was no news and it was time to assume he was lost to the disaster. Jarrod was a number to add to the growing list of unfortunate souls.

There was another call he had to make. He didn't want to speak to Greta, but it was the only way he could speak to his daughter. He dialled home. The panic in Greta's voice was gone. Thinking that Ste was dead had changed her. There was an unrecognisable warmth to her voice. Greta was being nice. To him. He couldn't answer the questions she rattled off because he wasn't listening. He was trying to figure things out and he was too raw to talk. He was struggling with everybody asking about Jarrod. The only person he had talked to about Irfan's death was the man's wife. No one else even knew about that awful chapter of yesterday and the last person he wanted to reveal this traumatic shit to was Greta. He had no words for her and shut down her attempts to engage him. He just wanted to talk to his little girl.

"Jarrod is gone. I will be home as soon as I can. There's nothing for me here anymore. Greta, I can't talk about it. Please, just put Amy on."

He sat on his bed acknowledging that, for the first time, he had actually said the words, 'Jarrod is gone.'

"I love you, Ste. I may not say it to you enough but remember this; I do love you. And I am sorry for so much. Please, just come home."

Ste paused to reflect. Nothing had changed with the events of recent days, even with this new display of affection. He could not give her anything in return. He was devoid. Greta waited for a response and when none came, she put their daughter on. Ste smiled with joy for the first time since before the disaster. He may have smiled in front of others, but this was the real deal. It wasn't an emotional fabrication for the benefit of somebody else. Amy calmed his soul and gave him a reason to live. They talked for as long as his little girl's attention span allowed, with the full array of silliness and loving affirmation. Her excitable energetic presence encouraged Ste to laugh. How he now longed to be home, just so that he could put his little girl to bed tonight.

Daddy and daughter declared their love and the call ended. Ste brushed away the elephant in the room and said a curt goodbye to Greta. It was thirty-six hours since he had slept and he lumbered to the bed falling into the deepest sleep of his life.

Chapter 59

He jumped up the moment he woke, aware of Isla staring at him from the chair by the window.

"What are you doing here? How did you get in?" Ste was grumpy and his questions were fired at her without warmth. This was an intrusion. She had no right to let herself into his room while he slept. They'd been on a few dates, but it already felt like she owned him.

"Morning to you, too, darling. I've been here a while; the maid let me in. That's okay, isn't it?"

Ste grunted a half response; not what Isla was expecting. He was being even less affectionate towards her and still hadn't opened up about his experiences, although she knew his feelings weren't just going to evaporate. He was locking her out because he was still unable to spill his soul. To anyone. And Isla was someone he didn't know well enough yet for that kind of intimacy.

"I'm sorry. If you don't want me here, I will go. But Ste, you need to talk about it. It's eating you up."

"I know I need to talk to somebody. Jarrod is dead. But I've got nobody to talk to." He almost spat out the final sentence.

In one sentence, Ste had crushed her. Isla's face fell and tears filled her eyes. Ste felt immediately sorry, almost regretful. He had no desire to hurt her, but right now he couldn't be responsible for somebody else's emotions when he couldn't control or even understand his own.

"What about me, Ste? Can't you talk to me?"

"You seriously expect me to talk to you about this? You can't help me! What insight have you got to offer? For fuck's sake, Isla, what are you, twenty-one, two, three? I forget. How the fuck can anybody that young offer me counselling for the experiences I have had?"

Today, Ste Lewis wasn't ready for love. They were only at the start of a new path together when things changed. And as far as Ste was concerned, in that moment, everything had changed. Nothing was the same. Her age and world experience had never been an issue before now, but this was not a normal event that a bit of informal psychological knowledge could support. It was not as though watching the first few series of *Frasier* could prepare somebody for counselling a partner through witnessing history's greatest urban massacre. He needed professional help.

And she wasn't even his partner—not yet.

"Doesn't everyone want to be loved, Ste? I think everyone needs to at least feel it."

He figured she'd been rehearsing words while he slept. But as she talked, all he heard was white noise.

"Everybody needs to know that there's someone looking out for them. I'm offering to be that person for you and want to help ease you through these awful days. There will be a time for us to begin again, and I know this isn't it. But, Ste, one day soon you will feel something other than hurt and loss. And right now, I don't know what will be strong enough to cut the block of ice encasing you, but I can help. I get that you're struggling. I don't know what to say to you though, at this moment, but might if you told me what happened. Maybe then I could help. I know you were near the Towers and your friend has gone. That's so shit. That's really fucking shit. But that's all I know. You could help me to help you by talking to me. We have a connection, right? There's no denying that. So please, just let me in."

Ste paced the floor searching for a response. His fingers gripped his hair, his face riddled with pain. He drew breath, deciding whether he had any words to give her. He crouched down, groaning with mental anguish as the images repeatedly swept through his mind. Ste removed his fingers from his hair, his hands forming tight fists and the whites of his knuckles were visible. Standing up, Isla could see that his eyes had taken on a rage. It seemed like the lovely, charming man now had a burning need to hit something.

It was not until Ste saw Isla's terrified face that calm returned, quickly followed by an avalanche of tears. His chin shivered, pockmarked with a thousand holes. Finally, he tried to speak.

"Okay, Isla, I'll tell you. Don't interrupt though, or I won't get through this."

Isla went to move towards him, her outstretched arms wanting to offer comfort. Ste put his hand up as if directing traffic. He had to get through this on his own. He reached for a bottle of water and drained it in one. Now he was finally prepared to talk.

"I watched my friend….. go into a Tower…. which a few minutes later…. was obliterated."

Every few words he stopped. This was harder than he had expected.

"I know Jarrod died because I watched people fall from the sky. They were trying to avoid being burnt or buried alive and I was covered in the shit of two falling tower blocks, one of which…. contained my friend."

He took a sip of water from a second bottle next to him, desperate to keep enough composure to get through this.

"I thought I had saved a man's life, but he died in front of me and I don't know if he would have survived if I'd done something different. He was in my arms, Isla. In my arms. I watched the life leave another human being and I couldn't do a fucking thing to stop it from happening. And the noises. Those hysterical streams and the crashing. The noises won't stop battering me. So, excuse me if I'm not all lovey-dovey right now, and am struggling to talk to people about it. And I'm sorry it's not the love story you want where I fall into your open arms and you're the only thing that can save me. This is real life, Isla. Yes. I'm angry. Good God, I'm fucking angry."

Isla drew a sharp breath as if to speak; but what could anyone say to that?

"I saw bodies everywhere and things that looked like bodies that I can't even describe. I can't close my eyes without seeing them. I didn't know who was dead and who was alive. Why was I chosen to survive? I wish I hadn't been. I'd rather be dead than have to live with this. I met up with the dead man's wife. That was what you walked in on. I left a note in his pocket, Isla, and I was talking to her about the last moments of her husband of forty years. Have you an idea how guilty I feel because I lived when he didn't? And then you walked uninvited into one of the worst moments in my life. It was private; you had no place to be there. Didn't I give you enough of a hint that I had to do some of this stuff alone? I can't share this experience with you. You weren't there."

"I'm sorry, Ste. I wish I had been with you."

"You wish you'd been with me? You wish you'd seen what I did? Grow up, Isla. You want to experience the things that have made me this person? You want to see what I saw? You wish you felt like I feel now?"

The rhetorical questions kept on coming.

"Seriously, fucking hell, Isla, what's wrong with you? Isn't this dark enough for you? Do you still think you have what it takes to get me through this? I'm the one who was there and by the time the sun came up this morning, I realised I was on my own, despite you being with me. I can't see me shifting this, ever. It's never going to change. For all our sakes, Isla, you need to leave and forget me. I can't be the person I wanted to be before this happened. Everything changed when those Towers came down. I can't go on as if nothing happened. I don't feel the way I did the last time we were together. Don't you get it? I don't feel anything! I'm damaged. You can't erase that kind of stuff. So please, go live in your world and allow me to die in mine."

Isla wanted to cut in. With what, she wasn't sure but knew she should say something. But every time her mouth opened to interject with kindness, Ste cut in. He knew he was going to hurt her but she wanted to hear the truth. At least he was calmer and finally talking.

"And, I miss my beautiful friend." It was only now that Ste lost this battle with tears. The mention of Jarrod was too much, and he let the emotion take over. As he closed his eyes, he recalled the breakfast meeting where life had been just fine. Jarrod laughing whilst nicking a Danish off Ste's plate; his larger-than-life smile was the window into his wonderfully whole-hearted personality. Their final goodbye. And the moment it all changed and had started to haunt him.

And Ste knew he was destroying Isla with every word. Although his heart was broken, he now just wanted her to leave.

"You're right, Ste. I'm sorry for trying to take care of you. And I'm sorry for fucking up, at least twice. But in case this means anything to you, I fell for you a long time ago. It felt like love, and when somebody is in love with someone else, they care enough to put themselves out for them. However bad the flames are, I want to help you put them out. So please, if ever you want to talk, let me know and I will be there."

Ste didn't move. Stood where he was, he was managing to partially still hold it together. But he ached for her to leave, giving him the moment he craved where he could fall to pieces in private.

"One last thing."

Fuck's sake, was she never going to go?

"Like you, I miss my beautiful friend. I never met Jarrod. But my beautiful friend is you and once again Ste, I'm really going to miss you."

He watched the door shut before picking up the phone and dialling a number he had dialled thousands of times before. It connected to voicemail.

"Hey. mate. Stop pissing about. Where are you? What happened? You must've got my messages, but I'm going to keep trying until you get back to me. So please call me back. Please, Jarrod. I don't mind doing the next tour without you if you don't want to do this shit anymore. So, we can just be friends. In fact, you're fired. You were holding me back, anyway."

Ste took a deep breath. Getting the words out was hard but Jarrod was the only person he could talk to.

"No hard feelings about the sacking thing." He tried to laugh but couldn't manage it. "We can finish our breakfast and get an early beer. I'll even listen to you murder American Pie on the karaoke. You really can't sing, pal. How did someone like you get into the music industry? You're tone-deaf. I'll even support the Yankees. I'll be the biggest rounders fan ever. I'll move here, we can get season tickets and I'll pretend I know what's going on. Just for you. Because when I close my eyes, I hear your voice and all I can see is you running off leaving me to pay the bill again. I wish you'd stayed or taken me with you. We could have faced those bastards together."

Ste stopped, unable to speak as the tears flooded down his face.

"I am so glad to have found you."

Ste hadn't realised that an automated message had kicked in. The mailbox was finally full.

"Call me back, Jarrod. I love you, buddy."

He had to put the receiver down, but it took an age for him to lower the handset onto its base. Hanging up was his acknowledgement that it was the end. With the phone rested, he knew it was time to go home.

Chapter 60

2011

He knew that one day he had to return, but after ten years, he still couldn't bring himself to fly back. He had managed fine by not going back to New York, despite the many work commitments that would have ordinarily taken him there.

It had taken a long time for Ste to find peace, but that had never extended to accepting the hospitality offered by either Mrs Shahid or Star. And since Star had remarried, the invitations to visit dried up. It no longer seemed appropriate. Quietly, he was relieved that he no longer needed to make the choice.

He made sure that the bands under his charge were given the opportunity to go Stateside, where they were looked after by the ever-reliable Devon and his growing team of capable acolytes. He trawled out the occasional joke to those who didn't know his history that he boycotted New York for cultural reasons. But there could be no replacement for Jarrod. Devon was reliable and diligent, but he didn't have Jarrod's flair or personality and they'd never bonded in the way he had hoped they would. He knew it was his barriers that were up more than anything Devon had done and it was hard to bond with someone you did everything you could to avoid seeing in person. However thick his skin had grown, he could never get to a point where a day could pass without some form of vivid recollection of 9/11. And that meant he would never return. He felt as though he would never really recover.

Ste had gone ten years without telling anybody else the details of that ghastly day. Tina had asked, Greta had demanded and his daughter, now a beautiful teenager, had tried to find out where the darkness had come from.

Ste couldn't open the darkest corners of his soul to anybody. He spent years in therapy, but he just wouldn't, or was it that he couldn't, open up. The first hypnotist couldn't even get him under, and the therapists were frustrated that their attempts to help him seemed so futile.

No one fully knew the extent of how 9/11 had emotionally dumped him on his arse. Although ten years had passed, Isla remained the only recipient of the full, gruesome picture which his mind continued to paint. Ste didn't want to be helped. He didn't believe he deserved saving.

Occasionally, he sent messages to Jarrod, although Star had gently asked Ste to stop with the messages. She said that every time the phone bleeped, a wave of optimism came across her before she was hit by the same realisation each time that they were both chasing the same, impossible thing. Ste tried to stop, but a nasty habit had formed where he called for his friend when drunk in the early hours of the morning. After the first few times, Star would ignore the call and allow Ste the opportunity to tearfully rant into the replacement phone she'd got. But after a while, the number was disconnected. Ste went back to texting and the service provider always sent him the same error message—at least two-way communication was resumed in a small way.

Jarrod never came home from work that day. Star eventually moved on. And Ste, comforted by updates from the New York team that Star was being cared for, removed himself from her life.

He continued to send his messages to a nonsense number that didn't exist, rationalising that the ether was as good a place to contact his friend as anywhere else. The messages weren't desperate anymore and were a friendly update on life from one mate to another. He just couldn't give up talking to his friend.

His internal torture continued. The loss of Jarrod, the death of Irfan, the way he had treated Isla. All these things weighed him down with guilt. The immovable shit continued to rip at his core. Ste chose to bury himself in anything that took his mind away from himself. The bands rolled around the world with familiar rates of success. The internet and digital comms opened the global market. He was still ahead of the game, moving the business into new regions which no longer had the historic accessibility barriers such as proximity. But it was tougher. There was more competition, less money to play with and a tougher landscape to navigate, regardless of the twenty-year reputation Ste now had.

Predictably, his home life never improved, and it was Greta who finally called time on their partnership—not Ste. She had tried her best, but life was too short to be miserable. For the year following 9/11, she loyally stuck by him and absorbed his frustrations. The psychotherapy failed to release the demons and the darkness creating the images tormented them all in the form of his often relentless screaming which would wake them most nights; she would hold him and give him her body as a release, but it killed the little of them that had survived. They put aside what happened before Ste flew to New York. They put their incompatibility aside because Ste was in no shape to be on his own, and for the good of their daughter, they vowed to do whatever it would take to hold him together.

Amy grew up not knowing the issues troubling her dad. She had a vague recollection of their late-night phone calls when he was in America, but never appreciated what 9/11 was until asking him to help her with a school project years later. It was this straw that broke Ste's emotional backbone. He was so angry and flew into a rage when she asked him to be part of a classroom show and tell. Her mum explained a little, but she didn't know why he screamed at night. Inevitably, the domestic side of Ste's world returned to the same wretchedness that had all but broken their family unit before it happened. After which, it was only a matter of time.

His colleagues accepted that the Ste they had known was no more. They hoped it was a temporary thing and that one day, things would get back to normal. But the years passed and those colleagues moved on, to be replaced by new ones. The more youthful office was less tolerant of the moody, unresponsive boss who often went days without talking to anybody. Ste was a changed man. They never knew Ste Lewis before the loss of Jarrod and the events of that September day, the time when Ste was first in the office, loudly playing the new pre-releases he'd been sent. Now he was drawn towards the dark 80s sounds of Joy Division and The Damned, sounds which pumped on an endless loop through his headphones as he stared blankly through the office. Whilst occasionally snapping himself into a more positive place, he would search for a more innocent sound, turning to the self-taped recordings of him and Ben messing around as teenagers in Ben's cellar. Ste Lewis was a mess. And Ste knew everybody knew, but he couldn't care less.

He took to the road as much as he could justify. He started to see his domestic life as a series of trial separations interrupted by occasional periods of being together, usually around Christmas when the bands didn't tour. Being at home with his daughter was where a father should be, but Ste rarely was. When there was no work to take him away, he'd disappear, hiding out with Ben's family miles away from his own. Ben had stayed in touch with Johnny, their childhood friend and intoxicated drummer from way back when. These were the connections to a happier past which helped Ste retain the smallest level of sanity. There can be no hiding it from people who have known you all your life.

Apart from the sympathetic noises that Greta had made in the immediate aftermath of the disaster, she had withdrawn. She'd returned to being someone who was no more than a stranger to him. But he had managed to keep close to Amy, and she to him. Technology helped, and it was by no means perfect. But of all the things that had dissipated, their bond was true.

Ste sat alone in front of the television to watch the ten-year anniversary service at Ground Zero. He was living alone, still in Islington and around the corner from his teenage daughter. The eventual split from Greta was amicable enough, to the extent that they could publicly describe themselves as 'good friends' without truly meaning it. While they had never been good friends, it was simpler and kinder than the truth. Greta was absolved of her responsibility to look after the man she'd spent too many years with, now happy to leave Amy in charge. Amy may have been his daughter, but theirs was different to the typical parent/sibling relationship because, without Amy, Ste was alone. It was almost an inverse relationship to the one it should have been. Ste meant it when he apologised for his up and down behaviour. He didn't want to be the surly, volatile man, but he was a distant character and often short-tempered and unkind.

His deepest regret was reserved for the way he'd treated Isla. He didn't regret deciding to not go after her when he got back to England. Apart from being ashamed of his behaviour, he was not the person who could love her the way Isla Kiely deserved to be loved; however, he regretted what might have been. Aside from his daughter, she was the only light that shone into his soul.

This morning's Sunday Observer carried a flattering piece about his twenty years in the industry. The article was accompanied by quotes from musicians and bands who offered their glowing tributes to his gravitas. The quotes from bands he had worked with in the early days were more about the person they remembered Ste to have been. The few commenting on his recent achievements were accompanied by words reflecting his diligence, professionalism and successes. Although this was just another article and these were just words on a page, Ste could read and easily understood the hidden meaning. He didn't bother reading the full copy. If it hadn't come out today, it might have meant more. Today was more significant than any article about him.

Chapter 61

The flag on the American Embassy flickered from its position at half-mast as the US Ambassador Louis Susman led the long moments of nervous silence from the Memorial Garden.

'For those here remembering someone close, torn from you in the most brutal way, deprived of some of life's most treasured moments, 9/11 has touched your life immeasurably. Yet, our societies are strong, our political institutions and justice systems function…'

Most people in the crowd outside the gates kept their heads bowed in thoughtful contemplation, although some there were keen to show that in a democracy, there will always be those who disagree. Although there, Isla wasn't listening and didn't feel reverent. She scanned the crowd for the person she hoped would be here. She wasn't looking for Prince Charles, David Cameron, or Judy Dench. What was this, a bloody film premiere? But despite repeatedly looking across the heads of the crowd, she never saw Ste and was starting to become aware that she was looking increasingly disrespectful to the commemoration for the three thousand victims of the terrorist slaughter. She tried to focus. She was always trying to focus.

I'll give you *'deprived of some of life's most treasured moments'*, she mumbled to herself.

Isla had left BA and the whole cabin crew business as soon as she returned from New York ten years ago. She'd stayed friends with Sally who had loyally stuck by her as she set about rearranging her life, and over the years, their friendship had become surprisingly strong. Sally had offered to come with her today; Isla was just grateful for the arm to hold as she focused on the screen relaying what was happening in the Memorial Garden yards away.

She couldn't focus on the words of the dignitaries. Isla's car crash of a decade left a litany of relationships that failed because they didn't hit those standards which had been set all those years before. The numerous jobs promised much but delivered little, and Isla continued to wander the world alone. The few good friends she had did at least understand her, but a decade on, she was a different person to the happy one in that more youthful, excitable time of life before 9/11. Then, she had been happy. The principal inhabitant of a world in which things were falling nicely into place. She was in love, and she had felt loved. Right up until the point when the tragedy, which the world had now stopped to remember, killed off whatever dreams had started to become a reality. The picture of that future which she had painted for herself had been suddenly shattered. That loss had haunted her. It continued to haunt her still.

There were some moments of happiness. Somebody would occasionally come into her life and make her feel special for a while. Work projects occasionally invigorated her. But those occasions were rare. She looked at her parents with respect, grateful for their unconditional love, more aware than ever of a parent's responsibility. But it triggered her to once again think about Ste. She'd staggered into her thirties without realising it and was emotionally self-medicating with unqualified advice from the books and magazines in which she took solace. She'd read advice that told her not to *waste her tears*. If she looked hard enough, she'd find that *she wasn't alone. Her tears were the product of her fears*, which was *nature's way of saying she had to let go of whatever she was holding onto*. Because what she was feeling would *dissolve* and one day, she would feel *strong enough to turn the hurt to love*.

Oh, Fuck Right Off. What a load of bollocks. She was angry, hurt, confused and alone and had ripped up too many magazines to read any more of their saccharine platitudes topped up by GCSE psychobabble.

Going to the ceremony was her way of drawing a line under the last decade; she could finally let go. After all, she had never had a relationship with Ste. During the two nights when they had shared a room, they had never shared the bed. But after all these years, and all those approaches from so many suitable men, why was her mind fixated on a man who she knew so little about? He had been so cruel to her. And still, however much this ceremony was about drawing a line, it was also about not drawing a line and hoping they could start again. If only he was here, maybe there was another chance.

She regretted her behaviour over those few days in New York, all the repeated attempts to force herself into the centre of his grief. She was young, naïve and in love with him. She'd sought out professional help, but at a hundred pounds an hour, and with her salary as a Travel Administrator being something she could barely live on as it was, that kind of therapy wasn't for her. There was no grief counselling for people who had not lost somebody. Friends were tired of her engaging them in discussions about her feelings and experiences. They'd grown up, moved on, had kids, and now lived in a world where the demands of nappies, blended food and sleep deprivation made Isla's ongoing lament a far lower priority than their own immediate challenges.

Her parents, loving as they were, didn't understand why she was such a lost soul. After she had quit cabin crew, her mum had a word with someone at Haven and Isla had agreed to join the company. However, she never showed up for her first day, something which caused a rift between them had that lasted years. Three months later, she was working at a different company doing the same thing. Her mum took it personally, unable to understand that it was nothing personal. Isla just wasn't coping. And they didn't know about Ste. Isla didn't see the point of explaining things that no longer mattered. They knew she was in New York that day, but it had been left at that. There was no point disturbing still waters.

The service wrapped up, jolting Isla from her daydream as had happened so many times before. The protesters held their ground, refusing to move until they could be assured that theirs was the last voice left bellowing into the London air. Sally made her excuses, racing home as she had to, to service the comforts of her family who would be waiting for their Sunday lunch. Isla stood alone in the dispersing crowds, her latest stab at closure. But without a conversation with Ste, closure would never come. He wasn't there. Why would he be? His life probably moved on years ago, while hers lay stagnant. Let sleeping dogs lie. He would still be a devoted father and probably a husband. If he was single, if he wanted her, then surely, he would have come looking by now?

She drew breath and decided that this was indeed her swan song; the line was now drawn. Ste Lewis was out of her life for good. She left in the direction of Soho where she'd find some company to take her mind away from where it was. She'd get a drink and hoped somebody she knew would show up. It was still early, but there was always a place to get a drink. Maybe she'd sing some sad songs to an equally sad stranger.

She picked up one of the few remaining papers on the newsstand, a copy of today's Observer. This would help kill some time.

"Big Issue, Ma'am?"

She put the paper back, acknowledging the engagement from the bloke in the day-glow bib.

"Thanks, mate. Keep the change."

Chapter 62

Right up to the morning of the anniversary, Ste hadn't decided whether to go to Grosvenor Square and join the crowd at the London memorial or watch the live coverage from both London and then New York, at home. He didn't have to be involved; maybe he would just stay in a darkened room and sleep through it. Amy had asked him if he had wanted her company, but if he was going to wake up and participate, he needed to experience it on his own. He cast an eye over the London ceremony, but after a hard week's work in Eastern Europe, he was barely awake. His late arrival home the previous evening came on the back of a Friday night session in Kiev which had dragged into Saturday morning, before his flight home had been chronically delayed. Not for the first time, Ste reminded himself that he was too old for this shit. He'd been doing this stuff for two decades. It was a younger man's game.

The build-up to the commemoration event dominated the news channels, even out in the Ukraine. Every time he turned on the television, Ste was immediately immersed in the old footage which he just could not switch off - everybody staggering away from the Towers looked just like he had, and he scanned the footage looking at everybody in case he found any footage of Jarrod. Pause, Rewind, Repeat. There was nothing new; every click of the remote darkened his already anguished mood.

He stood when the moments of silence demanded it, and he sat to listen to the speeches, waiting for any namecheck Jarrod may get. But he never heard it. Footage reading all victims' names was not broadcast live. Five hours of name-reading was not something the networks could carry, but he would watch it online another day, extending further his decade of closure. In his deliberately darkened lounge, he watched in silence, offering a prayer for the lost and the thousands who had survived but never recovered.

God wasn't part of his life and he had no belief in anything spiritual.

Despite reading that grief could stimulate a need for something bigger than *we* understand, he'd never fallen into the God-trap, rationalising that if God were so great, surely those planes would have suffered engine failure on the ground before they took off? Endless conspiracy theories dominated the internet. Tributes came from the great, the good and the bereaved. And then there was George Bloody Bush. Ste had no interest in the lamentations of a man who chose this sensitive platform to justify his actions, linking the actions of the Flight 93 heroes with his own liars' war raging in the Middle East. Just as long as the odious Tony 'BLiar' was nowhere to be seen.

Views of New York showed its people living their life ten years on. While many struggled with the cards life had dealt them, the sun shone on the joggers and bikers who exercised across Central Park. Life seemed to be good for the walkers on the High Line as they meandered down onto the pathway alongside the Hudson.

Typically, predictably, he once again thought of Isla. Her name, her image, the woman who was never far away from his thoughts.

His phone vibrated. It was a text from Amy.

'*RU OK? Love you Dad x*'

For the first time since he turned the television on hours before, Ste cracked a smile. The simple act of love triggered the emotion that needed to come out. As the tears flowed down his cheeks, he shook with the pain consuming him. But rather than message Amy back, he sent a text to somebody else.

'*Hey, mate. Long-time no speak. I still miss you.*'

A familiar error message came back. Jarrod wouldn't be getting that text either. Nothing ever changed. He sat back with nothing but his thoughts for company. How and when would this tormented existence become something that didn't feel so desperate?

Chapter 63

2020

There had been enough time to temper the havoc that would quickly devastate the world. With the 2020 New Year party balloons still half-inflated, events continued to unfold thousands of miles away, but the warnings came and went. Within weeks, it was part of the daily news cycle. Pictures from Wuhan showed just how forceful the authoritarian Chinese officials were in dealing with the dissenting minorities to Beijing's strict controls on movement. Even the images of residents being dragged into military vehicles disguised with stick-on medical signs, were not enough to wake up Boris, the PM, still riding the self-congratulatory wave of Brexit and the affirmation that he was temporarily the political King of the Union.

By early February, things were increasingly serious at home. With Italy entering the tightest peacetime controls of public movement Europe had ever known, it was only a matter of time before the rest of Europe followed. Despite a leadership that had won a mandate based on tougher border controls, Britain was surprisingly lax. Screening at airports and ports wasn't happening, and there was no process in place, or even the necessary equipment, to separate the potential carriers arriving at the numerous entry points into the Union. And when the inevitable first case was reported, it was clear things were getting serious and were quickly about to get a lot worse. Meanwhile, the government flippantly advised the public to sing Happy Birthday whilst washing their hands. Not really the effective governing the British people deserved from their government. It wasn't the strong leadership they thought they were voting for just a few months before.

Like most rational members of planet earth, Isla was frightened. This could potentially turn into a worse disaster than 9/11. The inevitability of its potential scale was obvious. This virus, like every virus before it, knew no borders; but aside from the public health issues, Isla had more pressing concerns. If the country was going into lockdown, being stuck with the man she was living with was something she knew she would not be able to get through. In normal times, without an order to stay together indoors, things were already volatile. There had been good times, but they were only memorable for their rarity. There was now no romance or affection and Isla had given up her plan to settle down and have a family of her own. The thought of dying alone – whether in four months, four years or forty years time – was enough to want something more than nothing. She had concluded that Jakob was a thoroughly unpleasant man; but the fear of being alone had forced her down a path that found her living with this somebody, even if he treated her badly.

As she walked by the canal that snaked around the old Olympic site in East London, her preoccupation was with herself. What state must she be in to see this relationship as a better choice than being alone? Isla was filled with self-loathing, continuing with her struggle to find any value in herself.

She recalled her fortieth birthday two years earlier. Her few remaining friends, who were largely happily partnered up and content as they skulked towards middle age, turned what should have been an old school party into a piss poor evening. They were at a stage in life where they had to plan to get a night out without kids, so much so that half the people who turned up only came to spend the evening liberating themselves from the shackles of parenthood. By nine, many of them were so far gone that they'd started to leave for home, and the other half were so unused to socialising outside of the confines of their middle-class, 'tapenade darling' dining tables, they'd forgotten how to have fun. The stilted, boring conversations about how Taliya was doing in Year Four, turned the event into a social disaster. In her life, the biggest challenge was not the availability of organic aubergines, or the cleaner either going off sick or going home to Argentina.

With her birthday party having prematurely disintegrated, Isla ended up going home with the pub bouncer many hours after the majority of her friends had disappeared. She had stopped seeing her beauty and the mirror was her enemy. The joy that freedom and self-respect brought continued to elude her. She was now older, heavier, lonely, and very unhappy; the sort of feelings that make you jump at the first thing presenting itself. And when Jakob took her for breakfast at a café in Hackney the next morning, he enthusiastically talked about his recent diving holiday. Maybe next time, they could go together? It felt like this could be the one to make the pain go away.

The first time he hit her, Isla convinced herself it was her fault. She'd had a drink and he was accelerated by something considerably less legal. He explained to her why it was her fault. She knew what she did wrong and it wouldn't happen again. So, she stayed with him, moving into his dingy one-bedroom flat soon after their first night together.

But the second time, Isla knew that it wasn't her fault. Jakob was an arsehole with a temper and when he couldn't unleash his temper at work, he took it out on whoever was closest. She knew next to nothing about him. He had no friends unconnected to work. Any attempts to connect with him about how he had ended up in East London, far away from his hometown in Lithuania, yielded nothing. He never discussed it, never went back '*home*' and sure as hell never suggested they visit together.

In fact, they'd never been anywhere together. There had never been further mention of a diving holiday and when Isla suggested they go away for a weekend in the New Forest, he reluctantly agreed but pulled out via a text message the day before. He had to work. There was no apology or regret. That was the end of it. No discussion; no explanation.

The Christmas that had recently passed had been joyless and her regular trips back to visit her loving parents in Hemel were now incredibly infrequent. She knew her lack of positivity was something her parents could see straight away. She hated worrying them. She also hated being questioned on her choices; choices she couldn't justify to rational, loving people such as her folks.

Remote from her family, and increasingly cut off from the friends who had outgrown her, Isla's attempts to make life better continued to backfire. She felt worse for trying. Her last flight out of New York in 2001, where she looked out over the devastation in the South of Manhattan Island, haunted her. She regretted her immediate decision to stop flying and pursue a different career. And the failure of her love life at that time underpinned the many failed relationships since.

Nothing came close to the feelings she had held for Ste nearly nineteen years ago. After nearly two years with him, Isla had never shared a spiritual moment with Jakob. In that first evening with Ste, she had established a benchmark to compare all future moments against, and inevitably, they had all failed to meet that mark.

As the never-ending news cycle rolled, it was confirmed on a minute-by-minute basis that the world had gone mad. The shops were being cleared of pasta and toilet rolls, with anything in a tin quickly becoming a new form of currency.

The government briefed the nation daily at five pm. Working from home was the new norm for anybody lucky enough to have a job. Isla and her colleagues were being furloughed. Pubs and clubs were closing; Jakob was going to be out of work. If she didn't get out, the prospect of being confined with a monster loomed. He was a threat to her, and she would be another nameless statistic on a domestic casualty list.

Although it was a long time since she had left home, the option of moving back to Hemel Hempstead was her best bet. She'd have to tell her parents the truth about her relationship to get through this and it would break their hearts, but, as the schools started closing, Isla knew she was running out of time to make her escape from the Hackney hell before public transport shut down. If she didn't leave now, she would be trapped.

She downed a second glass of vodka. That would be enough to find the courage she needed to ring her parents' house - but it rang out.

They're never out at this time of the evening.

She tried her mum's mobile but there was no answer.

Only one number left to dial. The number she wanted to dial least. Her dad's.

Chapter 64

It barely rang once.

"Dad. That was quick."

"Isla. It's your mum."

"What do you mean? What's wrong?"

"Isn't that why you are calling? I'm sure I left you a message."

She looked at her phone. No message. No missed call. For a moment, Isla thought her dad was going mad.

"Didn't I call you earlier? I'm sure I did. I left a message with that bloke of yours. Isla, your mum is sick."

"Dad, what's up with mum? Where are you?"

"She's been ill for days. We're at Watford General. She was acting funny but I don't know what's wrong. They think I'm ill too, but I've told them I'm okay. They think it's the Chinese thing everyone is so excited about. Where are you, my darling girl? Can you come?"

Her dad did not normally call her his '*darling*', not since she was little. Her dad was scared. Her dad was never scared.

"I'm on my way."

Isla only had time to pack a night bag, focusing instead on making sure she took all the important papers she'd need to start over, away from Jakob. Running away from the flat, she never once glanced back, jumping onto the deserted 253 bus to Euston, before a twenty-minute train journey to Watford Junction.

She texted Jakob; not for a confrontation, that would be pointless. But it would answer the question of whether her dad was losing the plot.

'*Evening J—Did my dad speak to you earlier?*'

'*Yes*'

'*Was there a message?*'

'Yes I forget what'

Pointless be damned. This wasn't something she could passively accept. There was no excuse for not passing the message to her. While she wondered how to respond, a familiar, but far older face stared up at her from a copy of the nightly 'Evening Standard' left on the seat next to her. Under the headline *'Kingmaker, Again'* Ste stared at her, the first time she had seen him in nearly two decades. He was sitting behind a desk with a castle in the sea some way behind him. It wasn't somewhere Isla recognised, but she had run out of time to read the article. Pushing the paper into her bag, she ran for the train to Hertfordshire. Her mind switched to the hospital as the panic in her dad's voice flooded over her like a wave. How bad was this?

Her phone beeped. A message from Jakob.

'Club closing tonight. No work. Buy food now.'

She was not going back. Isla had seen the last of that man. She just hoped she wasn't too late to see her mum before visiting time was over.

Watford Junction was an eerily deserted, vacuous place. Rubbish danced in the wind. At this time of night, there would normally be the daily gaggle of commuters queuing up for snacks on their way home, but, like everything else, the kiosks were closed. While London limped on, everywhere outside the sprawling metropolis was finished.

There were no taxis at the rank. Isla ran up Clarendon Road with her baggage. The town was deserted. Even Wetherspoons' hard-core weeknight pissheads had admitted defeat, unable to resist the international pressure for everyone to go home. Turning into Market Street, all the restaurants were closed; the ring road was deserted to the point that a murder of crows remained unmoved as they picked over the bones of a discarded KFC. This unique scene warranted the appearance of a cluster of zombies. In the distance, she could hear the piercing sounds of emergency sirens. She phoned her dad again, but this time, it rang out. She rang again, and a third time the phone rang without answer. It was an hour since they had spoken. What could have happened in an hour?

Chapter 65

Isla passed the Vicarage Road Stadium, approaching a mass of activity around the normally unguarded hospital entrance where all vehicles were now being directed. The dayglow-jacketed security staff were wearing masks as they engaged each driver at the front of the queue that snaked towards the main road. The absence of life across the rest of the town was in stark contrast to the chaos engulfing this small road. There were sirens, car horns and desperate yells all directed at the two blokes guarding the hospital entrance.

A security guard came up to her with a Watford FC scarf around his face, demanding that she stop.

"Where are you going? This is now a restricted area."

"My mum and dad are in here. I don't know where."

"You can't come in unless you have clearance."

"Clearance? What sort of clearance? My dad phoned me and said my mum is sick in hospital. What sort of clearance do I need to respond to that?"

The security guard softened his tone, but the rules were not changing.

"Look, love, I'm really sorry. No one's allowed in unless they are dropping someone off or need medical attention themselves. And there's no exceptions. I'm sorry, but it is for your safety."

Safety be buggered. Isla knew all the back ways into the hospital from all the times she'd staggered in and out of the all-night staff parties. But before she'd had time to move away, her phone rang. It was her dad.

"Dad, I'm outside and they won't let me in."

"Hi, Miss Kiely. I'm sorry, this is not your dad. I am one of the doctors on duty here and I am sorry to be the bearer of bad news."

Isla gulped. She suspected that this was the news she'd been dreading. Her mum had Covid-19 and was going to be isolated. Her dad was with her and wouldn't be able to phone her.

"I'm outside. I can come in right now and see my mum. But the security people won't let me in." She was begging; her parents were the only people she had in the world.

"I'm sorry. I don't know how much you know. Your mum is very sick with Covid-19 and she may not have long left."

Isla paused. In her heart, she knew what he was going to say.

"Thank you, Doctor. I'm prepared for this. Can I come in and see her now? Is that allowed? Thanks for letting me know. But where's my dad? Why are you calling? Can I not just come in?"

"Isla, I am sorry, but your dad collapsed. We think it was a heart attack."

"Was?" Isla dropped to the floor, her phone crashing from her hands to the pavement disconnecting the call. The guard in the scarf ran towards her, adjusting his mask before reaching her. She had fallen hard but wasn't hurt, reaching for her phone, desperate to continue the conversation. The phone rang again. As she pulled herself up from the ground, tears streaming down her face, she could hear her name being called down the line. Steadying herself, she took a breath and resumed the conversation.

"Is that the doctor?"

"Isla. I'm sorry. Are you okay? I don't know how much you heard. The line dropped."

"I'm by the main entrance and I think you are going to tell me my dad is dead, and my mum is about to die."

She didn't need it spelled out. The task was hard enough for the medical staff without her needing to be spoon-fed.

"Isla, I am sorry. Let me send someone to come and get you. Please wait where you are."

The security guard with her took a call on his radio and ushered her to the portable hut. He found a chair and offered her a spare mask which Isla put on, each of them applying hand gel as they waited for somebody to arrive.

Isla went through the motions of appreciation to the security man, unable to offer anything more than basic platitudes. Her dad was gone, and it was probably too late to see her mum. For the first time in her life, she was on her own. The darkness of the evening wrapped itself around her. She sat alone, oblivious to the lights bouncing off the security guards who had resumed their attempts to control the mayhem around her. She gazed at the back of the Graham Taylor Stand and the ground her dad had loved so much for his entire life. One of his only constants.

Had loved.

He was gone. He'd died yards from the stand dedicated to the club's most successful manager. In her head, all Isla could hear was the loud chanting from the stands.

"One Graham Taylor, there's only one Graham Taylor!"

As she struggled to hold herself together, a middle-aged nurse hurried towards her.

"Are you Isla?"

She slowly nodded in reluctant affirmation.

"I'm sorry to meet you in these sad circumstances. I'm Sister Siobhan, and I've been with your parents today. Would you like to come in with me?"

Isla put on the plastic overall, rubber gloves and surgical mask the Sister had put down two metres from her. They stopped at one of the rooms off the main reception area. Despite the chaos outside, this part of the hospital was empty.

"Where is everyone?" Isla enquired.

"Once patients are dropped off, everyone has to leave. We are trying to limit the exposure of this awful virus. Isla, I'm so sorry, but we need to protect you as well, so we won't be leaving this room."

Isla understood. Even the most emotional person would see the sense in containment. If the country had been locked down sooner, this may never have happened. She thought of Jakob, incredulous that the nightclub where he was working was still open tonight, when a short distance away, people were dying of this terrible virus. Her face gripped with rage. His lazy indifference had stopped her from seeing her dear parents before they died.

"Where is Mum now?"

"Isla, your mum is very sick. She came in earlier today but she has been unwell for much longer. She couldn't breathe and is on one of the Covid-19 wards. We've made her as comfortable as we can. Don't worry; she is being artificially ventilated, but there's no sign that she is suffering."

"That's not a good sign, is it? You've doped her up so she can die in peace!"

"I'm sorry, Isla, I don't want to give you false hope, but she's unlikely to make it through the night. Your mum is asleep and in a really peaceful place. It's the best we can do."

The Sister was a woman of compassion and warmth.

"What about my dad?"

"He was taken very suddenly. When he drove your mum in, she was seriously ill and the shock of how bad she was…. It just seemed to suddenly overtake him."

"When was this?"

"They got here at lunchtime, but when it was clear to us how bad your mum's condition was, he wouldn't leave. He was showing symptoms, although they were not as bad. We started to treat him for the virus as a precaution, but he got upset when he realised how bad your mum was. So, we let him stay after he called you as he said you were coming to get him. But then he suddenly collapsed about an hour ago."

"That's just after we spoke. I called to him and told him I was coming."

"I'm sorry, Isla. There was nothing we could do. We tried to resuscitate him. The shock was too much and just took him."

Isla had spent a lifetime believing her parents were just partners of convenience, quietly cohabiting a world of passive interactions rather than living out the epic love story she had sought for herself. But the evidence suggested that her parents' love was one that went further than any public display of affection could indicate. It was far deeper. Intrinsic. A private love just between them.

"Is there anyone I can call, Isla? Do you have somebody who can pick you up? I'm afraid we need to get you outside of the hospital grounds as soon as we can."

Isla looked at her open bag, the unread copy of the Evening Standard poking out of the opening.

"No. There is no one. I'll call a cab".

There is no one. I've got no one. I'm all alone.

Chapter 66

The Uber raced down the deserted A41. Despite being only seven miles, the journey back to her parents' house could sometimes take over an hour. But tonight, it went in an instant. Or maybe it didn't. Isla was in a blur, only snapping to as she recognised the familiar magic roundabout on the edge of Hemel's Town Centre. For a change, she felt no sense of dread at the prospect of going home. There was nobody there to upset because there was nobody there. Although her mum was still alive, Isla had already started grieving for both her parents. She knew that her mum was never coming home. As the taxi pulled up to her family home, Isla stopped; she couldn't go in. Her mum was hours from dying. Although she had nowhere to go, she also had no sanitiser or anything to stop her from picking up the virus herself. She asked the driver to take her to the twenty-four-hour Tesco up at Jarmans Park. Despite her sense of helplessness, at least she held on to the desire to be alive.

The driver waited outside without question, aware that something serious had happened to his fare. You don't pick somebody up from a hospital in that state, especially now, and expect them to be okay. And the chances of her getting another cab from this wasteland of activity were slim.

Isla came out clutching a bag of essential things to make her safe. The shop was out of hand sanitiser, so she'd gone overboard on alternatives that would probably make her skin bleed, but it was better than using nothing. She had plastic gloves and an improvised face mask made from a woollen scarf left in the clothing department's bargain bin. She could then use cotton wool pads as an extra barrier. The car returned to the house and tentatively, with a sense of disbelief, she walked through the front door. Her home felt contaminated.

The television was on. It was always on when her parents were at home, but in their rush to get to the hospital, her dad had not switched it off. Nor had he finished the half-drunk cup of tea sat on the table next to what had been his chair. The table next to where her mother would have been sat was now turned on its side, a broken glass of what looked like water smashed across the surrounding floor. This was where they had last been in the house before they'd left for the hospital. The room told her their story. She broke down. Nobody could hear her cries. She lay on the carpet, the bags from Tesco next to her and as the emotion took a firm grip, Isla looked at her father's chair. Without wanting to, she fell asleep.

It can't have been too long before Isla was woken by the sound of her phone. She had no idea where she was, or why she was lying on a carpet with a scarf around her mouth. It was a Watford number. The reality dawned. Her mum was gone. It was less of an emotional flood and more of a tsunami.

"Hello. Isla here."

"Isla, this is Sister Siobhan. I wanted to let you know immediately that your mum has just passed. I am very sorry. Can we do anything for you?"

It was four in the morning and, in the space of eight hours, Isla had gone from living with a partner in London and having two parents happily approaching retirement together to being a single, middle-aged orphan.

"Thank you for letting me know, Sister."

What else was there to say?

Chapter 67

There was nothing to do. With the country entering lockdown, there was a paralysis among officials charged with burying her parents. Nobody knew what was allowed or when things could happen. Isla cleaned the house. She bleached everything more than once, confident that there was now no chance the deadly virus would get her from inside the house. She contacted extended family and the few friends her parents had, methodically running through the list of names to contact, adding to them whenever one of the distant aunts or uncles she contacted gave her another name she should call. It was funny getting to know your parents after they had died by virtue of what others thought about them.

Their social circle was very small; she was surprised by some of the stories that people wanted to share. She never saw this side of her folks. It was a shame. She wished that she had taken the time to really know them. Shame on her. Their relationship might have been less parent and child, and more grown-up friends if she'd known some of the stories when they were alive.

As she went through the household paperwork, she found that her mum was meticulous about her accounting. There was very little that Isla needed to do with their affairs. Their intentions were clear and laid out in a will that she found in the bureau at the bottom of the narrow stairs. Despite her grief, she realised that for the first time in her life, she was free. Not just free from debt, but also free from the fear of disappointing her parents. She knew her parents had always loved her, but she also knew they saw her failings as their own.

And now she owned a house! And such was the scarcity of value in anything she had left with Jakob, she decided there was nothing worth going back for. Along with her bank bits, she'd left Hackney with her passport as a historic force of habit. All the other important paperwork had always been kept here or was backed up online. She didn't need to go back. Ever.

The daily tasks were a new routine. The cleaning, the paperwork, the phone calls to finalise plans for the funeral. Socially distanced forays for supplies became part of the routine, and the only hardship was not being able to see her mum and dad at peace. She wasn't even allowed the closure usually afforded someone by visiting them both in the Chapel of Rest. These were the rules in place to limit the spread of infection. Picking up her dad's car from the hospital was an ordeal. In his initial rush, her dad had parked it on double yellows over a week before and it was now long gone. The hospital had been kind in facilitating its return with no charges – after all, how do you fine a dead person? – but the process had taken several long, painful conversations with organisations that all now had much better things to be doing than sorting out the repatriation of a 2014 Honda Accord. Dad had always gone with the Japanese cars as he felt you could safely drive them until they died. Or you died. Whichever came first.

Their joint funeral came and went. Only five people were allowed to attend. There had been hundreds of deaths in every town in the land and services were limited to fifteen minutes before the puff of smoke. It was over.

I'm alone......

That evening, she relived the night two weeks before when things changed forever. She had not heard from Jakob. Not so much as a '*where the fuck are you*' text. He was sulking. Like the shopping, and cleaning and paying the bills—the finishing was down to her. She sent a text.

'*It's over. Sell my stuff if you want.*'

His response was demeaning and without any sign of regret or respect.

'*Fuck you Lisa*' – he didn't bother to override the auto-correction that had mis-spelled her name yet again.

She was livid that he had taken her right to say goodbye to her folks. The blackened eyes and bust nose were nothing compared to that. She would never forgive him. But she was going to have her revenge. It came in the form of never giving the bastard another thought. She wouldn't be bitter or turn herself inside out with hatred. That wouldn't affect him, but it would be toxic for her. He'd taken enough from her already and her ultimate revenge was being free of him for good. Mostly, she was angry with herself for allowing the situation to get to where it had. She was too proud to talk to her parents and let them help her. And she was angry with herself for waiting until they were dead to find out about them. She had only ever known them in one role—as her parents. She had never once seen them as people in their own rights. She regretted not telling the truth about what happened in New York, the few days which had underpinned so many of her subsequent choices.

They hadn't done a bad job of bringing her up. It wasn't until New York that things had started to go horribly wrong for her. Until then, she'd done well. Only after 9/11 did she dramatically fall, quickly becoming less than she was before. That was not their fault. That was not anybody's fault.

She drank from the glass of wine in front of her, looking at the spotlessly clean house. Her house. The only untidiness was the stack of papers on the coffee table. On top of them was the copy of the Evening Standard from two weeks before, the picture of Ste once again staring up at her.

She read the article by Jennifer Ruby. His picture, and his typically huge smile, filled Isla with the warmth that she had been missing. He was managing bands under his own label and, of course, was doing well. She remembered the band he was so excited to be managing when they met. *The Cormacks.* They weren't the success he predicted, but they played around the top ten for a couple of years, before dropping into obscurity to make way for the next big thing. She'd followed his career from a distance; it was hard to miss it, such was his profile and list of high-profile successes. She shuffled through her iTunes and found some of his signings in her playlists. There was no mention of family in the article, but he wasn't living in London. The view was from the Solent, and the castle was a fort surrounded by water between Southsea and the Isle of Wight. The article was not a significant piece of writing, just a plug for another new band that had been booked to start a UK tour before the lockdown kicked in. The timing of the breakthrough tour couldn't have been worse, and at the bottom of the article was a footnote confirming the tour had since been cancelled. But the album was already e-released and she instantly logged onto Spotify to listen to 'Maverick Road'. She heard the threads of the bands alluded to in the piece, remembering The Cormacks and their Celtic-Rock vibe which dominated the BBC 6 Music playlists and the jukebox in every Irish pub she'd since been to.

The music aside, she was only reading the article to find out about Ste. Were they both alone? It was such a long time since they had staggered through the dusty New York streets, irrecoverably traumatised by the events of 9/11. She was affected by proxy. But it had ruined her life. Her pain was real. And as the whole world struggled to function in its newly locked down state, Isla felt more alone than ever.

Nineteen years was a long time to hold onto lost love. They were the real thing in waiting and she had known in her heart that had it not been for 9/11, they would have made it. But she lost her man before he was ever hers to lose.

She switched on her dad's iPad and typed 'Ste Lewis music' into Google. It defaulted to something else. She did not want to find out about Steve the Jazz Pianist, or Stephen, the guy from the Big Band of Fun. She searched under management and found 'Southsea Records.' There was a fancy address in Charlotte St, London. But as London had been cleared of all but the most essential key workers, there was no chance he would be there.

Loneliness, memories, and the subsequent glasses of wine gnawed at her. *Surely it won't hurt to attempt to contact him. What's the worst that can happen?*

He had cast her away like used toilet roll the last time they'd met. She'd walked away from him without closure. If his life was complete without her now, he could ignore her message.

What harm could it do?

Looking at his bio and the contact details for the company, she took a chance on an e-mail address that followed the likely format.

Ste.Lewis@solentrecords.info

'*Hello.*

Are you there? It's Isla. From a long time ago. Ping me back if you can.'

She pressed send and waited. She had given the power to cyberspace.

Isla took another sip of wine and drifted off in her chair. It was her mum's chair, and she wondered whether her mum forgave her. She had been very clear to her all her life that it was the man's job to chase the girl. Here she was disappointing her again and chasing a man who had made it clear that he didn't want her. Isla was restarting her life. The rules were there to be re-written or re-validated. This was her time to take control.

Chapter 68

Logging on the next morning, Isla felt a rush of exhilaration. Her inbox contained a message from Ste. Her heart started to beat in a way that she remembered from the dim and distant past. This was it. Finally!

It took no time at all for her heartbeat to return to normal, as, on opening the mail, it was clearly an automated response. But it meant she had at least got somewhere.

Message: AUTO RESPONSE:

Thank you for your message.

At the current time, I am out of the office on essential family business. Please contact my PA, Rachel.Arthur@solentrecords.info during my absence.

This e-mail will not be forwarded.

Stay Safe!

Despite landing in the right inbox—a good thing—he wasn't there to read it—suboptimal. Isla sent a mail to Rachel. She introduced herself as an old friend trying to get in touch. It was the sort of message Rachel would have received many times at a high-profile time for an up-and-coming band. She guessed there would be fewer groupies these days, unlike the last time she approached Ste's company looking for him, and the subsequent fobbing off, labelled as just another hanger-on. Rachel responded quickly, promising that Ste would be made aware of her message the next time they spoke. While it might be just another fob off, just maybe it was more than that and her luck was finally changing.

The following days dragged by. Her constant refreshing of the inbox was like a psychological tick. It crossed her mind that she might not be as memorable as she thought she was. Ste could be partnered up and wouldn't want to open the can of worms that she represented. None of the articles she read about him gave away any personal information. There was no reference to a daughter or a partner despite her deep, stalkerish searches of the many dark corners of the internet.

Lockdown remained in full force, and it showed no immediate signs of being lifted. The illness that had taken her mother and accelerated her father's death, continued to sweep the country. Although only a few thousand Brits had died in March, it was clear this was the tip of the iceberg. A month after the first UK deaths, nearly a thousand people a day were dying across Britain, and that figure was being replicated across the world. It was a cowardly virus that took the weak and people who couldn't stand up to it. The severity of how widespread it was hit home when the Prime Minister himself was stricken. Propaganda showed him rallying and he made his recovery but had been given a real fright by the magnitude of it all. Some of the country cheered as tales of his heroic battle against the virus were leaked, but Isla felt sadness. She didn't want anybody else to die from it. But if it were a choice between Mum and Boris Johnson, she knew who she would want to win.

Nothing came back from Ste. He had a Twitter account, but it was one that the label used on his behalf. She figured it out because it was such a terrifically dull read. Isla knew Ste well enough to know he would not put his name to the tedious prose that the PR editor was pissing out for him. The days moved on and life showed no signs of returning to normal. She gave up on Ste and waited for the times to get better.

Chapter 69

It had been going so well. The bands were selling, and the company was making money. He'd relocated back 'home' to Southsea and had a penthouse flat overlooking both the common and Spitbank Fort, one of Palmerston's follies which had sat in the Solent since 1878. Ste was in a place where the one-hundred-hour weeks that he'd endured for a quarter of a century had paid off. At long last, he had a manageable schedule. At forty-eight years old, Ste could see the future. The business could sustain itself under his leadership team, allowing him to drift into semi-retirement. He planned to live part-time in the Caribbean where the vibe flowing through the islands invigorated him on each of his trips out there.

Amy was with him. She had grown into a fine woman and was working for his company. She had the inevitable flair that had come from a lifetime of watching her father creating music royalty. At twenty-one, she now managed the London office. However, as the nation watched the government press conference, it was clear that London was about to close. So, with just a few hours' notice before the city shut its doors, Amy raced to Waterloo, taking the train down to Portsmouth to stay at her dad's seafront apartment. The government-mandated controls gave her a quick choice—an abandoned city or the seaside. All bookings, recordings, press conferences and summer festivals were cancelled and their world was to shut down for an indefinite period. Amy had closed the office, grateful that as panic set in across the city, at least she had somewhere else to go.

Amy had lived with her mum all her life, but after her dad moved out, she would spend most weekends with him. It was so different being in the middle of the world her dad was at the centre of, compared to the dark, bitter place that her mum plodded through. Since he had come back from the catastrophe of 9/11, Ste had done his best to be a good father. Amy had wanted for nothing. And all these years on, Amy saw her parents' split as a blessing for them both. Her dad flourished and was happier with his life. Despite being better off alone, her mum failed to develop a positive outlook and left her confined within the parameters she set herself. It created a long-term resentment, Greta becoming increasingly convinced that her best days had passed her by and she'd given it all up for the loveless life through which she trudged. While she never used the exact words, Amy knew she resented what she'd given up for her. Greta fell in and out of destructive relationships with narcissistic men and gradually became impossible to live with.

Amy moved between their houses as she wished. Taking up the offer of a job with her dad was a no-brainer. She loved his business and loved the idea of being close to him as they worked. Although she enjoyed the energy that London generated, she was equally drawn to the comfort of family time on the coast where she could spend hours walking along Southsea front with the men in her life, her grandad and father taking great pleasure in regaling her with stories about their lives. Her dad's stories were ridiculous, funny and intoxicating. And as she got older, he drifted into revealing more of the darkness in his soul, using Amy as a therapeutic release in re-visiting the tragedy of 2001. He didn't go into great detail but had started to explain the images that still shocked him from sleep. And sometimes, he mentioned a girl called Isla as his great regret; but he never said much more. Walking past the old castle where Henry VIII watched the Mary Rose sink, she was glad that her dad was finally unburdening himself. Amy was tapping into the sealed emotions that Ste had never confided in anybody. She probably got further than the professional therapists who had supported her dad almost twenty years before.

Despite Covid-19, their business was going to be fine. The Government furlough scheme had helped with the costs of mothballing. The physical business had been put to sleep on that grim March day when the venues were all forced to close their doors. But everything would surely reopen sometime down the road, at the point when the restrictions were lifted. In the meantime, new opportunities emerged during lockdown. Livestreaming presented the opportunities which Ste loved so much. All good leaders embraced change with typical quick thinking, and Ste spotted the opportunities while much of the business still floundered. This was what continued to give him the edge. It was a new age and Ste was helping shape it. He was promoting the next 'Biggest Thing Ever' and Maverick Road would have their day. When the madness ended and it was safe, they would have their world tour. The 2020 tour was going to take in every major music city between Dublin and Moscow. It would just have to be shifted twelve months forward. At least, that was the hope.

Surely, there's no way this chaos will last longer than a few months?

They'd have to re-design the T-shirts, but maybe the 2020 ones would be collectors' items as 'The Tour That Never Happened'? Ste had never been content to rest on his laurels. The nation was a captive audience and his aim was to Livestream the band into every home in the country before lockdown was lifted. The kids streamed interviews and did their *'Daily Workout with Maverick Road'*. They streamed their own Live Lounge channel and even did a *'Cook with Maverick Road'* slot. Facebook, Twitter and other social media with photos, news pods, blogs and interactive Facetime, were drenched with the sounds of Maverick Road. They were everywhere.

He'd first found the band playing at the Wedgewood Rooms just around the corner from his home. He wandered into a Square Roots Promotions night after the promoter, an old mate from the school band, had asked him out for a beer. It was still incredible that in this Hi-Tec age, where image and online is everything, a five-minute walk to meet an old friend for a drink could still lead to chance opportunity. While the internet age made everything less personal, the intimacy of gigging was yet to be replaced. The old ways were still current, with the added bonus of musicians being more accessible than ever.

Amy was Ste's world. She was an acolyte at work, but by no means a deferential employee and never shy in presenting her ideas or persuading her dad that he did not know the youthful audience he targeted as well as he thought. She knew that once upon a time, if you did this, the consequence was that. If you created a buzz in NME or did an interview with the Evening Standard, you could guarantee it would add two hundred tickets to an audience at the Roundhouse. But if you were trying to get university students out on a Tuesday night in Huddersfield, the chances of the old ways working with a few posters around the Union was not enough. Viral didn't just mean a global pandemic. He had a media team in place, but he knew it took a certain type of management to really get behind things that he didn't always understand. As such, she was a terrific addition to his media team when she joined the company. Ste knew her value and was unapologetic in helping her career advance quickly. She delivered, and that was what mattered.

But his runny nose was not hay fever, and the cough was not because of the many spliffs he continued to enjoy after dark. The instruction was clear. He had to self-isolate and just hope that Amy hadn't picked up anything. God knows where he had got this wretched virus from. He had been careful. He'd shopped online and washed it when it was delivered. They hadn't left the house other than for the government-sanctioned daily walk. For the first time in his adult life, he had not been to a gig for a whole calendar month. Not that there were any to go to. Even when Amy was a baby, he still did three or four gigs a week. No wonder he and Greta had struggled.

There were still no tests available for Ste to confirm if he had the virus or not. But he wasn't getting any better, so after a few days, he turned on the Out of Office on his e-mail and hunkered down. He was far weaker than he could remember and was struggling with everything. While Amy did her best, caring for him in a mask and rubber gloves, cleaning obsessively and cooking the food that he couldn't face '*for your own good*', she finally phoned the hospital and arranged for her dad to be admitted to QA. Looking down on the city that her dad grew up in, the hospital complex was in a state of ordered panic as she drove through the main entrance. Ste was in the back of her car, trying to hold it together. He was scared. He was not ready to die; not even close.

The hospital staff were kind to Ste as he was admitted through the doors into the Covid section, and to Amy, who was required to leave after the formalities were complete. The hospital staff, who hadn't been home in days, were all heroes.

It didn't take long for things to change. For the better. Within a few days, Ste was calling over FaceTime and in constant contact through WhatsApp. She thought he was secretly enjoying his time off, watching endless crime dramas and ridiculous chick-flicks on Netflix without anyone to take the piss out of his TV choices. By the end of the week, she was told she could pick her dad up in the morning. Amy cooked, cleaned and enforced a strict

'No Work' policy. Ste had to rest and build up gradually and Amy was not letting her dad's inability to take direction get in the way of her enforcement of the hospital's rules. The laptop would not be switched on again until she said so. She could manage the business until he was ready to take over.

Chapter 70

Most of the calls for him were from the many industry contacts with whom he had built relationships over the decades. A few wanted to take the piss out of his photo in the paper, referencing Gordon Gecko and a sea view that screamed

'Semi-Retirement!'

The Kingmaker—that was a bad joke among a few old friends. But they'd run with it as the headline. Amy had reminded him that no publicity was bad publicity.

The article tweaked his brain cells. He was desperate to get back to it, and his strength had returned.

"I fancy logging on for a bit. Can you get me the laptop so I can touch base with things? I think I've finished Netflix!"

"Dad, the doctor said No! I've kept my eye on things and there's nothing that needs your attention. It's okay, please don't worry."

Amy had hidden the technology and continued moving it from place to place knowing her dad would be trying to find it; such was his stubbornness. But by the third day, Amy finally relented and offered to turn on his phone and pick up the messages for him.

"There's a few messages on here from Rachel. I'll listen to them."

"Can you play them? It will be nice to hear her voice."

She put the phone onto speaker and played the three weeks of messages. God knows how many text and WhatsApp messages there were to trawl through.

'Hello again, Ste. Rachel here. Sorry you're not well, and I don't want to bother you. But there was an e-mail that I'm just not sure about. It was unusual. From someone called, let me look again, someone called Isla.'

Ste sat bolt upright.

"Please give me my phone, Amy. I need to see this e-mail."

"Dad. No."

"Amy. Please give me the phone. This is not work. This is very personal."

Amy suddenly remembered the name. Her dad had mentioned Isla several times down the years and could see from the look on his face that it was important to him. She passed the phone over and left the room, wondering how much she still didn't know.

Ste looked at the hundreds of unread e-mails in his inbox. He searched for her name and found the mail. Nearly two decades had gone by without a word from her, but just the name, Isla, summoned up an exhilaration he had not felt in so long. Good god, it really had been nearly twenty years.

Wow! That girl. She still gets me every time!

He read the message and quickly typed a response to the woman who evidently still held a place in his mind. It was not just affection he had for her. There was also the regret.

'*WTF, Isla! I'm still alive and kicking. Just. Are you okay? This is a surprise. Want to chat?*'

Ste pressed send.

Ninety miles away, Isla's e-mail alert popped up prompting a tearful outburst. This time, they were tears of happiness. She had found him. And he clearly had no issue with being found.

Chapter 71

Within seconds, she replied with her mobile number. There was no pissing about; all the rules from the Dating Bible about how long you leave the e-mail replies were suspended. Ste might have taken weeks to reply, but she had no interest in a pre-coupling dance. She wanted to talk to Ste. She *had* to talk to him and after that, she knew she would want to see him. Twenty years was too long to piss about. She hoped he felt the same.

Her phone rang immediately, and Isla answered before the first ring had completed. The exchange from Ste picking up her email to now was a matter of minutes.

"Holy Fuck, is it really you?"

Isla burst into tears at the sound of his voice. Although deeper in tone, it was instantly recognisable as the man she once loved and still hung onto the memories of loving.

After a silence where Ste listened to Isla's weak attempts to regain her composure, it was clear this could turn into a long conversation.

"So, do you fancy shifting to FaceTime, Isla? It might make things more real. And besides, I want to see how you've aged."

"Can I be honest, Ste?"

"Well, there's not much point in chatting if it's not going to be an honest one, is there?"

"Well, rather than FaceTime, can I drive to wherever you are and we can talk in person? You've no idea how long or how much I've missed you." This was a conversation she had longed for, but the last thing she wanted to do was frighten him away. She wasn't sure whether he was married, partnered, or whatever people did in Portsmouth. If he was even in Portsmouth.

"There's a slight problem with coming to see me."

Oh no, he's taken....

Isla feared she had wandered into his life at a time when there was no room for her again. Had she misread the urgency she had inferred from his text message?

Ste was interrupted by a woman's voice.

Shit. He is with someone. I'm an idiot…. There was no way he was going to be available after all this time. Bollocks, bollocksy, bollocks!

Her heart dropped to the pit of her stomach and she felt like hanging up. The decision had already been taken away from her. He hung up. Ste had hung up. She was sure he was married.

What an arsehole. Calling her when his wife was at home.

Incoming FaceTime call from a number not in her book. She relaxed, smiling again, answering the call to see the Ste she recognised from his picture in the paper. Next to him was a woman. She was considerably younger, with a bemused look on her face.

"Isla, meet my daughter, Amy. She is not very happy with me because I'm supposed to be resting."

"Hello". Both women replied simultaneously. Isla smiled, looking upon the girl who had interrupted their boat trip plans all those years ago.

"I'm sorry for appearing rude, but my dad has not been well with this virus, so I've told him I will go back to my mum's if this conversation lasts more than five minutes. But nice to meet you, Isla."

"She's serious." Ste nodded in acknowledgement. "So, in the spirit of brevity and holding onto my daughter, please tell me this. Where are you and are you okay?"

He ushered Amy away, smiling at the beautiful woman on his phone.

"It was not supposed to be this way, but I am back in Hemel."

"You always wanted to leave there."

"I did. I did. I promise, I did leave. Fat lot of good it did me. I've only been back a few weeks because both of my parents died on the same day. So no, I'm not okay, but I will be."

"Isla, I am so sorry. Is there anything I can do?"

Isla thought for a moment.

"Well, that depends on the answer to the next question, Ste."

"And what's that?"

"Do you ever think about me? Because I have thought about you with sickening regularity for my entire adult life. And I wondered if, now and again, you ever found space for me in your mind. Because if you did, that would make me very happy indeed."

"Isla, I'm going to take a running jump at something. Were you serious about coming down to Southsea? Because if you were, I'd love to see you!"

"Yes, Ste. Yes, I was."

"My neighbour is away, and I have the keys. It takes about ninety minutes from where you are, and we can talk if my daughter is still talking to me after I tell her what's about to happen! Let's just hope she lets you in."

"Text me your postcode? I know we aren't allowed to leave our homes, but if this isn't an emergency to help a vulnerable person, I don't know what is. I'll pack an overnight bag and be there as soon as I can."

"Lovely stuff. But one thing."

"What's that, Ste?"

"Make sure you pack more than an overnight bag, Isla. We have a lot of catching up to do."

Chapter 72

"What do you mean, 'She's coming to stay?'"

Ste didn't know where to look. He knew what Amy was going to say and he couldn't disagree with any of the valid objections she was going come up with.

"Dad, before I leave here and go back to Mum's, I think it's time you told me two things. In any order. Firstly, what does the word 'rehabilitation' mean to you and secondly, who the fuck is Isla?"

Amy would need some convincing that this was the best rehabilitation Ste could ask for. She didn't feel it was unreasonable to be concerned by the unexpected change of pace in her dad's lifestyle, but she had a right to know more. What was inside his soul?

Ste couldn't justify not opening up any longer. Amy was his absolute world, and she deserved answers. Moreover, he wanted to tell her.

"My darling girl. I love you so much and being a father has been the most important thing in the world to me. You were the reason I held onto sanity after New York because being your dad is the best and most wonderful thing I have ever done. And since then, I have tried making the right decisions and doing whatever it took to firstly keep our family together and since I failed to do that, to keep you front and centre of every subsequent decision."

"I know that, Dad, you've been amazing. But where does this Isla come into it? Did you have an affair?"

Ste didn't answer her question. He needed time to think.

'No, that's not me. In fact, it's quite the reverse! When Isla and I met, your mum and I weren't even together. But the idea of not being the best Dad I could be when you were born, meant I made an agreement with myself that I had to do whatever I could to make sure we stayed together. I thought that it would be the best thing for you. And looking back, I still think that it was a good decision to make. Maybe it wasn't, but I stand by my choice."

"I figured all this out, Dad. This isn't news. But what has that got to do with Isla? Once again, who is she?"

Ste explained how they had met, why they spent time together and what had happened in New York, and how the tragedy of 9/11 had destroyed their relationship which had taken on such a significant role in his heart. Although their contact over twenty-three years covered a handful of meetings, with nothing since September 2001, there was a significance; a longing. It was unfulfilled and regretful. But Isla was the woman who was there when he was alone, desperately struggling with the haunting images of the crash, the dust, the smoke, the explosion and the bodies that he saw fall. The dust-covered, ghost-like faces wandering the streets of Lower Manhattan for eternity haunted him. The pain never left him. And Isla was at the heart of it.

Remembering that he needed convalescence, Ste lay on the sofa that was baked in the warm afternoon sun. Amy saw him drifting off and moved out of view so he could rest.

Isla would call when she got there, so she lifted her dad's phone off the coffee table and put it in her pocket. There was nothing more she could do, even if there was a case for her to interfere. This was more important to her Dad than the rules of convalescence. She found the spare keys for the next-door flat and went to check that it was indeed empty and if anything needed doing. The last thing she would allow was her father's medical isolation to be disturbed; and if that meant they talked to each other across the hallway between the flats, then that is how it would be.

Before she finished preparing the neighbour's flat, Ste's phone rang.

"Hello, Isla. This is Amy. Are you near?"

"I'm outside. Is your dad there?"

"You made good time. But look, he's been asleep for a while. You'll understand I won't wake him just yet. He's been really sick."

"I understand, Amy. There was nothing on the road so I raced here all the way. I'll take a walk for a while."

"Don't be silly, Isla. I'll come down and let you in."

Amy wanted to meet Isla. She was the most important thing in Ste's world.

Isla felt no hostility from Amy, but she didn't detect any warmth either. She had no idea what Ste had told his daughter about her; if anything at all.

Having let Isla into the building, the women walked upstairs, neither of them overly motivated to break the familiar silence that continued to envelop the country. While they were eager for this initial meeting to be pleasant, it was going to be awkward, and secretly, both were eager for Ste to quickly wake up.

Amy showed Isla into the neighbour's flat and they sat on opposite chairs, conscious of the distancing requirements that they had already broken.

"Dad said you, how did he put it again, '*shared time*' a while back?"

"Yes. Something like that. Not that much time. But back then, your Dad had a sudden and amazing impact on me. I've always cared very much for him, despite not seeing him for a long time."

Isla couldn't find the appropriate words to describe what happened in New York. How do you say,

'Since he went to pieces from seeing bodies fall from the sky? Since he lost his mind witnessing the deaths of three thousand people?'

How do you put that stuff into words?

"I know. Mum said he was never the same after that last New York trip."

The awkward reference to Greta was inevitably going to come, but Isla had not expected it so soon, or for it to come from Ste's daughter. It hung in the air like a noxious fart that wouldn't break up. It killed the pleasantries.

As the late afternoon sunshine turned to early evening dusk, the women found enough common ground to make small talk easier. Isla explained what had happened to her over recent weeks, saving the bits about Jakob for another lifetime. There was no reason to revisit that shit today. And the story may give the impression that she was a loser who was only one step away from the streets. Amy talked about the business, but their individual loyalty to the snoozing man in the adjacent flat meant neither wanted to give away too much.

Food was a guaranteed way to break any silence or period of awkwardness. Amy ordered in from one of the few takeaway places still delivering. And as Amy's phone buzzed with the notification from Dominos that the driver was downstairs carrying out a socially distanced drop off, they heard Ste calling. Amy wandered downstairs to get the pizza and told Isla to surprise Ste.

"Not too close though, Isla, please."

Having just lost both her parents, Isla was not taking any chances. She was so close to seeing Ste after all this time, she'd have worn a full Hazmat suit if Amy had asked. As she quietly opened the door, she looked around the spacious room which overlooked Southsea common, recognising the room from the article. She heard the voice from her past. His voice.

"Are you there, darling?"

"It's Isla, Ste."

"That's what I meant, Isla. Whether I said it or not, you've always been my darling."

For the second time in the last few hours, Isla burst into tears, this time at a loss for any appropriate words. Although he had lost weight since the picture in the paper was taken, Ste was an older spit of the man she met twenty-three years ago. He had the same warm smile, kind eyes, and was still so bloody attractive.

Amy appeared at the door with the pizzas and saw her dad and the virtual stranger in tears. She knew when to leave, and taking half of one pizza, disappeared towards the neighbours' flat.

"Again, Dad, please don't get too close."

Isla nodded, but Ste was more sarcastic in his response to the reverse parenting.

"Cheers, Mum."

Ste and Isla didn't hear her response. They were transfixed by the first view of each other in a lifetime.

Chapter 73

Asking them to follow the formal medical advice and common-sense direction demanded for the next two weeks seemed an impossible task. Since their reunion, the three of them played by the rules of isolation, but as the days went on, it was getting harder. The risk of them having the virus and being a threat was low, but they persisted, raw to the threat given Isla's loss and Ste's time in hospital.

Because one was symptomatic and the other two had been in proximity to people who were infected, there was no getting around the fourteen-day period of isolation. Isla struggled to contain her excitement as the days counted down. She hadn't had any human contact since her parent's death, including being able to accept a hug from any of the four relatives allowed to attend the funeral. She just wanted to hold Ste, to kiss him again and be close enough to feel that everything was going to be alright.

Ste told her he was desperately in need of intimacy; the hugs and kisses of his grown-up daughter were great but didn't replace the other type of love from a woman. Despite her threats, Amy stayed with them in Southsea and had quickly warmed to their guest. By the third day, she had bonded with Isla and could see for herself why her dad had a place in his heart for her. The time was coming when she'd need to make herself scarce. She could see how this was panning out and was happy for them.

The day came when Isla could wake Ste up in person. She wanted to be with him when he woke for the first time since the terrible morning in New York. None of them had developed any of the symptoms Ste had shown before his hospitalisation. They were free from the virus that continued to wreck so many lives the world over.

It was VE Day, and the sun filled the sky. Amy tactfully said that she needed some air and would take her outdoor exercise early. The flat took on a radiance that you could only get from being high up. There were no obstructions, and you could follow the Hovercraft on its trip across the Solent into Ryde. Isla got up early. Throughout the night, she hadn't slept for more than an hour at a time, and quietly let herself into the flat as soon as she felt was acceptable. Amy was already awake and preparing an Espresso before her long, circular bike ride around the island.

"I'll be gone all morning, Isla; back around lunchtime. Then there's some stuff going on outdoors for VE Day later. Could be fun, if you two are up for it. It'll be a change from what we've been used to recently."

"Thank you again, Amy. Thank you so much."

The last days had been some of the happiest Isla had ever experienced and Amy responded similarly when her dad had asked her how she felt about Isla. Isla and Amy spent a lot of time talking while Ste rested. And Isla had told Amy about the sacrifice her dad had made to do what he felt was right. Amy confided that if the boot was on her foot, she wasn't sure she would have signed up for the life he had with her mum, when his heart belonged elsewhere. She loved her mum but understood why there was so much tension. She tried not to be disloyal to her mum but said enough that Isla understood that Greta was a difficult woman. And Ste had put up with it. Amy gave them her blessing and said her dad had earned the right to chase rainbows with Isla. Isla assured her that this was the real thing—and a long time coming.

With their isolation from each other complete, the two women took a moment to embrace for the first time. There was a warmth in the embrace that neither could have predicted two weeks before. It was the first genuine feeling of love that Isla had felt since she had seen her parents for the final time, last Christmas.

As Amy closed the door behind her, Ste opened his bedroom door. Isla didn't want anything to jeopardise the plan they had made for their morning. It would end two decades isolated from each other.

"Good morning, Darling."

Isla was nervous for the first time since arriving at the flat two weeks before. So far, they had been in forced isolation; there had been rules. They couldn't even embrace. But now they could do what they wanted.

Ste moved to Isla who fiddled nervously with the Espresso machine. He took her hand in his and as she gazed into his soul as they held each other again. The intensity of the silence and the strength of feeling between them was electric. He could feel her next to him, the beat of her heart audible even to the deaf. Any other time, such a heart rate would be considered unhealthy.

He leaned in and felt Isla immediately move towards him, and a kiss that now released decades of bottled emotion. Their previous kisses had nothing on this. A full voltage electric shock of a kiss that was incomparable to anything else.

Amy had left the music playing in the background, and in the pause between songs, they parted to look into each other. The stereo tripped into a new song as Mandolin Orange, modern exponents of Americana, filled the corners of the room. Ste reached for the remote and turned up the volume, immersing the two of them in the sweet loving sounds of the North Carolina couple.

'Like Old Ties, and Companions, we never leave alone. So old man, give me endless time, never let these ties sever. So, Heaven knows and all this fooling around, these times won't last forever, after all.'

Ste was singing along with the words until Isla put a finger on his lips at the mention of forever.

"Hey, Ste, want a bet on that?"

"Shall we find out?"

"That would be agreeable. I've been waiting to listen to music with you for a long time. Last time you played a tune to me, you fell straight to sleep; and I haven't been able to get this song out of my head since."

Isla picked up her phone and connected it to the speaker.

'Hmm hmm hmm, hmm hmm, hmm hmm, yeah….. It is you…. I said Pressure Drop….'

Alone and together, really together, for the first time, they held each other close. The early summer sun blazed through the tall windows lighting up the flat. Portsmouth was not Bridgetown, and their 2020 selves were not the youthful kids they were in 1998. But their world was perfect.

"Hey?"

"What?"

"I love you."

"I love you, too, Ste."

'It is you……………'

The End